WITH A VENGEANCE

WITH
A
VENGEANCE

by Dell Shannon

William Morrow & Company, Inc.

New York

Revenge proves its own executioner.
—JOHN FORD, THE BROKEN HEART

WITH A VENGEANCE

One

I⊤ all began a long while before the boys in the Homicide Bureau at Central, L.A.P.D., knew one thing about it. Some of them weren't in Homicide when it all began. Mendoza was still new in Homicide then, and still Sergeant Mendoza, and it was long before he'd met Alison Weir or ever even contemplated matrimony, much less had any remote notion about the twin monsters arriving to upset his life. And it was long before Hackett—not then Sergeant—had met his Angel, and worried and wondered about her, and ended up loving her.

Bert Dwyer wasn't yet transferred to Homicide when it all began, his feet set on the path which brought him in the end to bloody death on the cold marble floor of a bank. And George Higgins was at Homicide then, but newer to the office than Mendoza, and even then pretty well settled in his bachelorhood and never dreaming that Fate had set his path alongside Dwyer's that in the end he should commit himself—gravely and solidly and efficiently as Higgins did everything—to Bert Dwyer's widow. Tom Landers was still riding a patrol car, and Galeano was still down in auto theft, and John Palliser was studying for the detectives' examination, still in uniform.

It was a long while back when it started. Matt Piggott

wasn't at Homicide, or Rory Farrell, and Sergeant Lake who nowadays sat at the desk outside Mendoza's office dealing with all the phones, was down in Forgery. Schenke wasn't there, or Thoms, or Glasser. Some of the men at Homicide then were since retired. And anyway, the start of it all wasn't any concern of Homicide's and they never heard about it then.

The men at Homicide then were involved as always in the endless routine, the sordid and violent and wanton and random deaths that happen too often in that section of any big city. With the junkies dead of the overdose, the stabbings during a brawl, the drunks dead of drink in the alleys, the bashings and muggings and armed assaults, they were busy.

And when the years-old motive started to operate, Homicide was routinely busy then, too. As per usual. Things were always coming along.

They had a fatal child-beating case, for one thing. Not much mystery about it, but a nasty case and all the paperwork to be done. Jason Grace was on that with Glasser. They were both seasoned cops but that sort of thing always did shake you a little, the purely Neanderthal thing—"I hadda stop her yellin', I hadda awful head on me, I just sorta slapped her a couple times, didn't go to—"

They had a liquor-store clerk held up and shot over on Main. That was being a bastard to work, not one single lead on it; probably they'd never get anybody for it. All they knew was the gun used, that nine-shot Harrington and Richardson .22.

They had a suicide: a straight suicide, twenty-year-old girl in a cheap rooming house on Temple, took an overdose and left a note. Boyfriend walked out on her, didn't want to go on, he'd know now how much she loved him . . . "People, people," said Hackett, shaking his head. "Poor pathetic little fool. Twenty, my God."

And Higgins said, "Maybe why, Art. Another five years, she'd maybe have grown some common sense. And then again, maybe not." But there was all the paperwork to do on it; and they hadn't so far found any relatives to pay for the funeral.

They had also an unidentified corpse, and all the paperwork on that: the flyers sent out with the description, man approximately 55-60 years of age, Caucasian, five-feet-eight, 150 pounds, appendectomy scar—and so forth. He'd been found alongside a derelict building on Second Street, not too good a section—dead of a heart attack—but his clothes were fairly good and he'd been clean and neat, no drink in him, so he probably hadn't been a bum and somebody ought to know him somewhere.

They'd just cleaned up a series of muggings in a couple of city parks, and got the nice evidence and seen the mugger arraigned. In fact, for an average week at Homicide, it was fairly quiet and slow, and this sunny Saturday in June, with the real heat not yet upon them, Mendoza had gone home early, leaving Hackett and Jason Grace and Higgins discussing, of all things, the contemporary novel.

"Just to point up the fact," the lieutenant had said, picking up his black Homburg, "that this is the deeply intellectual force we all know it is."

"Well, blame it on Virginia," said Grace in his soft voice. "She takes these serious kicks once in a while—joined this study club, you know, and brings the damn books home and—" He grinned, touching his hairline mustache, as precise as Mendoza's own against his coffee-colored complexion.

"Intellectual be damned," said Hackett sleepily, propping his feet up on his desk in the communal sergeants' office. "Half of 'em disguised pornography and the other half egghead political treatises disguised as fiction. I can't read that stuff."

13

"That's not a bad description, Sergeant," said Grace thoughtfully.

Higgins yawned and said he didn't try to read it. A cop had enough to do, he said, without keeping up with *The Saturday Review of Literature* for God's sake. And had anything come in from Missing Persons on the description of that corpse, or were they still pawing through their records by hand?

"I'll call Carey," said Hackett, reluctantly sitting up and reaching for the phone.

It had been a quiet day. So Mendoza went home, to the big Spanish house on Rayo Grande Avenue in the Hollywood hills. He found his house empty of all save the four cats: and, strange for the reformed man-about-town, he felt annoyed. When he came home, his household should be there to acknowledge him. He gave himself a small drink, talked to the cats, replaced the record albums El Señor inevitably dragged out of the cabinet while nobody was around, and investigating the refrigerator found some Roquefort cheese. He was scattering cracker crumbs on the living-room carpet when Alison arrived home from a day's painting visit to the beach, and presently Mrs. MacTaggart and the twin monsters from an afternoon's visit to Barnsdall Park.

The twins, tired out by the swings and sandboxes, were tucked away to bed without protest; dinner materialized under Mrs. MacTaggart's deft hands. And at eleven o'clock, Mendoza was wandering around the big master bedroom starting to get undressed, while Alison sat up in bed with a book, looking very fetching in pale-green nylon with her copper hair loose to her shoulders; she'd been letting it grow.

"I don't know but what it *is* a good description," said Mendoza suddenly, taking off his watch. "Mmh, yes. Contemporary literature. *¡Por mi vida!*"

"What?" said Alison vaguely.

14

"Just—what are you reading, contemporary literature?"

"Con——heavens, no. Most of the stuff all the critics rave over is terrible, honestly. No, it's a life of Landseer."

"Oh. The fellow who painted all those sad-eyed dogs and horses."

Alison bristled. "Well, I expect it's very old-fashioned of me—"

The telephone rang.

"—but I *like* Landseer. I really—"

Mendoza went out to the hall. "Mendoza here."

"We've got a kind of funny little thing down here, Lieutenant," said Sergeant Farrell. "Something that looks—well, Galeano and Piggott went out on it, and Nick just called in, said we'd better brief you. Kind of offbeat, you know."

"Oh? What kind of offbeat?"

"Well, it's a body, of course. Found about half an hour ago, under a tree in the Old Plaza. By, I gather, a couple of neckers. The man called in, Traffic chased a squad car out, and the squad-car men called us when they saw the guy was dead. So Nick and Matt went out to look at it. Offbeat you can say. Down there, and—well, we've got an ambulance on the way, see what Bainbridge says about the corpse in the morning, but Nick says it looks very funny, Lieutenant. A fellow about forty, ordinary-looking, but he's dressed to the nines—expensive clothes—and Nick says he's been strangled by something like a thin wire or a piece of clothesline, something like that—and there was a card tucked halfway into his shirt pocket—"

"A business card? I don't—"

"No, no. A card, Nick says, that's all, I don't know what kind, but it's got written on it, *The Vengeance is Just.* Just that. He thought it was offbeat enough that you ought to—"

"¡*Vaya por Dios!* Yes, indeed," said Mendoza. "Very funny, Rory. Did you—?"

15

"I told him to call back in five minutes, I'd find out if you wanted to have a personal look, and—"

"I think I do," said Mendoza. "Yes. Tell him to hold the corpse, Rory—I'm on my way." He went back to the bedroom, put on his watch, reached for a tie, telling Alison about it.

She laughed, looking up from Landseer. "You and your talk about resigning, and enjoying the money and maybe going round the world, after twenty-three years' service. ¡Cómo no, ni qué niña muerto! You'd die of boredom. Talk about born cops."

Mendoza grinned at her, putting on his jacket. "Fool that I am. Only a cop could be idiot enough to walk out on you already in bed. I don't suppose it'll take more than an hour. Can Landseer occupy you that long?"

"I'm taking no bets," said Alison darkly. "Not with you. Go and have fun with your corpse, amante."

And it wasn't that he had, then, any premonitions; nor did he think of himself as the dedicated cop. But, along with a few other necessary traits to the good cop, Luis Rodolfo Vicente Mendoza had a larger bump of curiosity than the average citizen, and anything a little offbeat that happened along he wanted to look at pronto.

The Old Plaza, he thought, backing out the Ferrari. A funny place for a corpse. On a Saturday night. True, very dark there under the few old trees: and later at night, there wouldn't be the old men occupying the benches as they did during the day, and on warm summer evenings. (So, the corpse not there very long?) But lights and people close around. He visualized it thoughtfully. The Union Station with its cab rank and blazing lights a long block down the hill. Olvera Street, the first street in L.A., preserved as a tourist attraction, a block away across North Spring. Of course, the old Mission Church right across the street from the

16

Plaza, and everything else right around, dark and silent at this time of night: no businesses or bars near. Still, a funny place. He didn't remember any instance of a body turning up in the Plaza, all the years he'd been at Homicide.

They'd held it for him. A black-and-white squad car, Galeano's old Ford, an ambulance, parked illegally at the curb on the Los Angeles Street side of the Plaza, and a spotlight up there under the trees. This was the original part of L.A. here, the little squarish Plaza and the old church up there, and the first little street of shops and houses which marked the beginning of this city. The Town of Our Lady Queen of the Angels of the Little Portion. Today it was not as it had been then; the city fathers had made a tasteful tiny park of it. There was green grass; the ground rose a little steeply in this small-block-square of park, to the spreading shelter of a few ancient olive trees, a bronze statue—Father Serra? Mendoza had never bothered to identify it—a few benches. Up the gentle rise to the center was the spotlight.

He came into the little circle, the interns from the ambulance standing around smoking, stocky dark Galeano, thin serious-looking Piggott, the two uniformed squad-car men— and the dead man; and Galeano greeted him sardonically.

"I thought you couldn't resist it. The vengeance bit. It's funny."

"It's funny," agreed Mendoza. "Let's see it. Any I.D. on him?"

"Oh, sure. He's Nelson Edward Jamison. Wallet on him all shipshape. Money too—forty-seven bucks and some change. And a lot of I.D. Social Security, driver's license, bank-account number card."

"You don't tell me. All the funnier," said Mendoza.

"I do tell you. He lives in Pasadena," said Galeano. "On Belvidere Street. And God knows I'm not the expert on fancy tailoring you are, Lieutenant, but if he paid less than fifty

17

bucks for his sports jacket or less than a quarter-century for his shoes, I'll eat 'em.'"

"You don't tell me," said Mendoza again. He stepped over to the corpse delicately—there wouldn't be footprints, though the grass was thinner under the trees; there hadn't, of course, in Southern California, been a drop of rain for months. There wasn't, in fact, anything very much around the body, and of what there was—cigarette ends, candy wrappers, a half-empty sack that had held popcorn—who could say whether they connected with the body? It was lying crumpled in front of one of the benches, as if the man had toppled from a sitting position. Mendoza squatted down to look at it.

"He's more or less as he was," said Galeano. "I just lifted him up, going through his pockets."

Strangled, yes. Strangled by brute force. See what more Bainbridge could say about that, but at first glance—any man at Homicide as long as Mendoza had been there picked up this and that—strangled not manually but with something. Cord, wire, whatever. "And," said Galeano, following his thought, "no sign of anything like that around."

Discounting the bulging eyes, the tip of protruding tongue, the man had not been a very prepossessing man. A low narrow forehead, a weak receding chin, a muddy sallow complexion: sandy-blond hair too long, tumbled over his brow, and a slack mouth even in life, probably. It was open, and the teeth were bad—discolored, one incisor half broken off. Sum him up, a fellow about Mendoza's size, call it five-ten, a hundred and fifty: between thirty-five and forty. And the clothes—yes. *Pues sí*, thought Mendoza. The spotlight showed the quality clearly. A shadow-plaid wool sports jacket, faint heather-lavender shading to gray. "It's a Brooks label," said Galeano over his shoulder. Pale-gray nylon slacks —a gray sports shirt, very clean and looking just pressed. Gray suède moccasins, silk socks. A leather *bolo* tie, and the

18

sliding clasp was, Mendoza decided with one accurate look, sterling: a sterling horseshoe. Very natty.

"Here," said Piggott gloomily, "is the card. Somebody had a grudge against him. When are people going to learn that vengeance belongs to the Lord, Lieutenant?" Piggott was a devout Free Methodist.

"At about the same time," said Mendoza, standing up, "that there ceases to be any need for police forces, Matt. All right, you boys take it away—see what Bainbridge makes of it." He looked at the card with interest, what he could see of it. Galeano and Piggott had, of course, brought a lab kit with them, and awaiting fingerprinting the card had been maneuvered into a small plastic bag. It was an ordinary three-by-five file card with lines printed on it. And diagonally across its face, in what looked like ball-point printing, very neatly ran the legend:

The Vengeance is Just

"Somebody with a grudge, all right," said Galeano. "But what was he doing down here in this part of town? In his fancy tailoring and all? Or was he strangled somewhere else and brought here? That I don't see."

"No," said Mendoza, "neither do I. He's no lightweight, Nick. Somebody'd have had to haul him up here from a car—it'd have taken some little while—and it's illegal to park on all four sides of this place. And down here the squad car comes around at fairly frequent intervals. Nobody would have attempted that—lights so near. Even as late as it probably was—I don't think he's more than an hour dead."

"I thought so too," said Galeano. "I sent the pair that found him back to the office in a squad car to give Rory a statement. Manuel Garcia and Rita Ortiz. Ordinary young couple—out on a date, come out of a movie, stop to have a malt, think they'll sit in the Plaza a while all cozy and smooch a little. That's another thing—I wonder if there's much of that. If X knew? If there is, he might have been interrupted by half a dozen couples after the privacy. Anyway, they're out—nothing to do with it. Garcia's an apprentice electrician, works for the city. Ordinary."

The interns were bundling the corpse onto a stretcher.

"Um, yes," said Mendoza. "I suppose you've looked all around here, as well as you could. Better rope it off, have another look in the morning. Just in case. So now we go to break the bad news to the family, if any."

"There is. One of those personal I.D. cards, in case of accident notify. A Mrs. Constance Jamison—wife or mother, I suppose, same address."

"*Lo siento tanto*. As long as I've been at it, I don't like breaking the bad news."

"You don't have to come along," said Galeano. "But I can see that long nose of yours twitching from here."

Mendoza grinned. "Just a glutton for work, that's me. I admit it, I'm curious about Mr. Jamison. What *was* he doing down here? His shoes aren't scuffed, and suède would show a mark—I trust you noticed that, playing detective. It looks as if he was killed right here, right where he fell. In—"

"His gents' fancy tailoring, sure. And with the wallet untouched."

"And just possibly," said Mendoza, stepping away from the place where the body had lain and lighting a cigarette, "just possibly, after Mrs. Constance Jamison has recovered from the shock, she'll tell us. It must have been Joe Doakes, he's been threatening to murder poor Nelson—over a girl, or a gambling debt, or an argument about politics."

"And also she might not," said Piggott even more gloomily. "Vengeance." He sniffed disapprovingly.

"All right," said Mendoza abruptly, "you see the area's roped off and posted, Matt—" He turned to the uniformed men. "And you see that somebody's stationed here to reinforce that. It'll come to nothing, ten to one, but we have to go through the motions. Nick, you and I'll go and break the bad news." Galeano handed over his car keys to Piggott silently.

And it was a little joke in the Homicide Bureau, about Mendoza's crystal ball; but whatever it was, it didn't always work. Clicking on the directional signal, making the turn onto the Pasadena freeway, Mendoza hadn't any dire premonitions at all. It was just an offbeat little thing that had turned up, and he fully expected that when they came to unravel it, it'd turn out to be the grudge over a girl, something like that. What made it a little funny was not only the card, but the fact of the strangling: grudge killings were more usually simple bashings or shootings.

When they found the Pasadena address, it suited the clothes Jamison had been wearing. A street above Orange Grove Avenue: a street of dignified old houses, big and expensive houses: manicured lawns. And it took a little while to wake the old house, and when at last the door opened to them, and they produced their badges, they got both less and more than they had expected. Breaking the bad news.

"For the *Lord's* sake," said the woman. "*Dead? Killed? By* somebody, not just a—that Nelson? You're *cops?* For the *Lord's* sake!" She shook her head at them wonderingly. "My God," she said, "the old lady'll go out of her *mind*. I just don't relish tellin' her, I tell you. Not *atall*. But I won't say I'm surprised. Way he ran around. Trouble he got into. What? No, I'm not Mrs. Jamison—I'm the housekeeper. My name's Madge Hooper. Been with her—I guess you might's well come in—a matter o' fifteen years. She's nearly eighty, y'know, and got the arthritis and a bad heart too—for the *Lord's* sake, let's hope it don't bring on an attack, *tellin'* her! Poor old soul—not but what I reckon it was her spoilin' him and all like that made him—"

It was a large, high-ceilinged, old-fashioned entrance hall, ornate plush-covered Victorian chairs all formal at either

21

side of the wide old front door, a faded oriental carpet, a crystal chandelier. "Mrs. Jamison—that's his mother?" asked Mendoza. "What do you—?"

"Didn't I say?" Madge Hooper was about fifty, a thin woman with friendly, curious eyes and a lot of defiantly ash-blond hair in bristling pink curlers for the night. She was clutching a blue corduroy robe around her, and she yawned, but her gaze on them was bright and interested. "Yes, that's right. She's an awful sentimental woman—nice woman, but kind of a fool too. If you know what I mean. There's a lot o' money—kind of substantial *old* money, you know—her husband was a banker. I been with her fifteen years, heard all about it. And seen some. That Nelson—Lordy, I can't get over it, him getting *murdered*, you say? It'll just about kill her, spite of all—well, he was a no-goodnik all right. Kind of the usual thing, you know, her bein' in her forties when he was born, and never expectin' any kids, married nearly twenty years—and him being a boy and all—and her husband dyin' pretty soon, and her spoilin' the kid rotten—"

"Mrs. Hooper, if you'd—"

"Oh, Lord, *I'm* not goin' to be the one to tell her! Like they say, as if she thought the sun rose 'n' set in him—and him no better than a bum, driftin' around, never any job, and in *police* trouble too—a real bad one he was, you could tell just by lookin' at him, nearly. I tell you true, when he was here—which he wasn't always, driftin' around like I say, the good Lord knows where or who with—and her pleased as a dog with two tails like they say when he *did* come home to stay awhile—I tell you true, I kept my rollin' pin handy! And he knew it too. After he got in *that* trouble that time. He'd *done time*. You know that? In San Quentin. For *rape*. And her sayin' everybody just tellin' lies about him! And now he's gone and got himself *murdered!* Lordy, I don't want to be the one to tell her—" Her eyes were avid, a little scared, desperately curious.

22

Mendoza and Galeano looked at each other.

San Quentin? Rape? *Vengeance.*

Even then, it looked fairly straightforward. A thing to be unraveled by time, patience, and hunting. It looked, in fact, as if there might be some good solid leads to be had.

Only at nine o'clock on Sunday morning, another squad-car man called in to Homicide with another corpse. They had had a routine call this morning from a Miss Alice Bremmer in Hollywood. Her brother, a Mr. William Bremmer who owned and operated a small shop on Spring Street downtown, had not returned home on Saturday night and Miss Bremmer feared he might have been taken ill, suffered a heart attack or something, and would the police check? They had. A routine call.

And the squad-car man chased over to Mr. William Bremmer's shop on Spring Street and had found the front door unlocked. Had found Mr. Bremmer dead in the rear room of his little shop—dead by strangulation, he said it looked like —and there was a kind of funny thing about it—

"Yes?" said Sergeant Lake efficiently. "I'll shoot an ambulance—address?"

"Right on his chest," said the squad-car man. "Just lying there. A little card, like a file card, and printing on it that says —crazy—*The Vengeance is Just.* And it looks sort of offbeat, and I thought—"

"What?" said Sergeant Lake. "What? Just a minute—" And he put down the phone to call Hackett's name.

Two

"Now just what the hell is this?" asked Mendoza. "What the *hell?*"

"Your guess is as good as mine, boy," said Hackett. "Is it a crusade of some kind? That Jamison I can see earning a grudge, but what we've got so far on Bremmer, he never did anybody any harm."

Mendoza looked around the shop. He'd come haring down here when Hackett called, pursued by Alison's anxious admonitions not to forget they were due at the Mawsons' for dinner at seven sharp, and she really couldn't give Sally *another* excuse after the last time— Vengeance? Two in one night? The card said it could hardly be coincidence; and having seen this one, he had to say it looked like the same printing.

"I will be damned," he said.

Hackett was looking around the shop too. "It kind of leaps to the eye," he offered, "how it was done."

"Oh, *conforme*," sighed Mendoza. That didn't go far toward telling them why, or who. Marx and Horder were busy in the stockroom past the door fifteen feet away at the back of the shop; it was doubtful if they'd pick up any useful latent prints there . . . Obvious, yes. This very neat and clean and rather snob-appeal little shop was called The Smokers'

Nook. It was stocked with everything for the smoker: expensive imported pipes, tobacco pouches, cigarette holders in sterling and gold, expensive cigarette boxes and humidors, exotic blends of tobacco. There were all sorts of imported cigarettes, Turkish blends: a large hookah occupied one corner; and there was a whole shelf of cigarette cases, another of lighters. According to the only man they'd talked to who had known Bremmer—the fellow who kept the newsstand at the corner, happened past on a morning stroll, noticed all the cops' cars and came in to ask questions—Bremmer had owned the shop for nearly twenty years, so he must have found it profitable.

The body was gone now, but it had been in the stockroom. Just inside the door, prone. Bremmer had been strangled with a thin cord or something similar, very apparently. Caught from behind, without much doubt by a pseudo customer who had asked for something in the stockroom, had followed Bremmer close and caught him there inside the door. A customer, obviously, who had been the only one in the shop at the time. And the intern had estimated that Bremmer had been dead about eighteen hours, and they knew from what Bremmer's sister had said that he usually closed up at five-thirty, so very likely it had been around that time, and the avenger—whoever—had just walked quietly out and shut the door behind him, and nobody had tried it until the squad-car man did.

Obvious. But it didn't take them very far.

"How could there be a link?" asked Hackett reasonably. "Bremmer and Jamison?"

"There doesn't have to be a link except for X," Mendoza pointed out. "Say he had a grudge against both of them and suddenly decided to pay it off." But he sounded uneasy even to himself.

"I can't say I like that much," said Hackett. He shifted his big bulk from one foot to the other, there beside the smaller

Mendoza. "What kind of fellow might know both Jamison and Bremmer? We know what the newsstand fellow said. Bremmer one of those all-for-routine, set-your-clock-by-him old-maid bachelors. Quiet, dull, fussy, lived alone till this older sister came from back East to live with him. Same routine day in day out. Off to Mass every Sunday regular, come home and have Sunday dinner and read the papers. And Jamison, Luis. *Jamison.* The ne'er-do-well drifter, despite the money—the rich bum—with a pedigree?"

"All right," said Mendoza. "Damn it. X thought Bremmer had cheated him, and then he had a fight with Jamison in a bar."

"Oh, now, Luis," said Hackett. "Enough for this vengeance bit. It's crazy. What have you got on Jamison yet? Known associates and so on?"

"I don't know. I passed on a request to Records last night. There's nothing more to do here," and Mendoza sounded annoyed. "Let's go back and see what Records can say, and then see the sister. Not, I suppose, that she can tell us much."

"Don't know. D'you suppose his books would turn up anything? A dissatisfied customer or—"

"Oh, for God's sake, Art! Let's keep our heads here," said Mendoza. "Vengeance, for—well, all we can do is look." But he cast another annoyed glance around the little snob-appeal shop as they went out. He didn't really expect Marx and Horder would find any useful prints.

They drove back to headquarters. Records had been prompt. Records usually was. This was a very coldly efficient force; but sometimes on the anonymous ones that really didn't matter. The best cop in the world can't make bricks without straw, and if Records didn't have anything to give them they started from scratch.

However, this was something concrete: the known record of Nelson Edward Jamison. They looked at it.

Caucasian male, twenty-three when first picked up, and

the record started in 1951. Which made him thirty-eight now. Five ten-and-a-half, one hundred sixty, etc., etc. Picked up on complaint of a woman that he'd raped her on the street, outside her apartment building, late one evening. Positive identification. He'd come to trial on that, but been acquitted (Mama paying a smart lawyer? very probably). He'd been picked up again a year later on a similar charge; that girl had dated him and (read between the lines) nearly got herself raped. But she wouldn't make a formal charge, so that was that. He had served his first and only term beginning a year later, when another assault-with-intent stuck: on another woman. He'd got a one-to-three and been paroled only eleven years back, so he'd served nearly his full term, which said he wasn't a model prisoner.

"Weedy fellow, rabbity sort of face," said Hackett to the official mug shots. "Does it figure he went in for rape?"

"Not necessarily. Other types do too," said Mendoza cynically.

Naturally, after that, Jamison had probably been dropped on for questioning in any local assault or rape that came along—that would be just routine—but there were no further serious charges on him. Still, there was something there: the woman he'd been charged with assaulting and got sentenced for. If he had been X there, which the evidence said he was, he could have also been X on the other case they hadn't made stick. And someone could have harbored resentment.

"For nearly fifteen years?" said Hackett to that. "*¡Pues hombre!* And what about Bremmer?"

"How do I know what about Bremmer? Let's go and ask. This is all up in the air," complained Mendoza, getting up. Jason Grace and Palliser were sharing Sunday duty with Hackett; Mendoza looked into the sergeants' office. "Suppose you two go and see whether you can talk to Mrs. Jamison." There'd been quite a little fuss about that last night—un-

27

derstandably. Madge Hooper had refused to wake up the old lady to have her told about Jamison until her doctor was standing by; and expectedly, she'd thrown a fit and gone into hysterics and been tenderly removed to hospital. Saturday had been Madge Hooper's day off but she'd told them Jamison had been there when she left the house at 10 A.M., so they wanted to know when his mother had last seen him and whether he'd said where he was going. And whether he was driving his car. Madge Hooper said he had a two-door Corvair and it wasn't in the garage, so he probably had been; they were awaiting the plate number from Sacramento.

"A part-time pro and *Bremmer*," said Hackett. "It's crazy, Luis. What connection?"

"Unless," said Mendoza, "it's a real lunatic, Art. Which it could be. Just out to take vengeance on anybody he thinks is wicked. By whatever tortuous reasoning."

"Oh, my God, yes. It could be, all right." Hackett looked dismayed. "All the kooks in a big town—God knows it could be. And if it is—"

"If it is, the chances are on our side. The lunatics aren't very smart. I'll tell you one thing," said Mendoza, thrusting the key into the ignition of the Ferrari, "we're soft-pedaling this to the press until we know more about it. *Dios*, yes. Two within twenty-four hours—and the vengeance bit looking at least slightly lunatic—can you imagine the headlines? *Avenger Stalks City—Who Will Be Next?*"

Hackett shut his eyes. "If he goes on like this it'll come out regardless."

"There's a saying," said Mendoza, "about not crossing bridges, Arturo."

"There wouldn't be anybody like that," said Alice Bremmer. She faced them quietly, a commonsensible woman with her feet on the ground, and her grief held decently in control, except that she fingered a silver rosary in her lap. She

28

was a big spare woman, with short gray hair neat and waved, a pleasant round face, faded blue eyes behind rimless glasses. She was properly dressed in a navy-blue shirtmaker dress, with service-weight stockings and plain navy pumps. "Enemies?" she said. "Will wouldn't have had any *enemies,* for goodness sake. People like us don't—ordinary people. He'd had his little shop there for nearly twenty years, started it on what Father left him. Before that he worked as a book-keeper, for a big chain of markets. He always wanted his own little shop of some kind. He came out to California over thirty years ago—we're from Minneapolis originally—they told him his throat trouble would be better in this climate. And it seemed foolish for me to go on living alone back there —there was just the two of us—when I retired from my job. I was in the library. I'm nearly ten years older than Will. So I came out to live with him."

It was a modest little house on Cole Avenue in Hollywood. The street was apartment-zoned and now was about half-and-half, brash new apartment buildings and small single houses, all well maintained. A very ordinary living room, this was: very neat and clean. Plain beige carpet, good, slightly old-fashioned furniture, innocuous framed flower prints and one larger religious picture.

"Miss Bremmer—"

"Why, how could anyone have any reason at all to want to harm Will?" she said suddenly. The rosary moved under her fingers. "Will—Will was a good man. He tried to live his religion, Lieutenant—did you say 'Lieutenant'? He wasn't grasping or mean or selfish in any way. He was pleased the shop did well enough—he had a lot coming in down there, the stockbrokers and lawyers and businessmen like that with offices around there, you see. But he never overcharged, and it's not as if he got rich from it. We were comfortable enough, with my pension, but that's all. And—"

"Have you ever heard your brother mention the name of Jamison?"

She deliberated. "No, I can't say I ever have. I knew a Mrs. Jamison in Minneapolis, she came to the library regularly. But that wouldn't be what you mean. No, I didn't, why?"

Neither Mendoza nor Hackett enlightened her.

"Do you remember your brother ever mentioning any trouble at his shop?—with a dissatisfied customer, an argument over prices or—?" Hackett shot Mendoza a sardonic look; but you had to ask. She was shaking her head.

"I said he didn't overcharge. He was a good man, a quiet man. I suppose," said Alice Bremmer equably, "a lot of people would say we were dull folk. Set in our ways. But that's how we are—were. Will was up at seven sharp every day, and we'd have breakfast at seven-thirty, and he'd be off on the stroke of eight. He never drove a car, you know—he had tunnel vision, as they call it, and couldn't get a license. So he took the bus downtown. I sold my car when I came out here, Will said there were markets and so on close, it didn't seem worth the—so he took the bus, as I say, and opened the shop at nine sharp, closed at five-thirty, and he'd be home about six-thirty. He'd never been late all the time I've been living with him, and that's nearly two years. We don't have too many friends—acquaintances. We both like to read. I'll be up to the market or the drugstore most days, and once a week down to the library, but I don't suppose we had anybody coming in once in a blue moon. Quiet. And you could always set your clock by Will. He'd never been late before. So I called the police—the station here. Wilcox Street. And they couldn't seem to understand just how unusual it was, for Will. I lay awake worrying, but—I don't know—I suppose it didn't occur to me sooner because Will's always been so well, apart from his little throat trouble, but after a while I did think—a heart attack or—so first thing in the morning I called the downtown police—"

30

"Yes." Mendoza regarded her in absent irritation. Ordinary people, she said. Eminently. Staid, solid, substantial citizens. William Bremmer not at all likely ever to have known one like Jamison personally. So where did that take them? Somebody with a grudge, real or imaginary, against both Bremmer and Jamison? And Bremmer had been killed first.

Vengeance, for God's sake . . . He told Miss Bremmer they would if necessary get a warrant, but they'd like to look here and at the shop—at all Bremmer's possessions. Just in case.

"Surely," she said. "Anything you need to do—that might help you. It wouldn't have been anyone Will knew, or anything he'd ever done. He was a good man, no one would have a reason to—do a thing like that. It must have been some crazy person, just not knowing what he was doing. I've just got to accept it was God's will. Whatever you want to do—"

They looked, and there was just nothing. At the house or the shop. A mass of confused prints, none clear, in the shop: naturally. The stock on hand quite undisturbed; look at his books; check it out, but provisionally there didn't seem to have been anything taken. Nothing personal at the shop except a little electric hot-plate in the stockroom where he'd brewed instant coffee. The sister told them he'd taken a sandwich from home, for lunch. Frugal, careful Mr. Bremmer. Bound volumes of a religious magazine, at the house; a lot of old books; his few neat, clean clothes, nothing at all significant in pockets or drawers. Nothing to say that William Bremmer had been anything but the quiet, respectable, rather dull little shopkeeper, living by precise routine. And unfortunately, the Homicide Bureau couldn't accept the same answer as Alice Bremmer—just God's will. They'd like something a little more definite.

They didn't get it. There or elsewhere.

31

Mendoza and Hackett got back to the office at ten to four to meet Grace and Palliser just coming in.

"Did you talk to her?"

"Poor silly fool of a woman," said John Palliser. He sat down, loosening his tie, his long dark humorous face looking serious for once. Palliser had been through a rough time recently: his mother's long illness, all the doctor bills, and then her sudden death; but he was looking a little happier these days. He had a vacation coming up at the end of next month, and Mendoza suspected he meant to make it a honeymoon with his schoolteacher Roberta Silverman. Alison said she was a nice girl . . . "I had a look at his record. She ought to be heaving a sigh of relief to be rid of him. Useless, dangerous sort of guy. Chancy, you never knew what he'd do. Yes, they let us talk to her. We listened to a lot of guff."

"Mother love," said Jason Grace softly, "is apt to be a lot blinder even than other kinds. No question, it does make trouble for us."

Mendoza laughed shortly. "Say it again. So?"

"So," said Palliser, "what we got after the guff is N.G. No use at all. She didn't know any of his friends. She never asked him questions, Nelson didn't like that. She didn't know where he went when he left the house. He left yesterday about four o'clock, driving, and that's all she knows. Oh, the clothes he was wearing, and that's it. We got a warrant and went all through the house. Nothing."

"*Absolutamente,*" said Grace. "That kind doesn't keep address books, Lieutenant. Or write letters, or get any. Fancy clothes, etcetera, and that's about it. Besides some more background, from the mother and the Hooper woman. Jamison'd been kicked out of various private schools up to age sixteen, and then Mama quit trying. Papa left a nice round sum in trust for him, works out at around ten grand a year income. So Nelson boy apparently just went his own way, with

Mama feeling grateful when he came home for awhile."

"*¡Mil rayos!*" said Mendoza. But a few minutes later the autopsy report on Jamison came up—Dr. Bainbridge wasn't a man to waste time—and that gave them a little something. Jamison had been drunk. Well beyond the legal count of incapability, by the percentage of alcohol in the blood. And they thought about that.

"He couldn't have traveled far under his own steam," said Hackett, absently lighting another cigarette. "And if he'd tried to drive, likely he'd have been tagged. So we go on a tour of the bars down there. Despite the money, maybe our Nelson had a taste for low company."

And that was the obvious thing to do, but Mendoza snorted. "And come up with some damned barfly he had an argument with? Who'd already, for God knows what reason, garroted Bremmer over on Spring?"

"Oh, don't be difficult, Luis," said Hackett. "You know as well as me it's usually the pretty crude thing. When you get it all laid out plain. We have to look in the indicated places."

Mendoza snorted again. "All up in the air—"

At six-fifteen a squad car called in; they'd just located Jamison's car. In a lot on San Pedro, no attendant there on Sunday, of course. Mendoza swore: all the tedious trouble of locating the attendant who'd been there on Saturday, and of course he wouldn't remember anything. The time, or Jamison, or whether he'd been alone. But as Hackett said, they had to look where they could.

The night crew was on then; he dispatched Galeano, Piggott, and Schenke to wander around all the bars within a six-block radius of the Plaza, with copies of Jamison's official mug shots.

And, marriage demanding some personal sacrifices, he went home, shaved for the second time, and took Alison—

33

elegant in topaz chiffon—out to the Mawsons' for dinner. Inevitably, Alison and the Mawsons talked painters' shop over dinner, and after dinner Mendoza grimly martyrized himself at bridge; the Mawsons were bridge players, and that was one card game he detested. But inevitably—there were people who maintained that Luis Mendoza had missed his vocation and should have been a cardsharp—he and Alison came out on top.

"My poor Luis," said Alison on the way home. "I don't really ask you to very often."

"Not really, *cara*."

"I never really expected to domesticate you all the way. You were a bachelor too long."

"Mmh," said Mendoza. "But what the hell *could* be the link? Between those two? Unless it is just the random lunatic. And that I don't think I buy, because—by the very little we've got—he's a little too canny. No prints on those damnfool cards"—that they knew now—"and the quick, sure garroting—very efficient way to kill anybody. No mess, no noise."

"Thugs," said Alison a little sleepily, sliding down against his shoulder.

"Well, your typical thug isn't given to—"

"No, no. *Thugs*. In India. You know. Sacrifices to the goddess Kali. There was—speaking of contemporary literature —a very good novel about it, by John Masters. I can't think of the title—*Nightrunners of Bengal*, was it? No, *The Deceivers* . . . That," said Alison, "was their exact m.o. Catching the victims from behind with a scarf weighted at one end. So it just flipped around the victim's neck and the thug caught the other end as it came back, and crossed ends and yanked."

"Oh," said Mendoza. "Is that so? *¿Verdad?*"

"Well, it seemed to be awfully well researched," said Ali-

34

son. "I suppose so. It was a good book. And it is so, isn't it, that sudden quick pressure on the carotid artery—"

"Oh, yes," said Mendoza. "Very efficient m.o. you can say indeed. Death within seconds, literally." And that had been in the one autopsy report they'd seen, too: probably death had been very nearly instantaneous. "Which does also not look like the lunatic. I'll tell you," he added suddenly, "what worries me about it—belatedly it just came to me—it looks planned. Organized. And occasionally the lunatics do, but not very often."

"Funny," said Alison through a yawn. "Funny-peculiar. You mean somebody must have had a motive—even if it's an offbeat one—on both Jamison and Bremmer. Very funny."

"That you can say again."

They had a break to begin with, because it had started over a weekend. A break where the press was concerned. Because the Sunday editions had been already made up, of course, and no real late news got into print until Monday. And a drunk found dead in the Plaza, and a shopkeeper some distance away who might have been held up and killed in the course of robbery—Homicide wasn't handing out much to the press—weren't important enough to get mentioned in the news broadcasts.

And Mendoza said, "If the damn press gets one whisper about those file cards—start a panic. Play it down, with both of them. An ex-con—an honest shopkeeper. Talk to the press about crime statistics and let it go at that."

Which was only sensible, until they had some glimmering of just what this was all about. If they ever did.

So the press wasn't, by Monday, raising a fuss. The press didn't mention Nelson Jamison at all; and William Bremmer got only a short paragraph. There was a lot of international news to report.

35

But on Sunday afternoon, the Wilcox Street precinct had got a call from a Mrs. Bernice Stewart, who'd seen that paragraph in the *Herald* about Central's still unidentified corpse, and Mrs. Stewart was afraid it just could be her great-uncle, one Robert Holland, by the description. So Sergeant Hawkins of the Wilcox Street station escorted Mrs. Stewart down to the morgue to look at the corpse. It wasn't Mrs. Stewart's great-uncle, but after Sergeant Hawkins had turned Mrs. Stewart over to a policewoman to be revived and soothed, he happened to run into Glasser, who'd come down to the morgue with a possible relative of the girl suicide—the city was under enough expense, they did like funerals to get paid for—and he and Glasser had been at the Academy together, so they went for coffee and chatted desultorily. And Glasser of course said something about Central's vengeance seeker, who had picked two such divergent victims.

And the upshot of that was, police officers naturally talking shop as much as practitioners of any other trade, that Hawkins passed along Central's latest news when he returned to Wilcox Street. And at 11:34 on Monday night the outside phone rang on Sergeant Farrell's desk and he picked it up.

"Homicide, Sergeant Farrell."

"This is Sergeant O'Conner, Wilcox Street," said a heavy voice in his ear. "One of my men was telling me something about one of your current cases—well, we've just got a thing that'll maybe interest your office, Sergeant. By what Hawkins said. About a couple of homicides down on your beat—funny little cards left about vengeance. Hah? Something kind of offbeat, I gathered. A nut or something. You know what I'm talking about?"

"Vengeance—" said Farrell. "Yeah, what've you got?"

"Well, a thing. A very funny kind of thing, Sergeant. I just thought somebody down your way might be interested, because if what I heard from Hawkins is gospel, it might tie up to your business, and we are all the same force after all, and God knows we get kept busy enough up here, and if it *is* your business—"

Three

By one o'clock they had the routine going up on Valley Oak Drive in the Hollywood hills, and Mendoza and Galeano were down at the Wilcox Street station with Sergeant O'Connor and the deceased's husband—Earl Varick. This killer was their boy all right, the same joker who'd taken off Jamison and Bremmer, so O'Connor was sitting back and letting Mendoza handle it.

Farrell had called Mendoza at home, and chased Galeano up to meet him at the Valley Oak address; and by the time Galeano got there he'd had a bright idea.

"So now a woman," he'd said as Mendoza got out of the Ferrari at the curb. "Look, I just had an idea. X being clever, see? The husband wants her out of the way, so he sets up like a series killing, and we never think about him. Picks the first two just at random, and maybe'll go on to do a couple more. I just thought—"

"*Dios mío*, you've been reading old mystery stories," said Mendoza. "Let's not reach, Nick."

In any event, that remote possibility got ruled out fairly soon. Mendoza called downtown for the mobile-lab truck, and that came and spotlights were set up, and they got a preliminary report from the interns with the ambulance, and now they were hearing what Varick had to say, back at Wilcox Street. Up in the old, drafty, discouraged-looking detective-squad room upstairs. The city fathers had built that fine new Police Facilities Building, Headquarters, downtown, and then shut the purse. The Wilcox Street house hadn't even been painted in years.

The husband was being good and quiet. He'd had a bad shock, and he wasn't a young man, pushing sixty, but he was a businesslike man and in control of himself, and the doctor had given him a shot. He said he wanted to talk to them, tell them anything he could. He could only think, he said, it must have been some kind of lunatic—with nothing stolen—because who'd have a reason to kill Edith? Mendoza started out asking gentle questions, concealing his impatience, letting Varick ramble a little. You never knew what might come out.

Varick gave them statistics readily. Edith Warren Varick, fifty-one, she'd been—"though she didn't look it"—no, no children, that was, he had a married son but—"We'd only been married six months, Edith and I. She lost her first husband many years ago, when she was only about thirty, I think, and she'd worked all her life. I can't get over it—it seems so damned *unfair*—only six months, and she was always saying what a luxury it was to her not to have to work—at the regular job, I mean. You know. She enjoyed fussing around the house so much—she'd been fixing it up, I'd been a widower since Brian was in high school, I'd kind of let things slide. And Brian and Margaret liked her so much—not *fair*. God, if I hadn't been out at that damned meeting—" Varick was a big florid-faced fellow, nearly bald, with a forthright gaze, but his face was drawn and his eyes bloodshot now. It had been a realtors' meeting: something to do with deciding jointly about a re-zoning matter. Varick owned his obviously prosperous realty company. He had left the house at seven-thirty. "It must have been getting on for a quarter to eleven, around there, when I got home—"

39

"Call was clocked at five to," commented O'Connor in the background.

"—and I drove into the garage as usual, and started for the back door. And I knew it'd be locked, we were both most careful about all the doors being locked after dark—the things that happen, and—" Varick passed a hand over his forehead. "That was the first—first thing that alarmed me, because the door was open. Unlocked, I mean. And I went in, and called Edith—yes, the kitchen light was on, the outside lights too but I expected that, she'd put the driveway flood-lights on for me, coming home—and she didn't answer, so then I looked around and finally—finally stepped outside again and that was when I—"

Edith Varick had been lying dead, garroted, a few feet to the right of the service-porch door, half-concealed behind a flowering shrub there. Not concealed by design, they thought. It was also pretty clear what had happened here. "Was your wife a timid woman, Mr. Varick?"

"T-Timid? Oh, no, not at all. She'd lived alone for so long, she was—she was very self-reliant," said Varick. "Used to—managing for herself. Not at all fearful or anything like that. And of course it's a quiet, nice part of town, we don't as a rule get much crime, but the way things are nowadays—"

So. Mendoza exchanged a glance with Galeano. They'd also heard, before, that Mrs. Varick knew approximately what time her husband would be home, and in the interests of thrift wouldn't have turned on the outside floodlights until a quarter of an hour or so before she expected him. And the intern had said, at about eleven-thirty, that she'd been at least two hours dead. Say nine o'clock. So Varick had an alibi—he'd been at the realtors' meeting. Check it out, but that was ninety-nine per cent sure. So it looked as if she'd heard some suspicious noise at the back of the house, a noise deliberate, or been otherwise enticed into opening the back door. There was a rear bell there. And somehow been lured

40

into taking a step or so from the rear threshold, and been neatly taken from behind—even as the drunken Jamison and the sober Bremmer.

She'd been wearing a very charming green brocade house-coat with a loose tie at the neckline, and the little file card with its cryptic message had been securely fixed in the knot of the tie. It looked exactly like the other two. This one might bear Varick's prints.

"I couldn't imagine—when I saw it, that was after I called you, I picked it up, I couldn't *imagine*—" He shook his head. "Vengeance? Somebody—vengeance on Edith? Edith never harmed anyone in her life! It isn't fair—when I think how happy we'd been, and her enjoying the house so much, and not having to go to work—she said it was like a dream, not having regular hours. All her life—and she'd held good jobs, earned a good salary, she was a legal secretary, went to night school and all to start with, years ago—and she was a good one too, she was efficient at everything—everything she put her hand to. She was with this one lawyer for a long time—I can't remember his name—" In his present state, Varick was troubled about this; he beat one palm gently on his forehead. "Mayse? Moses? Marshall?—I don't remember, it's silly but I just can't—she liked him, and then after he died she got a very good job with a firm of corporation lawyers, she'd been with them for a couple of years—that was how I met her, one of the partners, Fred Harkness, is an old school friend of mine—and, well, we just seemed to hit it off, I hadn't thought about marrying again, but Edith—well, we just—she was a very good-looking woman," said Varick painfully. "You wouldn't take her for fifty-one at all. Of course a—a business-woman, she has to keep herself smartened up as they say, but even so—"

"Yes, Mr. Varick," said Mendoza. She had been. They'd seen the photograph in the living room of the newly refurbished house in the hills: a snapshot, blown up, which had probably been taken on their recent wedding day: both of them dressed up, smiling and happy. Edith Warren Varick hadn't looked her age: a woman with a very nice figure, a smallish woman who'd once been very pretty indeed, and was still attractive, with a quick friendly smile, good teeth, large blue eyes, pepper-and-salt hair in a crisp brief cut.

"Mr. Varick, did your wife know anyone named Jamison? . . . Or Bremmer?"

He shook his head dumbly. "I don't think so, I don't remember ever hearing those—you could look in her address book, but I don't think—"

"Had she had any kind of—trouble at all, recently? Anything, such as a little argument with someone at the door, or even one of her friends, or—"

He was shaking his head again. "No, nothing—nothing like that. I'd have heard. Edith would have said. She didn't —didn't *have* arguments—she was a—a friendly, outgoing person. That—that thing, *vengeance*. I can't understand it. It just doesn't make sense."

They didn't tell him it didn't make much sense to them, either. Edith Varick just compounded the mystery. A quiet, respectable, middle-aged woman, recently and happily remarried. What possible connection to Jamison and Bremmer? Of course, the inference to be cautiously drawn—or was it?—was that X knew all three but they didn't know each other. Or was X choosing at random?

They gave Varick a cup of coffee and drifted over to the other side of the big room to kick it around a little. O'Connor said, "As far as I'm concerned, Lieutenant, you're welcome to this one. I'm not even having any guesses about it. Vengeance, for God's sake."

"He'll need his crystal ball all right," said Galeano.

"I only wish to God I had one," said Mendoza. "*Caray*, what the hell is this all about? Vengeance. I'll tell you what

42

Edith says to me, at least. It's not the random deal. He's picking them deliberately. I won't go so far as to guess why."

"And what says that?" asked Galeano.

"Well, we have to go by probabilities, ¿cómo no? All right. Jamison doesn't seem to have been a lush. Tied one on now and then, maybe, but not regularly. But he was drunk when he was killed. Did X get him that way purposely? So he'd be able to steer him up to that nice dark spot? It could be. And then look how he probably walked into Bremmer's shop just about at closing time, so he'd be pretty sure of being the last customer. Went on asking for this and that until he hit on something Bremmer had to go to the back room to get. But Edith Varick—even more so, Nick. That's a fairly big house, a family house—how did he know she was alone, unless he'd been stalking her deliberately? And—"

Galeano lit a cigarette. "I don't say I'm as smart as our star lieutenant, but I can't buy that one. I've worked with you long enough to know exactly why you'd like to think so"—he flashed his wide white grin at Mendoza—"but having a wide streak of peasant caution in me, I don't buy it. Say it's the nut, just the nut with an urge to kill people. Maybe with some nutty notion in his head that almost anybody he looks at is to blame for his being out of a job, or an orphan, or his wife leaving him, or like that. All right. He goes into Bremmer's shop to buy a pack of cigarettes—Bremmer had all the ordinary brands as well as the fancy ones—and he gets the urge. He pays Bremmer, and Bremmer thinks, well, that's the last sale of the day, and taking it for granted the nut is walking out he turns into the back room to collect, say, his lunchbox or his jacket before closing up. Nut follows him on tiptoe, *kaput*. And a while later that night the nut happens to be in the bar where Jamison is for once getting tanked up. He gets the urge again. He follows Jamison out, maybe makes up to him all cunning or maybe just follows him up to the Plaza, Jamison just wandering around the way a drunk

43

will. *Kaput* again. And the next time he gets the urge he just happens to be up on Valley Oak Drive and maybe sees Edith Varick through a window. Rings the rear bell, she comes to see who's there, *kaput.*"

"*Vaya historia*," said Mendoza mildly. "And why am I reading any continuity into it, *amigo?*"

"Because," said Galeano, "you've got such a damn strong sense of order. Just constitutionally you don't want to admit that a thing, or a series of things, can be meaningless. And I wish to God I could buy your continuity, because if there was any connecting link, any halfway plausible motive, any *order* to the thing, it'd make it easier to find out about. A little. Probably."

"Could it be," said O'Connor diffidently—he was a clerkly-looking man in the forties, and had obviously heard about Mendoza's reputation—"that these people were somehow tied up together in the past? I'm just thinking off the top of my mind, you understand, but could it be they were once— oh, involved in an accident together, or something like that?"

"Well, it's an idea," said Mendoza with a shrug. "But how that would start off a series of killings—" Nelson Jamison, he thought. William Bremmer. Edith Varick. They had nothing whatever in common that he could see. "And that being so," he added abstractedly, "I suppose we go looking—provisionally—for the lunatic." Query all the asylums, public and private: and that wouldn't make a dent. The double talk from all the head doctors. Have a look at their own records for all the known psychos. Look at the psychos. And probably come up with nothing, after a lot of heartbreaking routine. And if it was just a nut, this might be his first excursion into nuthood, so to speak, and he wouldn't be on file anywhere.

On second thought, had the victims anything at all in common? Jamison thirty-eight. Bremmer sixty-two. Edith

44

Varick fifty-one. Jamison certainly with no religion. Bremmer a Catholic.

Hell. He went back to Varick. "We won't keep you any longer, Mr. Varick. We're sorry to have—"

"It's all right. I just want you to find *out*," said Varick painfully. "Who. I want to help you however I can."

"Yes, sir. Did your wife attend any church regularly? . . . She didn't. Well. We'll want her address book, please. Can you tell me who her closest friends were?"

"Oh—I suppose I'd say Sarah Walker. Mrs. Walker. They'd worked together once. And Mary Canning, and a Myra Faulkner—I'd never met her—we had the Walkers to dinner—"

"All right, thanks very much, Mr. Varick. We'll have a car take you home—or to your son's?" Mendoza jerked his head at O'Connor, who nodded and went out.

"I'd better not—disturb them so late," said Varick. "The baby's been a little sick, and—thank you. You've been very —well, anything I can do—thank you." He went out stiffly.

There were things to do, but they couldn't get started until morning. Mendoza and Galeano were about to leave when the lab team reported in, expecting them to be still at the precinct. They hadn't turned up much. Only one thing of significance.

The rear yard of the Varick house was very meticulously kept up: a random-paved walk from the drive to the back door, a semicircle of lawn, bordered flower beds. And on that paved walk, about ten feet to the left of the service-porch door, the lab men had found an old tin can that had once held stewed tomatoes. They'd printed it: nothing useful.

And that showed Mendoza more of the picture. Mrs. Varick wouldn't have left that can there . . . "He rang the rear bell, and when she came, turned on the outside lights and unlocked the door, he tossed the tin can up onto the walk from where he was standing—behind that shrub. And she stepped out to investigate the noise—not a timid woman—and he caught her from behind."

"Yes," said Galeano. "I see that."

"And damn it, Nick, you can talk about the nut picking them by chance all you like—I'm still laying money they're picked because of who they are. Why, don't ask me."

"The orderly mind," said Galeano. "You're just wishful-thinking. Me, I'm just praying the press doesn't get hold of it."

The press hadn't, up to next day. Homicide was playing this one close to the chest.

They started, on Tuesday morning, the checkout of all known psychos, all recently released mental patients. It was very smoggy on Tuesday, with, as the newscasters politely termed it, Heavy Eye-Irritation. The men working outside the office cursed the smog, and those who could stay inside on the phones blessed the efficient ventilating system.

They had, on Monday, talked to the lot attendant at the parking lot where Jamison's car had been left. He didn't remember who had left it or at what time. He'd just noticed it was there when he locked up at six; and hell, he said, there was a sign, lot chained at 6 P.M., it was just the guy's hard luck if he hadn't noticed it.

Mendoza called Fletcher down in Traffic and asked whether the Old Plaza was a regular haunt of neckers. It wasn't. Too open really, said Fletcher. On hot summer nights people sitting there till all hours, just sitting. Or feeding the pigeons.

The further look around the Plaza, by daylight, had turned up nothing connectable to Jamison—or anyone else—at all.

The autopsy report on Bremmer came in on Tuesday, and told them nothing. He'd been garroted by a thin cord of some kind, possibly but less likely a piece of wire; he had

46

died within a minute or so of the attack. Time of death between 5 and 6 P.M. on Saturday.

The experts had been poring over the file cards all for nothing too. All they could say was that they were ordinary three-by-five file cards, available at any dime store for fifteen cents a pack; and the cryptic message had been printed with an ordinary ball-point pen which might have been one of a variety of brands. If ever they got a hot suspect, the experts could probably give them some handwriting evidence, but that didn't look likely to be happening very soon.

Mendoza was annoyed. He had, as Galeano said, the orderly mind, and he hated this kind of frustration. Ordinarily the patient routine got you somewhere, because what they were generally dealing with was the fairly unintelligent pro criminal; but either the lunatic thing or the perfectly anonymous kill could frustrate them forever—good as they were at the job.

The vengeance is just. Whose? What kind? Why? All up in the air. And just let the damned press get hold of it—

Mendoza was as annoyed as he had ever felt. This was the funniest thing, in the funny-peculiar sense, that had come along since he'd been sitting at this desk. Well, there had been that Slasher thing—and that damned offbeat rapist who'd so nearly accounted for Alison—he still turned a little cold when he thought about that; but by and large—

If it was a lunatic, of course, nothing personal about the victims would be relevant.

Or would it? Just very occasionally you got the cunning lunatic who could make rational plans. Witness that rapist. But in a series of lunatic murders, there was generally a category which embraced all the victims. X was appointed by God to destroy all prostitutes, or Christian Scientists, or Republicans. Like that. And certainly you couldn't by any stretch of the imagination make Jamison, Bremmer, and Edith Varick fit into one category.

Mendoza smoothed his mustache absently and stared at the desk calendar without seeing it. *Thugs,* he thought irrelevantly.

Tuesday was George Higgins' day off. He had made, he thought, just a little progress with Mary Dwyer—he'd got her calling him by his first name now, as well as the two kids, Steve and Laura. She asked him to dinner once in a while. He figured, Mary being female, she knew well enough how he felt, but he didn't know at all how she felt about him, that way. George Higgins wasn't much of a prize, he thought; and she probably wouldn't want to start worrying about another cop. He still hadn't got up nerve to ask her to go out with him.

George Higgins, thirty-eight and never exactly backward with the females.

But this was Mary.

He'd noticed last week that the latch on the driveway gate was stiff at the old house on Silver Lake Boulevard she was still paying for: out of the pension, and what she made. He drove up there after breakfast, spent a while playing with Brucie the Scottie, and carefully oiled the latch.

At intervals he ruminated about their avenger. That was a very funny thing, all right. Three people. Vengeance.

But having great faith (without thinking much about it) in the efficiency and intelligence of this force, he figured they'd untangle all the funny business eventually.

Maybe, he thought, Luis would have one of his brain waves about it.

"There's just nothing to get hold of in it," said Hackett. He leaned over Angel's shoulder and confiscated one of the hot cookies she'd just transferred to the paper plate, and Angel slapped his hand.

"They're for my party tomorrow, you big lummox—hands off."

"Good," mumbled Hackett. "Just nothing at *all*. You couldn't pick three more different people if you deliberately went looking. Nothing in common, and they didn't know each other. But there's a kind of feeling about it—I think I'm with Luis, that it isn't just a nut. That there is *some* kind of planning behind it, however offbeat." He lifted the cover off the casserole on the back of the stove and sniffed.

"Um," said Angel thoughtfully. Hackett's pretty brown-haired Angel had come round of late to firm support of the powers of Lieutenant Mendoza of Homicide. "Does he think so? He's probably right. But it is a very peculiar thing, what you've told—Art, *no!* That's my very special saffron rice for the party, *not* for dinner—Swiss steak tonight, about fifteen minutes—and have you weighed today?"

"Well," said Hackett guiltily, "it was only a pound over. A hundred and ninety-six. And I think that doctor's unrealistic—after all, I am six-three-and-a-half."

"Yes, well," said Angel, "you'd better stick to just a little butter on the baked potato instead of sour cream. Oh, damn, there's the baby, just as I—"

"I'll see to her," said Hackett hastily, and fled with a wistful backward look at the casserole.

And Sergeant Farrell wondered whether the night would bring them number four with the avenger's little file card left with it. As did Mendoza, who went home and sounded off in frustration to Alison. "Not one damn thing to get hold of—"

"Oh, I can imagine all sorts of things," said Alison. "How many more do you suppose there are he thinks deserve vengeance? It could be—"

"Don't say things like that!" said Mendoza.

"—all the people," said Alison brightly, "who were maybe in a crowd together when there was a—a fire, and his poor

49

old mother got burned to death and he resents their being alive. Or—"

"You should be writing popular novels, *cara. ¡Claro que no!* How would he know who they all were? *Dios,* if the press—"

"Don't fuss. You'll crack it. Or he'll stop, and you can bury it in Pending."

"Which I do *not* like to—I need a drink," said Mendoza.

And nothing turned up overnight for Homicide, except a brawl in a bar with one man stabbed and another shot and on the critical list: a good many witnesses, and it would take some time to get all the statements and, hopefully, prod the fellow responsible into a voluntary confession. There was also another holdup job, over on Figueroa, another liquor store, the night clerk shot.

Galeano said when he came that it looked like a .22. Maybe the same .22 they knew had already accounted for the other liquor-store clerk? If so, or if not, they had a description on this one: the clerk had lived long enough to tell. Which was helpful.

But by the time the day crew came on and Sergeant Farrell, folding away his current crossword-puzzle book, went off duty, their avenger hadn't pulled off number four.

As far as they knew, at least.

Four

A<small>ND</small> considering William Bremmer and Edith Varick, Mendoza didn't think it would mean much, but on Wednesday morning he started out to find the women Jamison had been accused of assaulting.

Jason Grace and Higgins were looking for something a lot more definite—an elevator man. The liquor-store clerk had given Galeano a good description. And by ten o'clock that morning they heard from Ballistics that that .22 was the same .22 they wanted for the other liquor-store clerk, so they'd have a nice case if they could connect him up with the gun—provided they could find him by the description.

They were looking for a man between eighteen and twenty-two, a Negro, medium-dark, small mustache, about six feet, thin, with a Southern accent. The first thing they did, of course, was go down to Records to see if there was one like that on file. More likely several like that, in a place this size. So they'd go look at them, and any really likely one bring in to question—always being careful to tell them about their rights to an attorney, etcetera—and see if they couldn't come up with X.

That was the kind of ordinary, deadly, efficient routine that they all understood so well: the kind that broke cases, time after time.

The avenger was something else again.

Mendoza hadn't any difficulty in locating the woman Jamison had done time for. Mrs. Rose Anderson. She was still living at the same address. Her husband, who was a cab driver, was inclined to resent the cops turning up just to remind her of that guy—Anderson was home nursing a sprained ankle, and interrupted the questioning. "Guys like that oughta get the gas chamber, ask me! Nuts—all nuts. Going in for rape, by God. Like to scared her to death—"

"Fought him like a wildcat," said Mrs. Anderson complacently. "And he was strong, too. My, I still just hate to think about it! I was coming home from work, I guess you know— I was working then, it was before Linda was born—we got two now, Bobby came along couple o' years later—at the phone company downtown, and you get real crazy hours there, I was on three hours in the morning and then four in the evening, got out at nine-thirty. It's on Olive, you know, and I had to walk over to Spring to get the bus to Hollywood. I usually went down Seventh. And it was after nine-thirty, o' course, everything closed mostly and not many people around except up there waiting for the bus at the corner. Waiting in an alley there he was, along Seventh. Lurking. I suppose, for any lone woman who came along. And before I *knew*, he had me—" She shuddered.

"Just remind her of it," growled Anderson. "Stash the bastard away for three years, my God. So how many more has he attacked since they let him out?"

They were both voluble in assuring Mendoza that neither of them had laid eyes on Jamison since the trial, nor wanted to, why in God's name they should go looking him up—

They were also ordinary people; Mendoza couldn't see any reason why they should.

The girl who had refused to make a formal charge he couldn't find. She had moved; she wasn't in the phone book or the city directory, and nobody seemed to know much about her. But it struck Mendoza as a little significant that her last address, the one she gave when she complained to the police, was within two blocks of the Jamison house in Pasadena. Jamison was not a very attractive character; did she know about the money and agree to date him on that account, and then find out he was even less attractive than he appeared? Very likely.

The woman who had first accused Jamison of raping her— the charge he'd been acquitted on—lived up on Clayton Avenue in Hollywood. She was thirtyish now, a slow-spoken, shy-eyed woman, Miss Miriam Foster. She told Mendoza all about it, only a little embarrassed. "I was a good deal younger then," she said ruefully. "I was only eighteen. And I *knew* it was him, even at night—I'd got a good look at his face and, well, it wasn't one you'd forget, was it?—but the lawyer confused me, tripped me up when I was testifying, and they acquitted him. I was terribly bitter at the time, but—" she shrugged. "These things happen."

And she had not seen Nelson Jamison from that day to this. Nor cared to. She was unmarried, and lived with her widowed mother.

And that was that. And Mendoza hadn't expected anything else.

But as he got back into the Ferrari and sorted out keys, he had one small thought. If Nelson Jamison had raped, and assaulted with intent to rape three women, over a period of years, he had in all probability assaulted or attempted to assault or actually raped others. If a man was built like that, he didn't go in for it just three times in fifteen years. And it might seem peculiar, but any cop knew it was so—a lot of women who got raped never reported it. Ashamed. Shocked. Embarrassed at the idea of publicity. And there were on the books a sufficient number of reported rapes they'd never got anybody for.

Only, if that was so and conceivably somebody wanted

53

private vengeance on Jamison for that, where in God's name did Bremmer and Edith Varick tie in?

"*¡Diez millón demonios!*" said Mendoza to himself.

At about the same time, Hackett was just striking pay dirt, and feeling surprised. Piggott, on night tour, had been covering bars down here, in Central's territory, in search of Jamison, with as yet no luck; and Hackett had started out this morning, with Jamison's mug shots, only because for all they yet knew Jamison might have been a frequent caller somewhere around here. And just now Hackett had turned up a barman who reacted.

It was a bar on Alameda, designated on the sign simply as "Al's"; and the bartender was Al himself, a big stocky dark man with powerful shoulders. Al Kafka.

"*Kafka?*" said Hackett. Contemporary literature—

"That's me. So it's a funny name—I heard some a lot funnier, mister. So it's my name, I play like I'm something I ain't and maybe change it to Vere de Vere? Like hell. All right, it's a funny name. Lots of people got funny—"

"Oh, sure," said Hackett hastily. "I was just—well, never mind," and he pulled out the badge and the mug shots.

Al looked at both and said, "I got a lotta respect for you guys. You do a good job. Once in a while I get a customer makes trouble, you know—some guys they got no sense at all, they get tanked up and sometimes they start a fight or something, so I call you guys, and never yet have I had one o' you in here wasn't a nice, honest, polite guy."

"Well, thanks very much," said Hackett. "We like to hear that, Mr. Kafka. We try to do the job right."

"You do," said Al emphatically. "I try to run this place right too, but you know some people just ain't got no sense. And likely never will have." He wiped his hands carefully on his bar apron and took the mug shot, fullface and profile, in both hands. "Oh, him," he said.

"You know him? You've seen him in here?"

"Yeah. Yeah, I have, and I don't particular want to see him again," said Al.

"You won't. He's dead."

"Dead, is he?" Al regarded the shots again and handed the print back to Hackett. The bar was a small one, and at this hour in the day only just open; there wasn't a customer in the place. "I know you won't take it, Sergeant, but I got to feel hospitable—you like a beer?" Hackett declined politely. "There, you see, all you guys got what they call integrity. That's what I mean. That's important. Especially dealing with the types you get down here. No, I don't know who this guy is—was—but, reason I say I didn't so damn well like him comin' in is a couple of fellows was with him sometimes when he come in. Who I do know, if you get me. And one of 'em is a fag, and the other's got a record some kind, I got that from listenin', don't know what kind, but guys like that I don't need comin' in to my place. Especially the fags," said Al with a grimace.

"Know their names?" Hackett took out his notebook.

"I do. The fag is Benny Ackerman, lives somewhere around, I think. The other one's name is Valdez, they call him Speedy."

"O.K., when was the last time you saw Jamison—this one —in here?"

"Saturday," said Al promptly. "Saturday afternoon he come in. I wouldn't be able to tell you, Sergeant, but I'd got in a bind. I don't, general rule, tend bar after five, see. Got a night barkeep. I go home, relax. But like they say, God moves mysterious-like. Bob, he's in the hospital. Saturday morning. This appendicitis—emergency, they cut him open for it. I can't get anybody on short notice—that I'd trust, that is. And it's Saturday night, I'm going to miss the Saturday night trade for a couple of TV programs? Like hell. I was here when that guy came and I was here when he left."

55

"What times?"

"He come in first about four-forty," said Al. "He was alone, yes. Two reasons I noticed him, every time he come. His fancy clothes—always all dressed up he was—and he wasn't—" Al paused. "You never knew about him."

"How d'you mean?"

"Most guys, you know about. They're regulars, they drop in for a beer or two after work. Or some just sit around talkin', over four, five beers, couple of hours after dinner at home. And a few regulars I got like any barkeep, who are the lushes. If you get me. Damn fools. Just pour it down as long as they got any money, till they pass out and I call you guys. Or in one case," said Al dispassionately, "this lush whose wife I feel sorry for, I call her brother and he comes haul him away."

"Yes," said Hackett, "but—"

"That one, you never knew," said Al. "Jamison, you say his name was? A real odd one, with his fancy clothes. Most of the time when he come in—which was not very often, maybe twice a month—whether he was alone, or with one of these other guys, he didn't do much serious drinkin'. Nurse along a couple of beers. And then again he'd come in—this would be maybe once out of six times—and really tie one on. You just never knew, see?"

"Yes, funny," said Hackett. "Did he ever pass out on you?"

"Not him. Always got away under his own power, though a few times one of his pals was helpin' him . . . He come in about four-forty, yes, sir, alone, and he stayed until around six, and then he went out—he'd had a couple o' beers—and then he come back again about nine, and that time he started on Scotch. Alone, yes. Now wait a minute, I was busy —Saturday night—but I kind of think that fag was sittin' with him later on. Yeah, I think so. I remember watching him —the other guy I mean—to see if he was about to pass out, in which case I would call you guys. They're a very nice couple

56

o' guys on this tour daytimes—don't know the night fellows so well, but the ones on days are good guys. O'Neill and Rodriguez, you know 'em? But he didn't, he got away on his own two legs."

"Alone?" asked Hackett eagerly.

Al thought. "Yeah," he said. "Yeah. I think—I'm pretty sure—the fag left a while before. He never has more than one beer anyway. Yeah, this Jamison was alone."

"So," said Hackett, "first, did anybody leave right after Jamison? And what time was that? And second, was there anybody here that night you didn't know, a stranger?"

Al brought out a short black cigar, sniffed it thoughtfully, offered another to Hackett, and lit it. "I would like to oblige you, Sergeant," he said regretfully. "I got a respect for you guys. But it was Saturday night, Sergeant, and I was tendin' bar alone in here. There's usually at least a couple of strangers drop in, this ain't too far from the station, you know. There was some that night. But when they came or went, or if one of 'em—or anybody—left just after this Jamison, I couldn't tell you, Sergeant. I was busy. I was only keepin' an eye on your boy to see he didn't pass out on me. I'm sorry, Sergeant."

"Hell!" said Hackett. "What time did he leave?"

"Some time after ten. Closer to after ten-thirty, I'd say."

"Hell!" said Hackett again. "If somebody from here did follow him out, Mr. Kafka, the chances are he's the one killed him—"

"Oh, he got took off, did he? Well, no loss," said Al. "I am sorry, Sergeant, but—" he shrugged.

And Jamison no loss, no, but what about Bremmer and Edith Varick?

Hackett and Mendoza landed back at the headquarters office separately just as Grace and Higgins came in towing a tall, thin Negro about twenty. He was eyeing Grace sullenly, and as they came to the door of the interrogation room past Mendoza's office, he balked and said resentfully, "I 'on't talk t'*you*. Fuzz, you got no call be fuzz. I 'on't tell you time o' day. Him, I got t', O.K."

"Well, well," said Grace. He sounded amused, a little sad, and not at all annoyed.

Higgins just looked annoyed. He waggled a finger at Hackett. "You like to oblige, Art?"

"Right with you," said Hackett, and followed him and the suspect into the interrogation room. Grace lit a cigarette.

"It's a waste of time getting mad about it, Jase," said Mendoza dryly.

"Oh, I know, I know, Lieutenant. It's also a waste of time," said Grace wryly, "looking at the entire matter from any viewpoint except that of just people. You take any cross-section of people anywhere, black, white, green, or yellow, and you're going to find smart and stupid and in-between, honest and dishonest, good, bad, and indifferent, which is only another way of talking about human nature. And the good Lord knows"—he grinned at Mendoza—"there are a lot of Garcias and Gonzaleses and Ruizes down in Records, hah, Lieutenant? But I will admit to you, that kind does annoy me and scare me a little bit. 'Whuh you doin', a cop?' he says to me. I shouldn't be a cop, on the side of the law, because I'm the color I am. A white cop he'll answer—if it will be like pulling teeth, and why should I mind getting out of the work?" Grace laughed shortly.

"No profit, Jase," said Mendoza. "There they are, the punks, damn what color they are. You aren't going to change them into angels overnight anyway, we just have to deal with them as they are."

"And, as I keep reminding myself," said Grace, "it does say, man He made a little lower than the angels. Some a hell of a lot lower, and damn the color again."

"You think he's X on the holdups?"

58

"Possible, maybe even probable. He fits the description. He's got a little pedigree, and he's been known to be violent. A little rough stuff. Never been known to pack a gun, but there's always a first time."

"So there is," said Mendoza, thinking about the avenger . . . Had his vengeance been accomplished? Three people. You could say, fast and furious. Bremmer and Jamison on Saturday; Edith Varick on Monday. And today was Wednesday. Well, he'd skipped Sunday. God, if there were more to come—

And what the hell else could they do on it, with nothing at all to get hold of, no possible leads—

Mendoza swore. "You like to turn your superior imagination loose on our vengeance seeker?"

Grace laughed. "I would not. Try your crystal ball. That is a queer one, all right."

They brought in four men to question, on Wednesday, who conformed to the description they'd got from the liquor-store clerk. Three of them had alibis of a sort, and the fourth one hadn't a gun and was very unlikely for that job anyway because he was mentally retarded. They had three more out of Records they were looking for.

They finally got the unknown corpse identified, on Wednesday. A young Greyhound-bus driver who'd just landed back home after a cross-country haul came in and identified the man as his uncle, one Rodney Hershey, who'd lived alone and hadn't been missed. Couldn't say what Hershey might have been doing down on Second, he lived near Mac-Arthur Park, but that wasn't important.

And Mendoza went home, and set up a card table in front of the sectional and began to play with the deck, shuffling, practicing the crooked poker deals, sleight-of-hand, and chain-smoking; and Alison eyed him and left him alone. It was Mrs. MacTaggart's day to visit her sister; Alison busied herself getting the twins to bed, Miss Teresa demanding "Loch Lomond" and Master John Luis the "Ave Maria." Mrs. MacTaggart, of course, was a devout Catholic.

"I don't know it, darling," said Alison. Heavens, Luis would have a *fit* if he—"I'm sorry, *amante*, won't 'Annie Laurie' do as well?"

"No!" said Master John Luis firmly. "*Ora pro nobis.*"

"Oh, dear," said Alison, glancing apprehensively toward the living room down the hall.

"Pretty please, *mo croidhe?*" said Master John coaxingly.

"*Por favor,*" said Miss Teresa, "Lomond. Bonnie."

Alison burst out laughing. "Well, we try to do our best for you, you terrors, but by the time you're ready for school heaven only knows what kind of English you'll be talking!"

She got them settled at last and went back to the living room. Mendoza, minus jacket and tie, with his hair up on end where he'd been running fingers through it, and at this time of day needing a shave, looked the prototype of the tough gambler as he sat laying out the cards. He had got himself a small shot glass of rye and unaccountably forgotten to pour an ounce for El Señor, who was sitting at his feet complaining bitterly; Bast, Sheba, and Nefertite were coiled in a complicated tangle at the other end of the sectional. "You forgot El Señor," said Alison.

"*¡Cómo!* Queen of diamonds," said Mendoza, and turned it up from the stacked deck. "Ace of clubs. Deuce of spades . . . That cat ought to join Alcoholics Anonymous. It's disgraceful . . . King of hearts."

"Just a little doesn't hurt him, and he does enjoy it so," said Alison. She went out to the kitchen and brought back a saucer of rye whisky. Pleased, El Señor began to lap.

"Shorten his life by five years," said Mendoza balefully. "Damn it, there has got to be some *reason* in it! The vengeance bit. If you went deliberately looking to find three people with not one damn thing in common—" He slapped the deck together and began to shuffle it.

"Maybe you're just dragging your heels and it is a lunatic," said Alison inattentively, looking at her watch.

"I'll be damned if I—what the hell is that thing doing here?" demanded Mendoza, noticing the portable TV in the opposite corner for the first time as Alison went over to switch it on. "I refuse, *absolutamente*, to have the idiot-box—" There was a color TV in the den, where he never sat, because Alison liked to watch Disney on Sunday night.

"It went *phut*," said Alison. "The big one. And the repair people said they couldn't come until tomorrow. This is Máiri's portable. I just borrowed it to hear the news." She turned to Channel five.

"I *refuse*—all this madly slanted damn stuff—"

"Oh, this one isn't. Really. Hugh Brundage, he's very good. I just—heavens, my watch must be slow," said Alison as the image of a nice-looking gray-haired man flashed on.

Mendoza sighed loudly and devoted his attention to stacking a new deck. He always thought better with a deck of cards in his hands.

". . . brush-fires raging out of control," said the modulated voice, "in Mendocino Canyon. Volunteer fire fighters are being brought in by air. It is hoped that the fires will be under control within twelve hours . . . On the local scene, as all the twelfth-grade classes of the city schools prepare for graduation night . . ."

Mendoza listened in long-suffering silence. El Señor finished his rye, stalked over and slapped his mother across the nose. Bast gave him a forgiving look and started to wash Sheba.

"Alcoholics Anonymous," muttered Mendoza. "That cat."

Jamison. Bremmer. Varick. Not the smell of any connection—just thank God the press hadn't got hold of it. The vengeance bit. And just what the hell—

"Still on the local scene," said the pleasant voice, "Glendale police are tonight investigating the mysterious murder of Frederick C. Millway, seventy-four, a retired state employee, who was found strangled to death in his apartment on Salem Street in that city. Mr. Millway's body was discovered by Mr. Wayne Loveless, the manager-superintendent of the apartment building. Interviewed by reporters, Mr. Loveless stated that the body might have lain unfound for days, as it had been unusual for him to enter tenants' apartments. Mr. Millway had asked the manager to repair a faucet in his apartment, and Mr. Loveless entered under the impression that Millway was out. Loveless stated that he could only believe the killer was a lunatic, since Millway was a quiet respectable man with no known enemies. Local police had offered no comment so far, except that Lieutenant L. M. Wheelwright announced that the full strength of the Glendale Detective Bureau would . . ."

"You see, you haven't got a monopoly on mysteries," said Alison.

Mendoza was systematically cheating at solitaire now. "*That* little hick force," he said.

". . . most curious and mysterious clue, said the lieutenant, was the small file card found on the body, a card which bore the cryptic message"—the newscaster glanced down at his notes—"'The vengeance is just.' Lieutenant Wheelwright expressed the opinion that . . ."

Mendoza dropped the deck of cards. "*¡Santa María! ¿Y ahora, qué?* For God's sake—" He leaped up. He said bitterly, "*Glendale!* This hick town—" And he ran for the phone in the hall.

". . . diligent detective work," said the newscaster pleasantly, "will soon discover the murderer . . . On the national scene, the President today . . ."

"For heaven's sake!" said Alison. Automatically she shut off the TV.

62

"This is Lieutenant Mendoza of the L.A.P.D., Homicide. Sergeant who?—Sergeant Foss, I want to speak with Lieutenant Wheelwright . . . What? Yes, it is urgent . . . Yes, a matter of—my God, *Glendale!*" said Mendoza aside to Alison. "This hick suburban—yes, Sergeant? . . . Central Homicide, that's right. About one of your—well, can you give me his home number, please? It's rather—he's not there," he hissed at Alison. "God, Glendale. I—"

"Well, after all, Luis, neither are you," said Alison reasonably. "At the office, I mean. You can't be, twenty-four hours a day."

"Two-four-one, one-eight-nine-one, yes, thanks, I've got that. Thanks." Mendoza slammed the phone down, picked it up and began to dial again.

"But how very peculiar," said Alison. "Frederick Millway. He sounds even more different from all the rest of them, doesn't he?"

"Lieutenant Wheelwright? This is—"

Five

"The most important thing is—you can see that, for God's sake—to keep it out of the press," said Mendoza urgently, forty minutes later in Wheelwright's office. "I know, I know—what's gone out on the air is past praying for, but let's for the love of God take it back, or say it's all been explained away—concoct some tale so they won't get hot and bothered about it. Look, you can tell them you've found out that file card was irrelevant, that—that this Millway liked to copy out Bible texts or some damn thing—"

"Well, I see that," said Lieutenant Wheelwright. "My God, what you tell me—four since last Saturday! I can hardly —well, sure, I see *that*. You'd have a panic, because just as you say there doesn't seem to be any rhyme or reason to how he picks people to kill. My God, I never heard of such a— and in a way, it all being one case, it *is* yours. And welcome you are to it, Lieutenant Mendoza."

"Yeah," said Galeano, "and when we do break it—then it'd make headlines too, and we'll get the whole bit all over again, about suppressing news—"

"Oh, for God's sake, worry about that later," said Mendoza. "You don't have to be an experienced cop to see how it'd set off a panic. We'll give 'em some soothing tale, to make

64

Millway look like the ordinary victim of a break-in artist or something. Rather you will," he added to Wheelwright.

"I do see that, Lieutenant, yes." Wheelwright stabbed out his cigarette. He was a big man with a square face and very curly gray hair, and both he and Glendale Police Headquarters had been a little surprise to Mendoza and Galeano. Who didn't, after all, get over this way very often.

Mendoza had got the address from him, and directions, and called Galeano at the office. They both landed there about the same time, Galeano taking the freeway, and the first thing that struck them was the building—a very handsome and very new building, about one-twentieth the size of their own headquarters, of course, but newer and much more decorative, of two shades of gray composition stone, broad shallow steps up to the plate-glass doors, and landscaped borders with floodlights in them. Wheelwright had been waiting in the big lobby, and brought them up to the Detective Bureau, which was a large rectangular room across the front of the building, with the newest of strip-lighting round the walls and the latest switchboard gadgets on the lieutenant's desk.

Wheelwright, catching Galeano's surreptitious glances around, grinned at both of them. "I know you boys've got the reputation," he said, "and we don't start to compare in size, but we do try to run a nice tight little force here, Lieutenant Mendoza. Of course it's a quiet town as a rule, even if the population's up—about a hundred and thirty-five thousand now . . . Yes, I see what you mean. Jack said there'd been some press calls—I told him to clam up from now on, until we come to some decision." He fingered his bulldog jaw thoughtfully. "So how does it go? You want to handle it?"

"Not necessarily," said Mendoza. Ten minutes ago he'd have said yes; but sizing up Wheelwright, he marked him as a good cop and a smart cop—which wasn't always necessarily the same thing. And Wheelwright wouldn't have

65

a bunch of morons working under him; not by this setup—or the calm-eyed desk man in uniform downstairs. "You don't," he asked curiously, looking around the big room empty save for the three of them, "have a night crew on up here?"

"Oh, yes," said Wheelwright. "Two men. They're out on an assault case. So what *do* you want?"

"I want to see everything you've got on this so far, and whatever else you get I want to hear. And—"

"Sure," said Wheelwright. "Easy enough." He opened the top drawer of his desk and brought out a big manila envelope. "I'd be just as happy to hand it straight over to you boys with the reputation. The funniest damn setup I've ever run across. It's all here." He upended the envelope and began to sort out the contents, handing over first a series of glossy eight-by-ten photographs.

Mendoza shared them with Galeano. "The trouble with us is," said Galeano, "we just hate to admit any other police force could even start to compare with us. You've got a good cameraman, Lieutenant."

There were eight shots: the body from several angles, the room, the file card. Frederick C. Millway had not been a handsome old man, and he looked worse dead. But it wasn't a weak face: high forehead, plentiful white hair, beak of a Roman nose, a lantern jaw. And not a small man; the statistics listed on the first report put him at six feet, nearly two hundred pounds. But it was, of course, an eminently satisfactory and relatively easy way to kill anybody. He'd been wearing black trousers and a white shirt open at the throat, black-leather slippers over bare feet.

It was an old apartment living room, but looked fairly tidy: overstuffed sofa and chair, a couple of other chairs, portable TV in one corner, glimpse into a kitchenette.

Millway was lying almost in the middle of the room—by the diagram sketch, eight feet from the door—with his

66

head toward the kitchenette archway at right angles to the apartment door.

"So," said Mendoza. "*Así, así.* The doorbell rang and he went to the door. X told him something all very plausible so that Millway asked him in. And as Millway turned half-around, X caught him with his little garrote. Very neat."

"That's how it looks. The doctor said right away, a thin cord or something like that. But for God's sake why? There wasn't anything taken, he had sixteen-odd bucks on him. Well, now you tell me all this, I guess that doesn't count in, but—*damndest* thing I ever ran across."

"What's your surgeon say about times?"

"He's usually pretty sharp," said Wheelwright. "Manager went up and found Millway about nine this morning. Doctor said late yesterday afternoon for time of death, call it 5 to 7 P.M."

"Oh," said Mendoza. "Yes, of course. The hours when most other residents would be in, getting ready for dinner and having dinner. Yes. So how does Millway stack up alongside our other victims? Anything at all in common?"

"Oh, for God's sake," said Galeano, who'd picked up a signed statement from the desk and been scanning it rapidly. "Anything in—!" He handed it to Mendoza.

It was the statement, three pages long, of Mr. Wayne Loveless, the superintendent-manager of the Salem Arms. Mr. Loveless was forty-nine and had been the superintendent of the building for fifteen years. "It is," said Wheelwright, "an old red-brick place—good-sized apartments, nice place if it is old."

Mr. Loveless testified that Frederick C. Millway had lived at the Salem Arms for eight years. He understood that Mr. Millway was retired, he'd worked for the state, he thought clerical work of some kind, but had never heard Millway say exactly. Anyway, the old man was on pension from the state, and he'd always paid the rent promptly and been a very good, quiet tenant. Never any drinking, that is, no noisy parties or like that—well, a man seventy-four— and what tenants did in their own places wasn't any of his business as long as they didn't disturb anyone else.

Mendoza cocked an inquisitive brow at Wheelwright. "A lush?"

Wheelwright divined the part he'd come to. "No, not exactly. If you read on—poor old fellow. Manager was there, being questioned, when we started looking the place over. Quite a little stock of liquor—Scotch. Millway wasn't a very happy old man, and evidently brooded on his troubles. Nobody ever saw him even high, by what we've heard so far, but it'd be my guess he quietly tied one on all alone every night, to sleep."

"Oh." Mendoza went on reading. Loveless did happen to know one thing about Millway. He probably wouldn't if it hadn't been for Mr. Kettler. Millway hadn't ever done much talking: polite enough when you met him coming in or going out, but not communicative—kept himself to himself. But for several years Mr. Walter Kettler had had the apartment next door to Millway, and they'd got friendly. The only other tenant, so far as Loveless knew, Millway had ever been friendly with. Old chaps about the same age—Loveless thought they'd played cards together, and as lone elderly men usually did, went out for dinner several times a week. And Mr. Kettler had been very friendly, a nice happy old gentleman, and he'd told Loveless this and that. He'd said once that Millway, when he retired, had come down to Glendale to live because his only relative lived here, a sister, but she'd died the next year. And once another time he'd said that they had to make allowances for Millway, his gruff manner and brooding and all, because he'd suffered a great tragedy in his life. Thirty years before, Kettler told Loveless, Millway's wife and four young children had all burned to death in a terrible fire, and he'd never got over it. And

68

Kettler had added that was was in confidence, Millway couldn't bear to have anyone mention it or sympathize, he'd only told Kettler on impulse. And now Millway hadn't any relations in the world.

"I'd like," said Mendoza, "to talk to this Kettler."

"So would we," said Wheelwright. "Because I saw that it just could be that this vengeance thing might indicate something that happened in the past—though that's kind of up in the air—and if Millway talked to Kettler that much, he might have told him other things. But it seems Kettler moved away. He was in an automobile accident, and in the hospital a long time, and then—Loveless says—he couldn't manage on his own any more, and went to a rest home or maybe to some relative, he isn't sure. Isn't sure where."

"*Qué mono,*" said Mendoza, going back to the statement. Millway, said Loveless, lived very quietly—very much by routine. As old people most often did. He didn't seem to have any hobbies or outside interests, you could put it. He usually went out about ten o'clock each morning, and, Loveless was pretty sure because Millway had mentioned it, when it was nice he walked down the five blocks to the little park opposite the Chamber of Commerce and maybe just sat, or watched people playing tennis on the courts there. Maybe he'd walk back to Brand Boulevard and have a sandwich some place there, or go across from the park to read at the main library; anyway, he usually came home in late afternoon, and that was really all Loveless knew about his habits. He was a good tenant. Quiet. And last Monday he'd knocked on the door of Loveless' apartment and told him the kitchen faucet was leaking and a new washer hadn't stopped it, and asked Loveless—and really the first free time Loveless had had since was Wednesday morning, he'd gone up and knocked, had no answer, so he'd thought Millway had gone out, and used his master key, and—

"It was kind of anonymous, that apartment," said Wheel-

69

wright. "A good many paperback books—he liked mystery stories, or maybe just read 'em to pass the time—didn't write or get letters, except the usual junk mail. Ordinary clothes. Ordinary things all over—except all the Scotch. Cheap Scotch. What he looks like—just a very ordinary old codger, retired civil service, like the post office maybe, or something like that—just marking time, waiting for the end. And now you tell me he's number four in this crazy series of killings! They sure as God don't match up very well, do they?" He rubbed his jaw.

"Oh, say it again!" said Mendoza savagely, slapping down Loveless' statement on top of the photographs. "¡Santa María! Of all the wild—four people, about as different types as you could find anywhere. And," he added to Galeano, "I still think it is the planned thing, and be damned to your lunatic getting the urge at random. You gave me a very pretty description of how his lunatic mind works —but I thought even then, it was a bit thin to place him down on our beat, getting the urge, and then arbitrarily move him up to the Hollywood hills. Why? What would he be doing up there if his normal beat is downtown? And on this one, I say it again even louder—it isn't reasonable to suppose that he turned up, with his damn urge, first down on Spring, and at the Plaza, and then up in Hollywood, and now Glendale of all places. They weren't picked at random."

Galeano looked uneasy and admitted it began to look that way. "And, hell, if it was something in the past—whatever crazy motive he thinks he's got—how in hell would we ever find out who?"

"I'll think about that later," said Mendoza. "Right now the important thing is to tell a pretty little tale to the press boys, so we won't have headlines about the avenger." He got up, looking at Wheelwright. "Because," he added wryly, "we can't win them all. With the best will in the world. And this is a bastard to work, all right. I just said it's not a lunatic, but

70

of course he's a nut of some kind, though it probably doesn't show. Yet. Whatever plausible motive he thinks he's got might be—we can't even guess—something very slight." He was thinking of Alison's tossed-off suggestion about the crowd and a fire. Something like that—not that exactly—it could very well be. "And on this kind of thing, the routine doesn't always pay off. And I'm all for a free press and the public being informed, but—what with all the other counts against us these days—if we don't manage to catch up with this joker, I would just as soon they all got quietly filed away under Pending—in your records, and Wilcox Street's, and ours, and God knows where else—as separate unsolved murders. Instead, my God, of one sensational mass murderer we were too dumb to find, brought up again whenever some punk yells we're not being nice to him."

Wheelwright laughed. "And how right you are," he said. "Trust me, I'll call 'em off. Sorry to have discommoded you this far, but of course I couldn't know—and I'll keep you briefed, whatever we turn up, if anything."

"Thanks very much. I'll do the same. Among us—" Mendoza picked up his hat. "I could bear to have copies of all that—photographs and so on."

"Will do."

"Maybe if I brood over what we've got long enough—"

"Once in a while," said Galeano, "he has a brain wave. Like female intuition."

"Is that so?" said Wheelwright. "Let's hope he does on this one."

But no visions occurred to Mendoza at all. It was like having bits and pieces of four different jigsaw puzzles on the same table, trying to fit them together.

Four such very different people. It took imagination to conceive any possible link between them, even a fleeting one.

The discouraging thought did come to him that X could

indeed be the only link. For there were people, and quite often they were the people who were on the way to going definitely lunatic—the incipient persecution complex—every man's hand against them. Practically everybody they met was out to cheat them, or injure them in some way, in their own minds. So take one like that, shove him over the line enough to start plotting murder, and you might get a thing like this. The four victims might be people he'd come across only casually. An argument with Jamison in a bar somewhere. Maybe he'd bought cigarettes from Bremmer and thought he'd been cheated. And—wait for it—yes, thought Mendoza (he was getting into his pajamas then, Alison sound asleep in the king-size double bed, her red hair loose on the pillow)—yes, if he was reaching into the past, maybe when Edith Varick had been the efficient legal secretary, she'd offended him some way—denied him an appointment or something. And Millway? Millway over in Glendale—and for eight years. Harmless old fellow. What about Millway, who didn't apparently get out of Glendale much? Well, X seemed to be mobile—downtown, the Hollywood hills—he could have come across Millway somehow.

He could even still be rational enough—or look that way —to be holding a job.

And if there was anything in that, thought Mendoza, getting into bed and turning out the light, they had a very small chance of getting him at all.

But he'd be interested in what—if anything—Wheelwright turned up from the other tenants in the Salem Arms, about anybody who'd been noticed there at the indicated times.

And it was a very small chance, of course, that anybody had noticed anything.

They still hadn't picked up any of the other three out of Records they wanted to look at on the liquor-store killings.

Grace and Landers had already gone out on that when Mendoza got to the office. It was Hackett's day off. He'd left a typed report and a statement by Alfred Kafka on Mendoza's desk.

As Mendoza came in, Higgins was reading that and Palliser stood looking out the window.

"Morning," he said. "No real heat yet. Hope it stays nice for my vacation."

Mendoza grunted. "Where you taking her?"

Palliser swung around looking mad and then, taking in their expressions, grinned self-consciously. "Well, school's out the seventeenth, and we thought we'd just go over to Vegas on a weekend and then when I'm off, maybe Tahoe."

"Should be nice up there," said Higgins, sounding a little wistful. "Listen, Luis, this thing, I just—"

"Before we kick it around any more let me brief you on number four," said Mendoza, and did so. He'd just finished when Sergeant Lake came in with a manila envelope and said somebody from Glendale-of-all-places had just left it off. "Well, quick work. We are not the only efficient force in the county."

"For God's sake!" said Higgins. "I will be damned. Retired civil service—"

"Or something like that. Who knows? And I had a very depressing little thought about it," said Mendoza, and relayed that. "You know the type. Sometimes they go over the line."

Higgins massaged his Neanderthal jaw. No beauty George Higgins, but a solid, dependable, good man: Mary Dwyer could do a lot worse. Which both Mendoza and Palliser thought, and did not say. "I could buy that, Luis," said Higgins, "and of course it wouldn't take us very far. But even if it is somebody like that, I say it doesn't stymie us *absolutely*. Because anybody who's gone over the line that far

—to do murder, maybe for a very small reason the way you say—isn't going to be acting exactly normal other ways."

"It happens, George. Sometimes they cover up a long time."

"But not forever. Look, this Jamison seems to have a couple of pals down there. Maybe, if we look them up and ask all polite, they'll tell us he told them about having an argument with somebody. Maybe we ask around where the Varick woman used to work, we'll turn up a little something there. And if we locate this Kettler, it could be Millway told him something—sure, roundabout, but *something* ought to show eventually, we do enough work on it."

"Not so necessarily," said Mendoza.

"But," said Palliser, and stopped, and went on. "Don't we all know the classic cases? From Jack the Ripper on. This is a very tricky sort of logic, but—well, take the nuts. The real nuts. That go berserk. They're apt to kill anybody, sure. Like that barber, back East somewhere, who all of a sudden ran out in the street with a shotgun and started shooting. But there are nuts and nuts. And when you get the ones who are technically insane but still managing to look all right on the surface—like some of the mass poisoners, Armstrong and so on—the ones capable of planning in detail, you know, and covering up after themselves—"

"Yes, well?"

"Well, with that kind," said Palliser, "which is what all this rather looks like, dooesn't it—with that kind, isn't there almost always a—a category? A certain kind of people they pick, or certain individuals? Not, at any rate, at absolute random."

"Mmh," said Mendoza. "Also a thought. That is perfectly true, John. A motive there is, a twisted lunatic one but a motive. But where does it give us to look?"

"They do say," said Higgins, "truth is stranger than—I had a thought, Luis. It sounds very damned corny, because

74

how many damn-fool old mystery stories, but—were all these people maybe once on a jury together? And convicted somebody of something? And—"

"*¡Salga de aquí!*" said Mendoza. "Get away, boy, you're really reaching! Or are you? Are you indeed? Hell and damnation, it won't do any harm to look . . . So you're with me?" He looked at Palliser. "You think they're tied up?"

"And so am I," said Higgins, sounding annoyed. "What else does that way-out idea say? And how the hell to go at it—"

"Routine," said Palliser. "Go back on all four of them and dig out every single little solitary thing. If they were ever all connected in any way, as a group—a jury, or a crowd maybe watching an arrest or a fire or any damn thing, or maybe witnesses in a court case, for God's sake, or they all attended the same state picnic or were on the same bus when it broke down, or—"

"Not a jury," said Mendoza suddenly. "N.G., George. Jamison had a police record."

"Not," said Higgins, "until he was twenty-three. He could've been a juror any time two years previous."

"So he could. We'll look," said Mendoza. "Just for fun. And would either of you care to estimate how many man-hours it will take? Or to follow up your bright little idea, John? And we've got a new one overnight"—he tapped the report Piggott had left on his desk—"man stabbed to death down on Temple, not one single damn lead. And are either of you taking any bets there won't be a number five turning up in the next twenty-four hours?"

"Oh, hell," said Higgins. "I know. We have to work it as we see it, Luis."

Sergeant Lake thrust his head in the door. "Call in from a squad car on Alpine," he announced succinctly. "Intersection Alpine and Cleveland. Guy run berserk—single house there. He's got a gun, maybe two, three guns by what they've

75

got so far, and a lot of ammo. He shot his wife—D.O.A.—and a neighbor, and he's holed up there firing at anything that moves. No cover. Three squad cars on it, five men, calling in for help—and shotguns, and tear gas."

"My God," said Higgins. He sounded resigned. But they started to move. Mendoza yanked open the top drawer and got out his gun, sliding extra ammo into his pockets; they went out to the corridor.

"Car waiting downstairs with requested equipment," said Sergeant Lake.

Detective Jason Grace was just coming in, towing a tall, thin, medium-dark Negro youth. "I think we're getting somewhere, Lieutenant," he said mildly. "Well, some excitement?"

"Excitement—" said Higgins, pushing past the suspect. "Drop him and tag along, Jase—we'll maybe need all our sharpshooters!"

Six

THAT turned out to be quite a little fracas, as they'd fully expected, and it took a while to get it cleared up. When the men from Homicide got there, there were six squad cars parked in the street and a milling excited crowd jabbering in English and Spanish, with one of the patrolmen using a bullhorn and reasoning with the man inside the house. No attempt had been made to get at the two ominously still bodies on the front lawn of the house.

"Name's Corregio, sir," one of the squad-car men briefed Mendoza curtly. "Joe Corregio. He's a nut—been up in Camarillo on and off. Suddenly goes into a fit or something and shoots his wife—and the neighbor who came to see what was up. Grace of God, all the kids are in school—they've got nine. We don't—"

"*¡Caray!*" said Mendoza.

"He's firing any time we make a move to—" Shots from the house confirmed this statement; the crowd ducked and jabbered louder. "All these damn people—we can't—"

They called up more men to get the crowd back, and a patrolman got himself shot in the arm and another one in the shoulder, and three people in the crowd were wounded, and time passed, before one of the uniformed men, covered by the rest of them, managed to crawl close enough to a side

77

window to lob in a tear-gas grenade; and it was a while after that they got Corregio in cuffs and took him away and in general started to get the mess cleared up.

That kind of thing was time-consuming, to say the least, and they could only be thankful that Corregio had a record of insanity, had spent time in an institution. So it wasn't necessary, as it would have been otherwise, to take all the tedious statements from the witnesses. Just stash him back in, it was to be hoped for good—and not at Camarillo this time, but Atascadero, for the criminally insane. However, a certain amount of paperwork there would be for some other people—the nine kids, unless there were relatives willing to take them, would find themselves wards of the court. The county tried but it was a little impersonal; where the nine kids would end up, in foster homes or an orphanage, wasn't certain.

They got back to base about noon, with the only casualty in Homicide a sprained thumb on Higgins' left hand when he'd dodged a shot and fallen against a squad car.

Mendoza said, "Jimmy can file anything that comes in for an hour. Let's go and have lunch."

Grace said plaintively he ought to start questioning his suspect, he thought he was the boy they wanted for those two homicides, but Mendoza said he'd keep. Higgins went down to First Aid and swore at the doctor who jerked his thumb joint back in place, and then they all went up to Federico's.

Mendoza had called Hackett last night, when he'd got back from Glendale, to tell him about number four; and Hackett lay awake trying to fit pieces together, and devising possible situations where four such very different people might have found themselves together. You could imagine any number of such situations, of course, but it was impossible to see how any one person like the avenger could have known who

78

they all were, or where to find them at home or elsewhere. It just made no sense at all.

He got up a little later than usual, his day off, and talked about it to Angel over breakfast, while she fed baby Sheila. Never any trouble about getting nearly-four-year-old Mark to eat; he was already out in the backyard chasing the cat.

Angel went out to market, leaving Sheila in her play-pen carefully in the shade, and Hackett got out the lawn mower. While he cut the lawn front and back, and emptied the grass catcher tidily into the refuse barrel, he thought about this very peculiar business some more, and the merest glimmering of an idea came to him.

If there was anything in it, he thought, it would make just a little better sense of the thing than any idea they'd had up to then.

He got a Coke out of the refrigerator and sat on the side porch with the big gray Persian, Silver Boy, on his knees, where he could keep an eye on the baby and Mark in his sandbox, and thought about it some more. By the time Angel came back, he'd decided it was good enough to pass on, so he went down the hall to the phone and called the office to see if Mendoza was in.

And Sergeant Lake told him about this fellow gone berserk, so Hackett hung up and worried. After worrying for thirty seconds he called back. "Had I better come in, Jimmy? Has anybody called you back since—?"

"I don't know," said Lake. "The boss didn't say, Art. I haven't heard a thing since they all barged out of here."

"Oh," said Hackett. He did some more worrying and then said, "I'd better come in. Just in case." A thing like that, bullets flying all around, anybody could get killed . . . He wouldn't soon forget Bert Dwyer dead on that bank floor . . . Would they be having a vacancy in Homicide again today?

He didn't tell Angel what was going on; just said they

needed him. She didn't ask because she'd just come across a new recipe brochure with something she'd got at the market, and only asked absently if he'd be late.

"I don't suppose so," said Hackett, and backed out the Barracuda and started for the freeway.

By the time he got to the office it was all over, and the rest of the boys had come back and then all gone off to lunch, and the only occupants of the office were Sergeant Lake and a sullen-looking, tall, thin Negro kid munching a ham sandwich.

Hackett felt rather deflated; and at the moment he wasn't hungry. He thought, being here he might as well do something besides turning around and going home.

Because he'd had another little idea too, on that Jamison. Which might tie in, in a way, with the big idea.

He went down to Records and got O'Brien to do some looking for him. Benny Ackerman, the fag Kafka had mentioned, was there all right: several counts, but of course they didn't get stashed away for long at a time. The other one was there too—Jesus Valdez, nickname Speedy. He'd done two terms for forcible rape and was currently on parole. Addresses for both of them—Elmyra Avenue and Boyd Street.

He went to look for Ackerman first. He found him at home, an old ramshackle single house with all the front windows broken, which hadn't seen a coat of paint since it was built around 1910. Ackerman was a fat, moronic-looking fellow about thirty, in old faded denims and a torn gray workshirt, and he shied away from Hackett and his badge like a nervous horse. He hadn't, he said, done nothing. Nothing at all. He was clean.

Hackett, eyeing him, might have argued the literal point. "Not saying you did. You knew Nelson Jamison, didn't you?"

"Oh," said Ackerman. "Oh. Well, sort of. Not too good, I mean. Just seein' him around."

"You knew he was killed? You were sitting with him at Al's the night it happened, weren't you?"

"Oh, Jesus, mister, you ain't sayin' *I* had anything to do—oh, Jesus, I never did! I seen him that night—sure, it was all over next day, I mean anybody knew him heard—but, mister, I only just hadda beer with him at Al's, he's still there when I left, honest, why'd *I*—I didn't really know him good. Only sometimes he'd buy a round. You know. Valdez knew him a lot better—or—or Manny Hersheimer—or Billy Fancher. Honest."

This Hackett didn't doubt. The ones like Jamison and Valdez didn't mix all-pals-together with the fags; it was in the cards that Ackerman had played up to Jamison a little because Jamison had money to buy drinks. And he'd had other questions for Ackerman, but looking at his stupid eyes he didn't think Ackerman could answer them. Jamison wouldn't have talked to one like that.

Valdez could be a horse of another color.

He left Ackerman, who immediately bolted inside the old house and slammed the door, and went to find Valdez.

It had warmed up a bit today, and he found Speedy Valdez sitting on his front porch drinking chilled red *vino* with his papa Gregorio and his old uncle Hernandez. They all regarded Hackett and his badge with cold-eyed indifference, and the old uncle spat on the sidewalk and muttered about dirty cops. This house on Boyd Street wasn't quite as run-down as the other one; its windows were intact; but it had a slatternly look that nearly amounted to a leer.

Valdez Junior assured Hackett that he was clean; he hadn't done nothing. Hackett could have reminded him that he was violating his parole by frequenting bars, but he had only Al's word and anyway that wasn't what he was interested in. He sat down uninvited on the second step, took out a cigarette and lit it leisurely. They all watched stolidly.

81

He was bigger than any two of them, and they couldn't tell him to go.

"You knew Nelson Jamison," he said casually.

"Oh—that," said Valdez. "Sure I knew him, cop. I don't know nothin' about how he got took off. Just heard he was. Up at the Old Plaza, hah? Well, I also heard he was fried that night, so I guess he just drifted up there and maybe got rolled by some bum, hah?"

"Maybe," said Hackett. "I wasn't fingering you for it, Valdez. You see him that night?"

"Nuh-uh. Not for a week 'r so . . . Well, I knew him like I know a lot of guys. Guys you run into, around . . . Yeah, I knew his old lady got some money, he was always with a roll. But nobody never tried to take him for it—he could be a mean one. Man, yes. Do I know, some stories he —" Valdez, starting to grin, stopped abruptly and retired into his wine.

"Mmh," said Hackett. "You know where he lived?"

"Why?" asked Valdez cautiously.

"It seems a little funny to us," said Hackett, "that a fellow like Jamison, nice house up in Pasadena, money and all, should be wandering around down here so much, that's all. Was he down here much, Valdez?"

"Some," said Valdez shortly. "What's wrong with down here, cop?"

"Nothing, I guess, if you don't want anything better," said Hackett. "Me, I live in Highland Park."

The old uncle gave a crack of laughter. "Cop on his nice big salary they pay him come shove us poor folk around! Give us no chance atall, poor, poor, grinding our faces—" He swallowed wine and spat again.

"First I've heard of it," said Hackett. "You graduated from high school, Valdez. Learned something about mechanics there, didn't you? How come you haven't got a job? Every

82

day I see ads in the paper for jobs you could do—and down here, enough people willing to hire an ex-con, give him a chance."

Valdez looked at him and shrugged. "We're on the welfare. Pays as good as any job I'd take."

"Valdez, why did Jamison come wandering around down here? Why? You and he were pals, weren't you—he talked to you! Two of a kind, you and Jamison—the ones who like it by force. And don't think we don't know the ones you got caught on weren't the first or the only! And that went for Jamison too, didn't it—didn't it?"

"I don't know nothin' about what he did or didn't do, you can't tie me in—"

"How many times have you caught a woman alone somewhere, Valdez?—but I don't care about you right now. Just Jamison. *That's* why he hung around down here, wasn't it? Where there are back alleys and little dark side-streets, and girls and women walking alone at night—women who are just like their men, leery of the cops, who wouldn't call 'cop' for anything short of a murder! That's why, isn't it? Did he talk to you about it? I think he did—because he knew you were safe to talk to. How many did he boast about to you, Valdez?"

Valdez was on his feet quick as a cat. "You can't tie me into th—you're tellin' the story, cop! How do I know why Nels come around? Maybe he liked the company better than up in Pasadena, cop!"

Hackett stood up too, and Valdez stood three steps above him on the porch but their eyes were on a level. "Maybe so," said Hackett. "Maybe he had a taste for low company all right. But I think he had a better reason than that, Valdez, and if I wasn't so sure of it I might just have your P.A. officer haul you in and persuade the truth out of you. But I guess you've told me all I want to know."

83

"I ain't told you nothin', nor I—"

"Oh, yes, you have," said Hackett with a grin.

He had a belated lunch and went back to headquarters to see if Mendoza was in. This time he found all of them there except Landers; they'd just ended a tedious but successful questioning-in-depth of Grace's suspect, who had finally come apart under their patient prodding and admitted he'd been the one who'd shot those two liquor-store clerks. Never done it, he said aggrievedly, if they hadn't tried to show fight; why'd they had to go and do that? It was an academic question, since they'd found the right gun under his mattress and the fellow who'd sold it to him two weeks ago; still, a signed confession was always nice and he'd have trouble repudiating it later with the old complaint of brutal cops, because they'd carefully brought in a lawyer from the Public Defenders' Office to hear all that went on.

Who said, nodding to Mendoza at the door, "Rather my job than yours, Lieutenant. Any day."

"Quite often I agree with you," said Mendoza sardonically. He smoothed his thick hair absently, from the widow's-peak. "What the hell are you doing here on your day off, Art?"

"Well, first I got a little worried about that nut with a gun —I heard about it from Jimmy—I might've known it was a fool's errand, but I came down to help out. And then as long as I was here— Well, I've got a little idea. Just call me a dedicated cop."

"On what?"

"Oh, the avenger bit. I thought—"

"Come on in and sit down. Jimmy, can you get us some coffee? Any new idea on that I could use."

They all went into Mendoza's office, the two big ones, Hackett and Higgins, seeming to fill all available space left by the slenderer tall dark Palliser, Mendoza, and Grace. Sergeant Lake fetched coffee.

84

"I was just thinking," said Hackett, stirring in sugar, "let's look at it the simplest way, Luis. We know the same one did them all—Jamison and Bremmer and Varick and now this Millway—on account of the m.o. and the cards. But nothing at all says all four were tied up together in any way. Why should they be? Look, here was my idea. Suppose our avenger is a puritanical crank of some kind, shoved over the line. He's appointed by God to wreak vengeance on sinners, say." They were all listening interestedly, Higgins absently massaging his thumb. "Sinners, wherever he finds them. Well, Jamison doesn't need explaining there. And I had a little idea on Jamison too—" he outlined that, and his interview with Valdez. Mendoza nodded, agreeing, and said he'd had that stray thought too. "Anybody might say Jamison deserved vengeance. The other three, by what we know, perfectly honest respectable people. But I ask you, what *we'd* say was respectable, would the puritanical nut? It just occurred to me, if he is that kind, could it be that he was all wild-eyed about the Catholic Menace, for instance? Bremmer was a Catholic—if the nut came across him somehow, I mean, to single out that particular Catholic—and who knows what else he's hipped on? Edith Varick—maybe he's also got a thing about hard-boiled career women with no children. Millway—who could say? Maybe he's got a thing about useless senior citizens taking pension money from taxpayers. What I'm saying is," said Hackett, "it could be he has a different reason on every one of them. See? That, according to his nutty logic, they're all sinners of one sort or another and deserve the vengeance."

"Now that," said Mendoza, folding his long hands into a steeple above his coffee cup, "is quite an idea indeed, Arturo."

"I like it," said Palliser. "It makes a little more sense than anything else we've thought up to now."

Higgins flexed his thumb. "You do get that type," he

85

agreed. "And I'll say something else, Art. It gives us something more concrete to get hold of, if that's so. Because—"

"Yes, sure," said Hackett. "I was going on to that. Because we can only make wild guesses on what his actual reasons might be—to think Bremmer, and Varick, and Millway, deserved the vengeance—well, say it was because Bremmer was Catholic, there had to be some reason he picked that particular Catholic. ¿Cómo no? And on Varick, say it was her being a career woman, well, my God, how many thousands are there in the county? But if it is like that, our boy's got to have had some personal contact with all those people at some time, in order to mark them down as individuals."

"Yes," said Mendoza dreamily. He swiveled around in his desk chair and stared out the window. It was smoggy again today. "Yes. I'm thinking something else now. Two of them —Jamison and Bremmer—on our beat. Not exactly the best part of town. But, you come to think of it, that was by chance. *All* of them actually lived in fairly good residential sections. Good to best."

"I'll be damned," said Higgins, sounding startled. "That they did."

"Jamison in an old-snob part of Pasadena. Bremmer, good middle-class street in Hollywood. Varick, exclusive area in the hills. Millway, good middle-class in Glendale." Mendoza swiveled around again. "Does it say anything?"

"It just could," said Grace. "Some kind of salesman covering those areas? Some—"

"But," said Hackett suddenly, dismally, "it doesn't, Luis. Bremmer. Bremmer wasn't at home except on Sundays—and evenings. He was down on Spring Street. If our boy had marked anybody, for his lunatic reason, at the home address, it'd have been the sister."

"*¡Porvida!* Yes. Damn. Well, it was just an idea. I like the rest of it," said Mendoza. "I like it very much. It makes just a

86

little more sense. That could be the answer—a big part of it."

"So where does it send us?" asked Higgins.

"We're going to poke around the victims a lot more," said Mendoza. "Ask questions and keep on asking. About every contact they'd had recently, and if that doesn't pay off, further back. Because there must have been some contact, damn it. A nut looking for vengeance on sinners doesn't pick them out of the blue, for God's sake. You do occasionally use that big brain of yours, Art. And remember that you majored in psychology at college . . ."

And July was coming up, when the homicide rate always climbed; Mendoza would just as soon have this one off his mind when that started, and besides, he was curious. As hell, about the avenger.

Of the victims, Millway was certainly the most anonymous; but he felt more curious about the woman. That night after dinner he went to see Mrs. Sarah Walker. Who had been described as Edith Varick's closest friend. He thought cynically of Varick (any cop knew this and that about human nature), even at his age, only six months married: the female friend would know more.

Edith Varick sounded a bit too good to be true. Had there been something about her, some area in her life, which had made her look deserving of vengeance to such a type as Hackett postulated?

Mendoza was always good at getting the females to talk. Sarah Walker talked very readily, coherently, and sensibly. She started to cry once, but stopped immediately. She seemed to be a nice woman—another one much as Edith Varick had been described; a middle-aged woman who had kept herself up in looks, kept her figure, dressed well. She was dark, with a fine olive complexion and expressive brown eyes. Her husband, a taciturn bald fellow, was an

87

M.D.; they had a rambling big Spanish house in the Los Feliz district.

Sarah Walker had known Edith Varick for years. Thirty years at least—"We met when we were both going to night school. But I married Adam a few years later, and Edith went on working—" She said, like Varick, that it wasn't fair. "Just as she'd got married again, could quit her job— she was quite domestic, she'd always have preferred to stay home, if her marriage—I'd been so happy for her—we both had, hadn't we, Adam? And I simply can't imagine—there was nothing, *nothing*, anybody could hold against Edith— such a cheerful person, so—and she hadn't had an easy life. But what you're asking me, Lieutenant, any little thing that anyone might have thought was wrong about her—it's crazy! She was absolutely honest and reliable and dependable and —and truthful—" She stopped with a little gasp.

"Um," said Dr. Walker. "My dear—do you think—?"

"What? Oh," she said, looking up at him. "Oh. But, *Adam*, how ridiculous. To say she wasn't truthful just because of a little white lie! She wasn't—"

"Not that. Husband."

Mendoza shot a glance between the two of them. "What about her husband, Mrs. Walker? Do you mean—"

"Oh, not Earl Varick," she said. She looked suddenly uneasy and then alarmed. "But I never *thought*—it's so long ago! Adam, do you think it could have anything to—but he must be dead by now! Oh, it couldn't have been—" She was agitated.

"Mrs. Walker—"

"Better tell 'em, anyway," said Dr. Walker. "Hum! That card Earl mentioned. Very queer. Smacked just a bit to me of"—he sneezed and brought out an immense handkerchief —"Atascadero."

"Good heavens, it never *occurred* to me!" said Sarah Walker. She stared at her husband, back to Mendoza. "It

88

must be all of twenty years ago—more. Oh, my God, if it *was*—! Yes, I had better tell you. You see, Lieutenant, as—as dear a person as Edith was, she was just—just a little bit old-fashioned in some ways—"

Not, reflected Mendoza, a very hopeful beginning, when he was hoping to hear about some, however infinitesimal, black mark on Edith's record. "Yes?" he murmured.

"—about just a few things. She—I suppose Adam and I are the only people who know about this, because—well, the fact is, you see, she—she married this man, Richard Warren, a year or so after Adam and I were married. And of course as her closest friend I heard all about it at the time, in strict confidence of course—and I never mentioned it to a soul, of course, Edith just needed someone to talk to. And if I thought she was a little foolish about telling that lie, well, we're all made the way we're made, Lieutenant." Mrs. Walker smiled very faintly. "She was—old-fashioned about such things."

Dr. Walker put the handkerchief away. "Superstitious," he said mildly.

"Maybe. But I respected her feelings, I never told anyone."

"Told anyone—" prompted Mendoza. What now?

"Why, he didn't die," said Sarah Walker. "The way she told everybody that he was killed in an accident. She went over to Reno, quietly, later on, and got a divorce. She'd had a perfectly awful time with him, almost from the first—she didn't know he'd been several years in an asylum, before. He didn't die—he went absolutely raving mad, even attacked her a couple of times, and she finally had to get him committed to an institution. She felt just awful about it, she didn't want anyone to know."

Mendoza stared at her. And this gave him most furiously to think.

Seven

WHEN Hackett came in on Friday morning he found Higgins idly talking to Sergeant Lake and glancing over a report at the same time. "Morning, Art. The autopsy report just came in on that corpse down on Temple."

"That one," said Hackett. "Anything useful?"

"Did you expect anything? Of course not. Man was stabbed seven times in the body from the front, and died of it. No, we haven't identified him yet. And it's an ordinary enough description—about sixty to sixty-five, five-nine, a hundred and fifty, poor-quality clothes, laborers' hands. Flotsam."

"Yes," said Hackett, "he could have been just a drifter. We do get 'em. Hit for what he had on him by another one." In the big city, in some sections, they got that kind of thing. The animals preying on each other. "I sometimes wish," he said thoughtfully, thinking of a certain columnist, "that some of these bleeding hearts so anxious for the brotherhood of man could spend a few weeks at the thankless job, George. In the jungle. The notion that mankind has progressed much from Neanderthal, on the whole, and is all ready for Utopia might sort of evaporate from their minds."

Higgins laughed. "I've had the same thought."

"Boss in?" Hackett asked Lake.

"He's on long distance. To Atascadero."

"Why the hell? Turned up something?"

Lake shrugged. "Don't know. We'll be doing without Jase this morning—that child beater's being arraigned and he's testifying." It was Landers' day off.

Hackett and Higgins went on into Mendoza's office. Its owner was swiveled around in his desk chair talking on the phone. As usual, his suit was a poem in silver-gray Italian silk, his white shirt snowy, his tie discreet; every hair in place, he was idly straightening out things on the desk with his free hand, aligning blotter and desk basket, pen stand and clock and ashtray.

"—you'll check, then. Well, as soon as you can—I'd be much obliged, doctor. Yes, doctor. Thanks very much." Mendoza put the phone down, swiveled around and said good morning.

"Atascadero?" said Hackett. "Why?" He'd left the office door open and John Palliser wandered in.

"Where are we going today?"

"Sit down," said Mendoza. "Let's have some opinions. I've turned up a very funny little something," and he told them about Edith Verick's little white lie. "First husband criminally insane, not deceased. At least, that we know of. He could still be alive. He could be loose. And she's the one who committed him."

"Well, for God's sake, Luis," said Hackett, "you're not thinking it means anything? How could it? If she was the only corpse we had with the little file card on it about vengeance, I'd jump at that. But she's not. She wasn't even the first in line. This I don't see at all—it's just a side issue."

"I'll go along with that," agreed Higgins. "It's kind of tempting to think, but there's not really much to it, is there? Coincidence? We all think this avenger is a nut, all right, but there are a lot of them running around—just because we come across this one, it hardly says he's the same nut."

"What possible connection," asked Palliser reasonably, "would Edith Verick's first husband have with Jamison or Bremmer or Millway?"

"Yes." Mendoza sighed and lit a cigarette with a snap of the desk lighter. "Yes. I had a little shock when I heard about it last night—I thought hard about it—but on second thoughts all that occurred to me too. Still, if it is damned thin, I thought we ought to check Warren. First rule of detective work, isn't it?—be thorough. Or at least the second. I've asked Atascadero to look him up—Mrs. Walker was pretty sure it was Atascadero. Oh, I know it's thin—but it just *could* be. We don't want to miss any bets because a thing looks obvious one way or the other. Because whatever else it is, this is not run of the mill and we can't work it exactly as usual. And God knows you never know *what's* going to be important when you get an offbeat one. Like that thing last March."

"Oh, God knows that," said Higgins. "*That* business!" Reminiscently they all grinned.

"No, I still think Art's brain wave about the different motives is the likeliest thing. We'll check Warren, as we can—just see. But meanwhile, let's get out of here before anything new shows up to sidetrack us. John, you take Bremmer. Go talk to people about him—his landlord, people who knew him. Find out what made him tick, any special interests, any groups he may have belonged to even a while ago—you know the kind of thing. Art, you do the same on Varick. And George, you can go over and hobnob with the Glendale boys. We haven't seen the actual terrain on Millway—and while, having met Lieutenant Wheelwright, I'd guess that's a bunch of fairly efficient cops, still I'd like you to poke around a little there, see if anything occurs to you or you can turn up something they didn't."

"I've got one idea already," said Higgins. "Somebody said Millway used to go sit in a park over there. Well, there are probably other old people around who did too. Did he talk to any of them? I'd like to take a picture along and ask. One of the close-ups wasn't too gruesome."

"Which is an idea. So, ¡Vamos!" Mendoza got up.

"Where are you bound for?"

"A long session at Records. I, just for fun, am going to look up all the counts Jamison collected. We've only seen it in capsule. I know everything won't be there, damn it. How many times, after his first pick-up, do you suppose he's been brought in to be questioned on the same sort of thing?"

"I remember one time," said Higgins. "I was thinking when I saw his mug shots I'd seen that face before somewhere, and all of a sudden it came to me. On account of his record, he was one of how many dozens we fetched in for questioning three and a half years back on that Wood case that—"

"My God, was he? He would have been," said Mendoza. That one had been something, all right; they were all silent, remembering it, Hackett briefly living over that terror-ridden dash through the night with Mendoza alternately cursing and praying beside him, and the eventual capture of their boy.

"And that kind of thing doesn't get into Records," said Higgins.

"Unfortunately, no. We'd be swamped with all the paper —it's bad enough now. We'll just see what is there," said Mendoza. "Let's get with it. You know what you're looking for—something, anything, about these people that makes them show as not quite so virtuous. And about who might have known, if there is anything, and all recent contacts, casual or otherwise."

They started out at that. It was the tedious kind of routine they were all familiar with; but that didn't make it any less tedious.

But it was the routine that so often broke a case.

93

By three o'clock that afternoon, Sergeant John Palliser had reached the conclusion that William Wilfred Bremmer could be a candidate for sainthood. The man, if he had been—by all Palliser had heard—abysmally dull and stodgy, apparently had no vices at all. Palliser talked to his landlord, from whom he'd leased the shop on Spring Street; to his sister again, to the neighbors, to the three people the sister had designated as their closest friends, and to the Bremmers' mailman (sometimes the mail a person received was revealing, and mailmen usually knew a good bit about the people on their routes), the Bremmers' doctor and the Bremmers' dentist. Nothing, but nothing, turned up; Bremmer had been the soul of virtue, if deadly dull. He paid his bills on time, he didn't cheat people or argue with them, he was very religious, he loved animals, he was kind to children. A lot of people had said indulgently that old Bremmer was the typical old-maid bachelor, but they said it kindly.

Now, just to round the hunt off, Palliser was about to see the priest of Bremmer's church, and he fully expected it would be more wasted effort.

It was the Holy Family Church on Hollywood Boulevard, and as he went in past the great carved-oak doors Palliser straightened his tie and resettled his jacket; it was hotter today and he felt tired and dirty after all his chasing around. A verger or something told him that Father O'Ryan was in his study and very probably not to be disturbed, but for a policeman he would ask. And presently Palliser found himself sitting facing Father O'Ryan, who was a round-faced happy-looking man with very blue eyes, across a wide desk.

"I know you can't tell me anything Mr. Bremmer may have told you at confession," said Palliser, "but you see, Father, we want to know everything possible about him—I'm sorry I can't tell you why, the full story, but it's important. And I understand he's been a—a faithful attendant here for a long time, and anything you can tell me about him—"

"Oh, dear, yes," said Father O'Ryan. "Since before I had this parish, in fact. I've been here only five years, since dear old Father Stephen was forced to retire. I must say, Sergeant, you do arouse my Celtic curiosity! It was astonishing and tragic enough that a man like Bremmer should get himself murdered—of all things—but now you asking questions about him, the victim—" He cocked his head at Palliser and smiled gently.

"Well, you know, Father," said Palliser, "what a man is like in himself—his essential personality—sometimes tells us quite a bit about how and why he came to get murdered."

The priest sobered. "I can see that would be so, Sergeant. Yes. In many cases. Somehow, I doubt that in Bremmer's— well, well. Just between the two of us, Sergeant, he was a terribly dull little man." O'Ryan's blue eyes twinkled at him. "I've always understood quite how the Lord feels about that one sinner redeemed as apart from the ninety-nine good sheep!" Palliser smiled. "But I only wish I could say that all my parishioners were as good Christians as Bremmer. As faithful in attendance, and as charitable, and—er—burdened with as light and trivial sins." O'Ryan suddenly produced a charming Irish grin and added solemnly, "He did have one secret vice, Sergeant—which I can tell you about because he asked me about it several times, you know, not during his confession."

"He had?"

"He had," said O'Ryan, "a secret liking for a little nip of good Scotch whisky now and then. Just a nip, you know. I assured him that so had I, and indeed there's a bottle in the cupboard there this minute. I *rather* think," said O'Ryan, "that it was the price which made him feel it must be sinful—and there I could agree too, what with all these iniquitous taxes the price of it *is* sinful. He used, you know, to go across the street from his little shop downtown, to a small bar there, for a quick drink before going home, after he'd

95

closed up. Did I think it was unjustifiable expense? The poor fellow worried about it. A little drink of good whisky never hurt anybody," said Father O'Ryan comfortably.

Palliser grinned at him. "I'd say the same. Well, if that's all anybody can say against Bremmer—" he sighed and stood up.

"It's a very curious thing. Poor Miss Bremmer—" the priest shook his head. "I suppose I mustn't ask you any questions, Sergeant."

"Well, I'm afraid—"

"Yes, now a thought does occur to me. I've been here only the five years, as I say. Father Stephen knew Mr. Bremmer much longer. He drops round to see me now and then when his arthritis is better—and I'll ask him if he remembers just any little thing about the man you might care to know."

"Thanks very much, Father," said Palliser. They shook hands.

"I'll pray for you to catch the fellow, Sergeant. We've not so many good Christian people about, we can afford to have them killed off."

Outside, Palliser looked at his watch. It was after three-thirty, and he felt he'd wasted the day. Just nothing. He began to wonder if there was anything in this idea of Art's at all. He dropped into the drugstore on the corner and had a Coke, and decided to call Roberta—she'd be home by now. Maybe cheer himself up a little, take her out to dinner to-night.

Hackett was having much the same frustrating experience with his researches on Edith Varick. He'd tried the neighbors first; she'd only lived there six months and in that area the neighbors didn't fraternize too much, but everybody he talked to said she'd seemed a very nice person. Of course, that Latin tag—*de mortuis* something or other. But they all seemed sincere.

He'd gone down to the firm she'd worked for, a big and busy firm of lawyers on Hill Street; and Harkness, the partner who'd introduced her to Varick, couldn't say enough in her praise. Not only efficient, but so pleasant to have around— cheerful, and all the girls working under her, stenos and file clerks, liked her too.

Hackett took that with a grain of salt, begged to be allowed to talk to them too and was told eagerly, *anything* Harkness could do to help. Talking to them—under, of course, the staid gray eye of Edith Varick's successor, a Mrs. Ferris—he singled out one, a pert redhead named Marge, and on his departure cunningly lay in wait for her below, hoping she wouldn't take off for lunch all chummy with one of the other girls. But she didn't, appearing in the lobby alone, and had hesitated only a moment before accepting his offer of lunch; and now he had her en- sconced across the table from him in a booth at a tiny coffee shop down the street, eating a three-decker bacon-tomato- and-avocado sandwich and drinking milk, while he ab- sently envied people who could eat anything and never gain a pound—like his Angel—and drank black coffee.

"Off the record," he said. "Just between us? Was she such a paragon?"

Marge looked at him over the sandwich. "What are you getting at, anyway? It's Mrs. Warren—I mean Mrs. Varick— who got murdered. Honestly, it doesn't seem possible— somebody we all knew. So well. I always think of her as Mrs. Warren—"

"You liked her? Honestly?"

Marge smiled at him and laid the sandwich down. "Well, I don't know what you're trying to get at, Sergeant, but if you think we were all fibbing before, maybe just because Mrs. Ferris was there, we weren't. Mrs. Warren was head secre- tary when I started to work here, that was only two years ago, of course—she hadn't been with the firm long. I know I heard Mr. Harkness say once, when she applied, and he read on her application she'd been Mr. Wendell Mays's secretary for so long, he just grabbed her up, didn't look any further. Mr. Mays had a big practice, he was very well known, and Mr. Harkness'd known him and said he'd heard him say what a jewel his Mrs. Warren was. And she *was*," said Marge.

"She was? Really?"

"Off the record and *on* the record," said Marge. "Of course she was a lot older than the rest of us, but she didn't seem so. She was so—so brisk and cheerful, and never cross or unfair in any way. Sometimes there'd be overtime work, something coming up at the last minute, and she'd always apologize for asking us to stay on. She was nice, Sergeant. And why you should want me to say anything else I can't imagine, with the poor woman murdered by a burglar!" Marge looked a little indignant.

"I didn't exactly," said Hackett.

She finished her milk and crumpled her paper napkin. "Just between you and me, Sergeant, we all liked Mrs. Warren about a thousand per cent better than this hellcat Ferris woman."

And despite himself Hackett laughed.

Over in Glendale, about three o'clock, Higgins was hitting a minor jackpot. He'd got, up to then, nothing. He'd politely checked in with Lieutenant Wheelwright by phone, to let him know that L.A. Homicide was in his territory, and been cordially welcomed. Somewhat enamored of his little idea, he'd gone first to the little park which occupied the square block between Harvard and Colorado, Kenwood and Louise. There weren't many people there, though it was a nice day, but he approached all of them with his badge and the least gruesome shot of Millway and asked questions. He drew blank. None of the park sitters, male or female, acknowledged knowing Millway or even seeing him there.

So Hackett went across the street to the main public library on Harvard, and there he got a little something. Indeed they knew Mr. Millway, said several of the librarians including the brisk, cheerful, black-haired Mrs. Thompson who was assistant head librarian. He'd come in quite a lot, often sat here reading a good part of the day. They had been terribly shocked to read about his murder. The things that happened these days—and in Glendale, such a quiet town as a rule!

Higgins, depressed, went back and sat in the park for another hour, approaching all newcomers—some dog walkers were showing up by then—and got tentative identification from a middle-aged man who thought he remembered seeing Millway here but had never exchanged any conversation with him. Higgins walked down to the Colorado Street side of the park and asked the two morning tennis-players there, and drew blank again. Then he went up to Police Headquarters and kicked it around a little with Wheelwright, and read the further statements the Glendale boys had got from the tenants. There was a lot of verbiage and no solid meat at all. Higgins began to wonder if there was anything at all in Art's idea. He took himself out to lunch presently, at a place recommended by Wheelwright, and then went back to the park. There were different people there now, and he asked them all, and got another tentative identification from a middle-aged woman who thought she'd seen Millway in the park but had never spoken with him.

Well, thought Higgins. In this peculiar business, the victim's nearly as elusive as X. His mind wandered to Mary Dwyer . . . Bert had been dead nine months. He ought to get up nerve to ask her to go to dinner with him some night. Thank God she hadn't suspected the little ruse by which he was paying for Laura's piano lessons. He didn't know what she felt about George Higgins *at all*, damn it. Mary, with her crisp black hair and cool gray eyes. And two nice kids. He'd like to take care of them all. And maybe it had all started because he'd liked Bert, but Mary—

Well. Not what he was getting paid for. Higgins went back to his car, looked up the address in the County Guide, and drove up to Salem Street.

The Salem Arms was an old but dignified red-brick apartment house. About forty apartments, he thought: four stories. Millway had lived on the third floor, apartment 312.

He went in, just to look at the terrain—sometimes that told you something. All that occurred to him was that X must have cased the place, must have known something about Millway's routine. The general age and quality of these apartments, in this neighborhood, would naturally attract the older and more settled people, not the newer, younger transients with their transistor radios and young children. About ninety to a hundred a month, he thought. And as Luis said—between 5 and 7 P.M.—ten to one, everybody here in, and having dinner.

He plodded up the stairs to the second floor. Stairs carpeted. No elevator. Closed doors all around except for one, the one immediately facing the landing. It was open, on an ordinary collection of living-room furniture. Higgins wondered if the tenants left it open much. If they'd been questioned.

A plump woman of middle age appeared suddenly in the living room with a shopping basket on one arm, came out, and banged the door behind her. She looked at Higgins there six feet away, and a little alarm showed in her eyes from the mere size of him.

"Did you—were you looking for somebody?"

Well, no harm to ask. Higgins produced his badge and asked. "Oh, my goodness, *that!*" she said, the alarm disappearing. Of course a cop would be big and ugly and wide-shouldered. She didn't notice the "L.A.P.D." "My goodness, that awful thing, that man murdered right upstairs! Why, we'd only just moved in, you know, first of the month, and if we hadn't already paid the two months' rent, I said to Bill, I'd feel like moving right out! But the manager said it'd never happened before, nice quiet neighborhood, and there are good locks and we're careful, of course. In Glendale, of all places—nice quiet town like this! And do you know, I said to Bill when I heard, *I might have seen him!*" She looked triumphantly at Higgins.

"What do you mean, Mrs.—?"

"Trapp, I'm Mrs. Trapp. It could have been the one. What it said in the paper. After that first clue, they thought it was, about the vengeance petered out. It said, probably between five and seven P.M. And it *could* have been him I saw!"

"Didn't the police—?" He understood all the tenants had been questioned. He got out his notebook. Just a fluke?—and if he hadn't been here, after those hick suburban boys missed a chance—he felt a little indignant, and a little hopeful.

"Oh, I wasn't here then. They talked to Bill, sure. He couldn't tell them anything. See, we hadn't been moved in three days when my Aunt Anna had the stroke. I had to go and see to things, over in Eagle Rock it was, till her daughter got here from Phoenix, my cousin Rhoda. Not that I minded —family duty. But I wasn't here on account of that. And I never saw a paper, two, three days, so busy and all, but when I did—when I got back, and Bill told me all about it, I said right off, he might have been the one."

"I'd like to hear all about it, Mrs. Trapp," said Higgins. Something?

"Happy to oblige. I'd forgot I was out of coffee. That very day the man got murdered, I mean. It was about a quarter of six, and Bill's due home at six-thirty, he's a mechanic at Art Frost's agency, and he does expect a good hot meal when he comes home, *which* I've never failed him yet. And there I was out of coffee, but that nice new Better Foods market's only a block away up on Central, so I just slipped my change purse in my pocket and nipped out to get some. And just as I came out the door, here," said Mrs. Trapp, "there was a man going up the stairs, there. And it *could* have been the one, being that time, couldn't it?"

"Possibly," said Higgins. "What did he look like, Mrs. Trapp?"

"Oh, I couldn't say. I didn't see his face, you know. Just noticed him climbing the stairs, from the back."

"Could you tell me anything about his clothes?"

"Well—uh—" she looked vague. "I didn't notice really. I mean, why would I, *then?* He was just a man going up the stairs."

"Do you think you'd ever seen him before?"

"Oh, I couldn't say. Really. I hadn't any call to notice him, *then.* But when the paper said between five and seven—"

Higgins shut his notebook and thought, people. And then his sense of fair play told him that she was perfectly right, why should she have taken any special notice, then? She was new in this building; it could have been one of the other tenants, for all she knew. And it still could have been. Nothing said that was X.

"He had on a light jacket," she said suddenly. "Trying to think back, it just came to me. Almost white, it was—whity-gray. And gray trousers."

Well, that was something. Go to all the trouble to check the other tenants—no, only the ones on the two top floors—to see if one of the men had been dressed like that?

It didn't sound like much, but you never knew what would pay off.

So now he was up in the Detective Bureau at Glendale Headquarters again, sitting beside Lieutenant Wheelwright's desk and giving him all these odds and ends.

"Funniest damn business," said Wheelwright interestedly. "We'll check those tenants, just to be thorough, Sergeant."

Looking around, Higgins decided this might be an up-and-coming little force after all. "It's nothing," he said. "Even if nobody there was dressed like that and hadn't any callers dressed like that, so we surmise that *was* X, it gives us nothing on him, nowhere to look. And we've had these offbeat ones before, God knows—" He thought about some of them, even a little nostalgically, that Slasher thing, and Art getting assaulted, and the bank robber, and that really crazy thing last March— "But this is just a handful of nothing. Nowhere to look. At least, thank God, you've scotched the press on that file card." Wheelwright had done that, announcing that it was just part of some contest Millway had been entering, looking up quotations: nothing to do with the murder, which was probably triggered by a burglary attempt.

"Yes, but—" said Wheelwright, and lights flashed and the phone burred discreetly on his desk. He picked it up. "Wheelwright . . . Oh. Oh, yes, he is, Lieutenant. You want —O.K. It's your boss," he said, handing over the phone.

"Luis?"

"Come to Papa," said Mendoza. "We've got number five."

"For God's sake!" said Higgins incredulously. "Number—who?"

"Owner of a gas station out on Beverly. One Ray Atwood. Discovered by a customer thirty minutes ago," said Mendoza tersely. "Come home, George."

"On my way," said Higgins. "My God!"

Eight

I<small>T</small> was a Richfield station on Beverly out the other side of Rampart Boulevard. When Higgins got there, he spotted the big black Ferrari parked around on the side street. Mendoza and Hackett were standing by the pumps talking to two men, the ambulance was parked near the grease pit, and the squad car just taking off to get back on tour. Probably the mobile lab was on the way.

Higgins parked ahead of the Ferrari and walked up to the group near the pumps. It was a smart, clean, new-looking station, as decorative as they tried to make them now, with cement-curb triangles of colored gravel and a Japanese-looking tree in the middle of the one on the corner.

One of the civilians, a short plump little man in untidy sports clothes, was talking loudly and compulsively, and tears stood in his eyes. The other one, a tall thin man in a rumpled suit and no tie, was just staring at the ground.

"—not *possible*, and my God, why? Why? A young man like Ray—good upstanding young man, ambitious, good, friendly, and he's got three kids, my God, how'll Sandra be left? Thirty-three, he was thirty-three. Just like my own son that I lost in Korea. Just like my own. And if it was a holdup, my God, why?—Ray always said, people told him about that, he always said he wouldn't be fool enough to

104

put up a fight to a holdup man. He's insured. There weren't any shots, my God. My God, a young man, three kids, him so proud of that boy of his, come into my place to buy a birthday present for the boy just last week it was—my God—"

John Palliser backed out of the ambulance and came up to Higgins. Higgins moved toward him. Palliser was looking angry.

He said, "This is one for the books, George. Come see. In broad daylight, with hordes of people all around. He may be a lunatic but he's a damn canny one, all right."

"How in the name of God could he take anybody here?" Higgins had been wondering about that ever since he'd laid eyes on the place. The station was on a corner of busy Beverly Boulevard, and across the side street was a TV-and-appliance store. Next to the station lot was a whole block of small stores under one roof: an arts-and-hobby shop, a hardware store, a music store, a dry cleaners', a coffee shop, a stationers'; then an alley, and more stores. And another block of stores across the street. People all around, within hailing distance.

"Oh, this was a beauty," said Palliser. "I will be damned. I will be damned. Just as easy to read as print, and this bastard—come up here."

There was, about the middle of the station lot, the small composition-stone and glass building where the books, cash register and so on would be: right next to that the grease pit, and over at one side of the lot, built of white stucco and partly faced with composition stone, the one small building housing the two rest rooms, back to back. *Gentlemen* was facing the street, about forty feet up from the sidewalk.

Palliser said, "Here. Right here." There was a partial head-high baffle built round two sides of the building, screening both doors. The door into *Gentlemen* was propped open with a brick. "Until it gets printed—but there won't be any.

105

He was right there." An outline in rough chalk on the beige vinyl flooring, inside the door: by the outline, Atwood had fallen prone, feet toward the door nearly touching it. Not much space here. Two cubicles, a washbasin, about seven square feet of floor space aside from the cubicles.

"I don't—oh," said Higgins. "For God's sake. What a diabolical—was he garroted too?"

"Damn right. It is," said Palliser, "the goddamned *arrogance* of it that gets me! In broad daylight—here! The intern said he wasn't an hour dead, or thereabout. You see the m.o.?"

"I see it," said Higgins. And diabolical you could call it. On the face of it, quite a problem, to murder a man in a place like this, people all around, without calling attention to yourself. Really only one way it could be done, quick and sure, and Higgins—a good detective but not having a murderous turn of mind—would never have thought of it himself. Probably. But he could see it now.

If Beverly Boulevard was crowded, well, there was a certain safety in crowds. You were anonymous in a crowd. Drive into the station, just a car stopping for gas. Maybe tell Atwood to fill the tank. And stroll across to the rest room meanwhile. And presently step out and beckon Atwood casually. There's a faucet running, won't shut off: one of the toilets is stopped up: there aren't any paper towels, you'd tell him. And Atwood comes, and you let him go in first, maybe still talking, and as soon as he's screened by the baffle and the door, out comes the garrote.

"But why the hell? That fellow out there said a young man—he can't—"

"Have any of them anything in common?" asked Palliser savagely. "You tell me! One thing I will say—"

"Yes," said Higgins, automatically functioning as a detective, "I see that. He must have known Atwood was alone in the station. Was he always? Not likely. He wouldn't have risked being seen by another attendant. As it was, even if somebody around noticed that—him beckoning Atwood over to the rest room, Atwood going in—it wouldn't matter if they saw him come casually out and drive away in his car. They'd just think Atwood had stayed to fix something. But what a nerve, John! To take the risk that nobody *would*—"

"It's a busy street. Probably a busy station. Who would take notice of another car driving in? But, you know, on this one maybe he's taken one chance too many," said Palliser. "Just possibly. Somebody might have noticed something."

And on this one, there were plenty of people to ask. Higgins looked across the street. On the corner there, a delicatessen: next to it, a photographers' shop, a four-entrance discount house, furniture and appliances; a liquor store; a bakery; and a drugstore. Somebody certainly might have seen something, on this one. And then again, they might not. It wasn't as if there'd been any shots, anything to draw attention to the gas station.

"But there are," he said, "a lot of places to ask."

Palliser agreed. "Taking any bets?"

"Uh-uh," said Higgins. "Having been a cop a long time, and knowing how blind people can be." They moved toward the pumps.

The plump man was running down a little and getting more coherent. "My God, who'll tell Sandra? I can't get over it—Ray! These damn hoods, these damn murderers running loose—every day you see it in the paper, crooks, holdups, shooting—what's *happened* to this generation? And always the ones like Ray—good, respectable, honest, ambitious!" He wiped a hand across his eyes.

"This is Mr. Seidenbaum from the hobby shop," said Mendoza to Higgins. "And Mr. Folsom who found the body."

Folsom was looking gloomy. "I'm sorry about it," he said in a bass voice, "but I didn't know the man and here I am delayed God knows how long and I had a five o'clock appointment. No offense."

And, on what the intern said, Folsom had just been unlucky there: the one man who'd pulled into this station in the last hour or two, who went over to the rest room. How many had driven in, waited, sworn, and gone on to the next station?

They were busy there, of course, for some time. The little crowd collected when the mobile lab arrived, most of the store owners on both sides of the street came over to see what had happened. Most of them had known Atwood at least casually, if not as well as Seidenbaum, and from piecing together what they could tell, the Homicide men came up with a picture that said their boy had cased this one all right. And yet, he hadn't had to know much but a few things which in theory he could have got from casual conversation with Atwood himself.

Ray Atwood had leased and managed the station for the last five years. He had a good reputation: hard-working, cheerful, ambitious, all the rest of it. Of course he wasn't alone on the job, most of the time. He hired another man, one Chuck Weaver, who was at the station from noon to nine at night when it closed, and an extra mechanic two days a week, Tuesdays and Thursdays. Weaver was currently on vacation, and Atwood had hired a young kid to fill in temporarily, but only from four o'clock on, the kid being in high school.

"He cut it fine," commented Hackett to that.

"Don't know. The intern said two-thirty to three-thirty," said Mendoza. And of course even if Weaver hadn't been on vacation, X could have found Atwood alone at the station in the morning.

The young kid had shown up by then, of course, and he didn't know a thing. Mr. Atwood just the same as usual yesterday, and he'd been at school till three today.

The mobile-lab unit didn't find anything but a mess of unclassifiable prints in the rest room, no physical evidence at all. It was, undeniably, a very efficient way of killing anybody.

And it got to be six o'clock and there wasn't anything more to be done here—statements to take later, at the office; Mendoza called in for Galeano and Piggott to come down and help start sorting that out, which statements might be important enough to get down in black and white. Seidenbaum hadn't seen anything. Hoeffler at the delicatessen across the street said he'd noticed "a big white car" in at the station, glancing up once, but he was very vague on times. One of the salesmen at the discount house said he'd noticed a tan car, could have been a Dodge or an Olds about five, six years old, at the station, when he went out for a cup of coffee about a quarter to three. Who would take any special note of a car pulling into a gas station? A thing that happened a hundred times a day. And nobody at all in the little crowd—of all the storekeepers both sides of the block—had noticed a strange man on foot in the station lot, any time today. But again, that wouldn't be so unusual that anybody would take notice.

Anonymity in a crowd, all right. Everybody along there had his own business to mind. Cars pulling in and out of the gas station all day. And X, of course, would have taken care not to draw attention to himself. All the same, this one had been pulled off with an arrogant recklessness, and it annoyed them considerably.

They'd give it to the press as a probable attempted holdup (nothing missing from the till, of course) and ask all public cooperation: would anyone who'd been on Beverly Boulevard at such and such times, who might have seen anything significant, please communicate with the police? From that, they'd probably get a few calls, but everything would have to be checked out, however vague the information was, because you never knew when something apparently irrelevant would turn out to be helpful.

Mendoza swore. "This bastard I would like to get. Laughing in our faces—"

"I don't suppose he is really, Luis," said Hackett slowly. "I don't think he's thinking about us at all. He's taking the precautions, sure, out of habit maybe because he started out that way. But we've said from the start he's a nut of some kind—has an obsession of some kind—and my guess'd be, he's so obsessed about it, being this far along, so to speak, he's beyond worrying about us at all."

And Mendoza said, "You could be absolutely right, Arturo. But I'd give double this year's income tax to know just what the hell his obsession is." The body had been taken away long ago, but he looked up at the little discreet rest room there. "Ray Atwood. What the hell put him in line for vengeance along with the rest of these people?"

There being no immediate answer, they went on to what came next. Which was breaking the news to the widow, and probably they wouldn't get any coherent answers out of her for a day or two. Palliser, still feeling angry—which he didn't very often—took off at ten to seven, drove over to South Pasadena and picked up Roberta Silverman, apologizing for lateness and explaining.

Roberta said she'd gathered what she was letting herself in for, marrying a cop; Alison and Angel had told her this and that. Palliser said "Yes" absently, and unusually for him talked shop over dinner at The Barristers' Inn. This one, he said—pulling off a thing like that, broad daylight on Beverly Boulevard—and the poor young fellow only thirty-three, a wife and family—somebody had said three kids. And Ray Atwood— "My God," he said, "if you went *looking*, Robin, for five people who were all utterly different from each other! There's nothing to get *hold* of on it. No possible connection."

"It's queer, all right," said Roberta, looking at him with her quiet eyes. "You don't often get the—the offbeat thing like this. It worries you. There was a card, just like all the others?" Policemen's wives and girl friends get trained not to talk secrets; policemen, even as other men, have to blow off steam to somebody.

"Oh, what else? Dropped on the body. Now just have a guess what this is all *about!*" said Palliser.

"A lunatic," said Roberta. "Haven't you got anything from checking with Camarillo and so on?"

"Nothing remotely useful. And how could there be, unless some known nut had pulled off this kind of thing before? They can tell us about patients recently released, they give us capsule reports on them, but—considering the head doctors—can they say with any certainty who's likely to do what? Nobody can. A handful of nothing—and only God's grace some nosy reporter hasn't ferreted it out and made headlines. I don't know, Art's idea about the different motives sounded plausible, but the more we look into backgrounds, the less sense it makes." Suddenly Palliser smiled —an hour of Roberta's company, and a couple of drinks before dinner, had restored his normal good humor. "I like that priest," he said. "On Bremmer. Little stodgy fellow—his one secret vice the little nip of good Scotch at the bar across the street . . . But I do ask you. That's the one thing we came across. I suppose you could say that's another unusual thing —all of them, except Jamison of course, such paragons of virtue. Such nice respectable people. But there they are, dead. Because somebody thought they deserved the vengeance."

"A little brandy after dinner, sir?" insinuated the waiter.

"Yes, thanks," said Palliser recklessly.

"But—*five* of them," said Roberta. "No leads at *all*, John?"

"It's a very anonymous way to commit murder," said Palliser.

"Yes, but—yes, I can see that." Roberta leaned on the table, chin cupped in one hand, smoking lazily. "I was just reading something a while ago—a very good novel by John Masters. About those Thugs. That was the way they went about it, garroting."

Palliser said he hadn't time to read fiction. Roberta opened her eyes on him wider and said severely she could see he needed his habits changed, and after they were married—

Palliser said he had no doubt of that. And the seventeenth *was* a Friday, wasn't it, and unless they were swamped at the office he could beg the Saturday off at least, and they could fly over to Vegas to make it legal. And then on his vacation have a proper wedding trip. And with any luck, he'd have a salary increase next year, and she could quit work and—

"Yes," said Roberta contentedly. They held hands across the table and sipped brandy and forgot about Ray Atwood who lay on a slab in the morgue awaiting the official identification.

It was a very funny thing, and probably had something to do with getting older, or possibly with Alison; but Mendoza had never minded breaking the bad news until he'd turned into a husband. People were people, they came all sorts, they had their own problems and griefs and opinions and lives to lead; and it had never meant anything to him, as Mendoza or as a cop, to ring the doorbell and show the badge and say, "Sorry, he's dead. You'll have to come down and identify the body." People died, a turn of Destiny's fixed roulette wheel, and that was that.

Until there was the house on Rayo Grande Avenue, and red-haired Alison in it, and later the twin monsters. Then, all of a sudden, he started minding when he had to break the bad news.

Breaking the bad news to Mary Dwyer that day, with a sudden vision of Hackett ringing the doorbell of the house on

Rayo Grande Avenue and saying gently, reluctantly, un-happily, "I'm sorry . . ."

There was a thing called empathy.

Hackett went with him, and they called in at headquar-ters and picked up a policewoman, Daisy Janeway, a veteran sergeant who was always a tower of strength.

Sandra Atwood, of course, wouldn't have been expecting him home until about nine-thirty.

They told her, the only way they could tell her—blunt and factual. She was a pretty woman about her husband's age, blonde and slim, and there was a ten-year-old boy and a seven-year-old girl and another girl about four, and only the boy really understood what they were talking about.

It was a rough one.

"No," she said. "No. There was so much we meant to do—so much we'd planned. You don't understand, that just can't be. He's only thirty-three. We were married in high school. They said, foolish, but we knew—we had it all planned. Ray's ambitious, but he knew college and a job like that were not for him—he's a very good mechanic, he likes to work with his hands. We saved and planned so long, for his own station—he's done so well. He went to night school, he took accounting so he'd know how to manage—we both worked, we said, not to start a family until we could afford it. Do it right. You don't understand," she said earnestly.

It was a modest newish house up on Tracy Street in Hollywood, the furniture rather sparse, everything polished and shining.

Sergeant Janeway murmured soothingly and stood pa-tiently holding the aspirin, the glass of water. "Mrs. Atwood, if you'd—"

The boy just stared, leaning on his mother, her arm around him fiercely—a nice-looking boy, tall for his age, brown-haired, brown-eyed; he stared at them and his chin quivered.

"You don't understand," said Sandra Atwood quite politely to Mendoza, to Hackett. "It can't be. We've been lucky. So lucky. But we planned it all. I worked too, when Ray went to school. He got that job at the station down on Spring, and Mr. Ring was good to him. Ray's very ambitious. He thought, manage a whole chain of stations eventually. Nothing can happen to Ray, he's lucky. Of course, you have to work and plan to be lucky. We have, you know." She looked up at Sergeant Janeway, and her blue eyes were quite blank, and she smiled. "Do you know, neither of us ever dated anybody else? We knew how it'd be for us, even in school. Three kids, we said—when we could afford it— and Ray'd get places. He's a good mechanic, but he's good at managing too, everybody likes Ray. And we worked for it—we saved. We really scrimped to get that money together, for the lease. Poor Ray"—she smiled at Mendoza—"Saturdays when he got off work at nine—that place downtown— before Glenn was born, of course, that was—he liked to stop in, have a beer before he came home, and he felt so guilty about it—as if it mattered! I didn't mind—he said—every spare penny, hon, we ought to, because we'll get places— and nice things for the kids—that silly bed jacket he got me when Glenn was born—"

"Mrs. Atwood," said Sergeant Janeway gently, "won't you—"

"The station's doing so well," she said. "You're just trying to frighten me, aren't you? I don't know why. It can't be, what you say, because you see Ray'd never leave me alone— it's been sixteen years, nearly seventeen, and what would I do without Ray?"

"Mother," said the boy in a whisper. "Mother. Is—is Dad *dead?*"

"Of course he can't be," she said reasonably. "He's only thirty-three. You're telling me—" And quite suddenly, as she tried to say *lies,* her pretty face crumpled into age and un-

114

believing grief and a kind of dissolution, and she said as if it was her last hope of faith or God or life, "*Ray!*" and fell across the arm of her chair.

"I don't think you'll get much out of her for a few days," said Sergeant Janeway compassionately. "I'll see to her, and the children. I expect there are some relatives. You might as well go."

And Mendoza went home, and was met at the door by Alison, who told him she thought the twin monsters had inherited all the worst traits of both sides of the family, they'd been perfect *devils* all day and both she and Máiri were completely worn out coping with them and she thought she'd been a complete fool to marry him at all.

"*No hay tal,*" said Mendoza. "*Vaya despacio, cara.*" Suddenly he hugged her very hard and close. "Let's thank the powers that be we've so much to complain about. We're here, together."

"Luis—" Alison held away and looked up at him.

"Never mind," he said. "*No metan tanta bulla.*"

"I kept dinner hot for you when you called—"

"I'll have a drink first," said Mendoza.

And Hackett went home, and found Angel peacefully stirring things on the stove, the baby serenely asleep and Mark absorbed with crayons and shelf paper, and said bitterly, "Why in hell did I ever want to be a cop! Harbingers of doom and disaster!"

"What?" said Angel. "Darling! The stalwart upstanding protectors of law and order! What prompted that?" Her cheeks were flushed from the hot stove, and she smiled at him. "I kept dinner hot for you, when you called."

Hackett looked at his house in order, the peaceful children, the great smoke-gray Persian cat curled asleep in his basket, and suddenly he pulled his Angel around from the stove and kissed her soundly.

"Goodness, Art! What prompted—"

"Just," he said, "for being here, Angel."

Cops—in spite of all the propaganda—were still human beings.

Nine

WHEN Hackett woke up on Saturday morning, there was something just on the edge of his consciousness that he couldn't pin down. It was, he had the distinct impression, something somebody had said to him, that had rung a faint bell—but he couldn't to save his life remember who, or what. It was just *there,* a tantalizing something that he felt might be important, but the more he tried to think about it, prod his memory, the further away it slid into his subconscious.

"Damn," he said, sitting on the edge of the bed. He yawned and scratched his head. Like trying to remember a name, he philosophized. Let it go, stop trying to remember, and when you least expected it, the thing would suddenly come to you.

It bothered him, because he had the definite feeling that it *was* important, but he tried to put it out of his mind in the approved manner. He washed and shaved, and found breakfast ready in the kitchen, and at seven-thirty-five backed out the Barracuda and started downtown on the freeway.

When he got to the office, he found some new business had come in. Overnight they'd got the stabbing victim identified: a man named Ruiz had come in and at the morgue identified the body as one Carlos Orvidez, his wife's uncle. He gave them an address, but Galeano had let it lie over for the day crew; it had been nearly midnight. Also they had a new body, an elderly man found dead of a bullet wound in an apartment on Second Street, and something would have to be done on that; the call had just come in as the shift was changing.

Higgins and Palliser drifted in with Landers behind them, and Sergeant Lake came in, took off his hat and sat down at the desk. Sergeant Farrell went out. The night men went out. Mendoza, spruce and natty as ever, appeared in the doorway of his office. "Art, you and George want to start the routine on this Orvidez? Tom, hang around a while, will you? I've got Sandra Atwood's father coming in to make a formal identification of the body—I want to talk to him first, and then you can take him down to the morgue."

"I still cannot get over that damned thing," said Palliser. "You'd think somebody would have seen something—on the other hand, of course—well. Had I better go out and talk to all those store owners again, try to pin down whatever they do remember?"

"No harm," said Mendoza. He laughed shortly. "Any little thing we can find out for sure—I've just had Wheelwright on the phone. The Glendale boys checked out the two top floors of Millway's apartment house. After hearing what Mrs. Trapp told you, George. Result, none of the male tenants own a very light, 'almost white' sports jacket, and as far as anybody remembers, there weren't any salesmen or visitors dressed like that coming around at that hour. So that could very well have been our boy, so we know he owns an almost-white sports jacket."

"Big deal," said Palliser. "I'll go poke around some more." He went out.

The thing, whatever it was, was still gnawing away at the back of Hackett's mind. He tried to forget it. Don't pay any notice and it would come to him eventually.

And both he and Higgins were a good deal more inter-

118

ested in the avenger and his latest victim than in the elderly Orvidez stabbed to death and left on the street, but some attention had to be paid to it, of course. Lake gave them the address—Beacon Avenue—and they headed for it in the Barracuda.

Mr. Arthur Dover came in at a quarter to nine. Sergeant Janeway had contacted Sandra Atwood's parents last night, and they'd showed up to take over right away. Nice people, she'd reported, very much shocked. Their doctor had taken Mrs. Atwood to the hospital, and they were staying with the children.

Dover was a smallish man, very dapper, quiet and sensible; he talked to Mendoza sensibly, after saying all the expectable things. He was taking it for granted that Atwood had been killed by a holdup man, and when Mendoza started to question him about Atwood's history he looked a little bewildered.

"But what has that—? Well, I want to help you in any way I can, Lieutenant, of course. Of course. This is the most shocking—we were against the marriage at first, they were so young, but it worked out just fine, you know. Sandra never wanted to go on to college, she's always been domestic, and Ray was such a steady, responsible boy—even at seventeen. A good boy—a good father. It's just a wicked thing, Lieutenant." Dover took off his glasses and started to clean them, his hands trembling slightly. He was a bookkeeper in the business offices of a big department store, a steady responsible man himself. "We were so proud of the grandchildren," he said. "I don't know what Sandra will do. He couldn't afford much insurance . . . But really I don't see why you'd be asking about—"

"We're thinking," said Mendoza, "from this and that evidence, that it could have been a grudge killing, Mr. Dover. Anything you can tell me about any trouble Atwood may have had with someone—at any time. Anything at all like that you can think of—I understand you saw your daughter and son-in-law regularly, he'd probably have mentioned anything—"

"Yes," said Dover mechanically, "yes, we nearly always had Sunday dinner together, I—we were so fond of Ray—such a—but that's just impossible, Lieutenant! There couldn't be anything like that! Ray was very easygoing, he wasn't given to quarrels with people—or any *trouble* of any sort. He hadn't a hot temper at all. Oh, he was strict with the children, both he and Sandra believe in *discipline*—but outside, why, that was one reason he was doing so well with the station, he had a very friendly manner with people, he was always putting himself out to give the little extra service, he had a good many regular customers just on account of that. I don't see—"

Mendoza said his piece all over again and jogged Mr. Dover into reminiscing. The Atwoods had married when they were still in high school. Such sensible youngsters, planning ahead—and so much in love. When he graduated, Ray had done his army service, had further training as a mechanic in the service, and Sandra had worked—office work. Then he'd got a job at a service station downtown, that was when he'd got out of the army and they were back home. And they'd started saving all they could, Sandra still working, for the start of their family and also for Ray to have his own station. They'd been married six years before Glenn was born, and by then Ray had a better job up in Hollywood; and about five years ago they'd finally got the money together for Ray to take up a lease on a chain station, and he'd never looked back since. Been doing fine. And—a little indignantly Mr. Dover said it—in all the years he'd known Ray Atwood, and no man could ask for a finer son-in-law, he'd never known him to have any kind of trouble or argument with anybody at all. "Ray was a very easygoing fellow," he said. "Everybody liked him. There just couldn't be anything like this grudge business, Lieutenant. Ray never did anybody down or anything like that."

Mendoza sighed and aligned the desk blotter with the edge of the desk. Another paragon of virtue, he thought. All these people couldn't be lying. And he'd thought Art's brilliant idea about the different motives sounded a good bet; but now he was wondering.

And what he was wondering about was the little notion Alison had tossed off. Somebody—O'Connor up at Wilcox Street—had offered the diffident idea that all this rigmarole might have its roots in the past somehow, and that was in his mind now. Something akin to Alison's fire, and X resenting people just being alive—because, always excepting Jamison, there just wasn't one solitary thing about the rest of these people that the most puritanical or fanatical lunatic could judge as deserving of vengeance.

"It just couldn't be," said Dover earnestly. "I thought— a holdup—"

Mendoza shifted the desk lighter in line with the basket. *Caray*, he thought, what the hell *was* all this, anyway? He'd been collecting a few statistics from the various statements they'd taken. And try as you would, you couldn't match them up any way at all: they just didn't jibe. Jamison, no religion, no politics, thirty-eight, money, a record. Bremmer, devout Catholic, Republican, sixty-two, a modest income. Varick, no religious affiliation, Democrat, fifty-one, had just married money. Millway, unknown, seventy-four, a modest pension. Atwood—what the hell did it matter? They didn't link in any of those ways, so it had to be something else.

So, was George's crazy idea about the jury possible? Only just, he decided. And if it was triggered by something like that, some incident in the past (and how far back?) in which all of these people had figured, he did not see how—even with all their resources these days—they could ever find out what it had been, unless they got very lucky and caught up with X and he told them.

And just who else around here, of the approximately seven and a quarter million people in L.A. County, did the avenger feel was deserving of vengeance?

God, he thought, if we could spot it—if it *is* a thing like that, spot the incident that, how long after the event, had triggered it off—and ferret out a couple of intended victims, stake them out—

That was just wishful thinking. Mendoza felt frustrated and annoyed. They'd had tough ones, and anonymous ones, before; and as he'd said to Wheelwright, some they had to file away under Pending. But he couldn't recall another quite so amorphous business as this. Lunatic—there couldn't be a sane reason behind it; but the lunatic very canny. Up, he thought suddenly, to a point. Yes. A very simple method, and really the canniness was rudimentary, wasn't it?

"Well, thanks very much, Mr. Dover," he said, getting up. "I'll want to talk to your daughter when she's feeling up to it, but—"

Dover shook his head. "She's just prostrated. I don't know what she'll do. We'll help all we can, but—and Ray hadn't any people, you know. His father died when he was just a kid, and his mother was killed in an accident a few years ago." He blinked at Mendoza. "You just find out who *did* it, Lieutenant. I'm not a vindictive man, but this is a wicked, wicked thing."

"So it is," said Mendoza. "Detective Landers will take you down to the morgue, Mr. Dover. It's just a formality—I'm sorry."

"Yes, sir, I understand."

And Mendoza, watching him out, thought about what Art had said further—an obsession of some kind. They could cover up for years, the incipient lunatics; but when they

122

started acting out the lunacy, quite often it started to show on the surface, and they got spotted.

But, five people—and that had been a very slick little operation, yesterday, at the gas station in broad daylight.

Sergeant Lake looked in and said he had another corpse. No mystery—thank God, the real mystery seldom came into Homicide—but some more paperwork. Elderly man dropped dead in front of the Biltmore Hotel.

Mendoza sighed again and said he'd get on it.

Hackett and Higgins had gone to the address on Beacon Avenue with the expectation that they would spend some time waiting for the relatives' shock and grief to expend itself, before they could ask questions. There was one little thing, of course—it might seem just a little funny, if Carlos Orvidez had a family, that the family hadn't missed him before and maybe mentioned it to the police; he'd been killed several days ago. But both Hackett and Higgins knew that, while the majority of Mexican families down here were honest, respectable people, there were others, and the Orvidez family might be one of them. People who, though they might never have broken any law, were just naturally leery of authority; and others who had been in cop trouble and felt the same way.

But as soon as they got inside the place, both of them as seasoned cops smelled something funny. Something wrong.

It looked like a typical family, and the funny thing was that, whatever smelled wrong, though neither of them could have explained that, was not pro-criminal wrong. It was just something funny.

There was Orvidez' daughter-in-law; Mama, about fifty, still pretty; and two younger kids still at home, a boy and girl in their teens. Probably a few more grown-up between those and the married daughter, who lived on the other side of this little frame duplex with her husband, Jim Aradores, and their three kids. They were all there except Aradores, who was, of course, at his job: he worked for the city as a professional tree trimmer and parks-maintenance man.

And they were all of them thoroughly American citizens; even Mama hadn't any accent on the English, the kids were sharp-eyed American kids talking the latest slang; and, oddly, there wasn't any emanation (overt or any other way) of the leeriness of cops. They hadn't delayed mentioning Grandpa being missing because they were scared of the brutal police. The five-year-old boy, belonging to the married daughter, stared at Hackett's badge and grinned at him admiringly.

And yet, it was an act. Mama bursting into tears. "My poor papa, the innocent old one, he is killed by some thief for the little, little money he has in his pockets! It is terrible —wicked—Margarita, you know we have told him not to be out at night alone! The terrible things that happen—"

"Um, Mrs. Orvidez," said Hackett. "We understood from Mr. Ruiz, who identified the body, that Mr. Orvidez was your father-in-law? Your husband is dead, but Mr. Orvidez lived with you?"

"Yes, that is so, but exactly the same as my own papa!" Her chins quivered pathetically. "A good man, we had worried—and now he is dead! Ah, we had told him—Margarita, you can say—not to go about at night, alone—even for the little, little money, these terrible wicked thieves—Jim had told him—" She gestured dramatically, a hand to her heart.

"Yes, but he was killed, probably, on Tuesday night," said Higgins. "He did live here? Why hadn't you reported him missing? Was he in the habit of staying away for several days at a time?"

"Yeah, he did sometimes," said Margarita Aradores. "He'd done that, all right." She was a shapely female in her late twenties, full-breasted. "Yeah, that's right."

"You said you never did like that fool Ruiz," piped up the

124

five-year-old brightly. "Why, Mama? He give me a candy bar once, why—?"

"You shut up! Kids, they—get things all twisted." She gave Higgins a nervous smile. "I—just like Mama says, we—well, we were just waiting for him to come home. Like—like he'd done before, see? Yeah, we'd told him not to go roaming all over, *some* people down here take a knife to you for a couple of bucks, but—gee, I wish Jim was here, he'd—well, you can *ask* him, he'll tell you too! It must've been just one of these bums, after what the old man had on him. Poor Grandpa."

The other kids, Mama's teen-agers, Margarita's other boy about ten, and a girl about twelve, watched the scene silently, with opaque dark eyes and impassive expressions. The girl was going to be as pretty as her mother.

"Well, when did you last see him?"

Mama shrugged. "Tuesday afternoon? I guess. Terrible, terrible. And we are thinking he's off enjoying himself with his friends—ah, these wicked people!" She shed a few more tears. "Why should we worry? He's lived sixty-five years with no harm, he's got the little money in his pocket from the state pension, why should we think terrible things happen to him? Like Margarita says, you can ask Jim, her man, he'll say—the poor Grandpa go off, stay two, three days enjoying himself with his friends—drink a little wine maybe—why should we think harm?"

"That's right," said Margarita. The five-year-old opened his mouth and she shook him hard and he shut it.

And it smelled very funny. Very funny indeed.

They went out and sat in the screaming-scarlet Barracuda and Higgins said, "They're nervous. Why, Art? They look like all-right people. The husband with a job. Kids look clean —house looks clean. Religious people—there's a crucifix on the wall, and that statue of the Virgin. Grandpa. For God's sake, why are they telling lies about it?"

125

"I think they are, all right," said Hackett thoughtfully. "I wonder why. I think we want to see this Jim Aradores, George, and I also think when we do we're going to hear some very much more plausible and glib lies backing up Mama and Margarita."

"Why?" asked Higgins blankly.

"Right now, I'm having no guesses. I also think," said Hackett even more thoughtfully, "that I'd like to talk to some of the neighbors about them. And do you know, George, I think we'll put the night crew on that—so Mama and Margarita don't notice, with any luck—and it could just be that we'll want to get a warrant and look through that house."

"You're ahead of me. For God's sake, you don't think they did it?"

"I don't know. I think they know more about it than they're saying."

"So do I, but to jump to the conclusion—if what I gather from the warrant bit is what you're doing—that he could have been killed closer to home—"

"I wasn't jumping exactly," said Hackett. "Just wondering. And I think I'd also like to talk to this Ruiz who identified the body. As his wife's uncle."

Higgins agreed to that, so they went and found Salvador Ruiz. He worked at a pool hall down on Fourth. And what they got there made the whole thing smell just a little more wrong. Ruiz was very reluctant to talk. Well, he'd seen in the paper about this body, and way it was described he just thought—no, no, he hadn't talked to any of Orvidez' family about it—some bum knifing the poor old man for what he had on him—he couldn't tell them anything else.

Hackett and Higgins, outside, looked at each other and headed back to base to query Records. They drew blank. None of these people had the smallest pedigree.

"Funny," said Higgins. "Let's lay it in front of Luis."

It was twelve-thirty, and the office was empty. They went

126

up to Federico's in search of Mendoza, but it was to be some time before they laid the funny smell about Orvidez in front of the boss, for just as they came in, and spotted Mendoza and Palliser at a table, Hackett's subconscious mind delivered the goods, and he clapped a hand to his forehead and said, "My God! My God, *that* was it! My—"

"What?" said Higgins.

Hackett charged up to the table and pulled out the third chair. "John," he said urgently. "You said something about that priest you saw—the priest of the church Bremmer went to. He told you about Bremmer liking a little nip of whisky now and—"

"That's right," said Palliser, looking a little surprised. "Why?" He put down the menu as the waiter came up. "Scotch and water, and then the minute steak, Adam. French fries."

"Listen," said Hackett. "Listen—my God, it just came to me—been at the back of my mind ever since I woke up, and I couldn't pin it down, but—what? Oh, the steak's fine, O.K., yes, Scotch and soda—listen—"

"What," asked Mendoza, "has bitten you? Don't tell me, an inspiration. Steak sandwich, Adam."

"Insp—"

"That'll do for me," said Higgins. "Scotch and water."

"*Listen!*" said Hackett. "If I remember right, he told you that Bremmer used to go across the street from his shop to a little bar there, for his nip of Scotch, before going home?"

"That's right," said Palliser interestedly. "Why?"

"Well, my God," said Hackett, "it just came to me—Luis, you'll remember—when we went to break the news to Sandra Atwood last night, how she was, talking about their life together, how they'd saved and so on. She said something about Atwood once having a job down on Spring, didn't she? A while ago?—we can sort it out just when. And about how they were saving every penny they could, and how he felt so guilty because he liked to stop and have a beer when he got off work. You remember that?"

"I—*¡Porvida!*" said Mendoza softly. "I do. Are you leaping to a wild conclusion?"

"Leaping be damned," said Hackett. "It was Spring Street that rang the little bell in my head, boys. It's possible, damn it. Isn't it at least *possible* that, when Ray Atwood had a job —of whatever sort—on Spring Street downtown, and liked to stop in a bar for a beer when he got off work—and Bremmer used to go 'across the street to a little bar' for his nip of Scotch—isn't it at least possible that it was *the same bar*? For God's sake, I know it's leaping, but—" The drinks came and he swallowed Scotch and soda thirstily.

"*¡Diez millón demonios desde infierno!*" said Mendoza very quietly. "It could just be. It could just be indeed. Leaping, *Dios*, yes. There's a good deal of Spring Street, but come to think not as many bars along there as some other streets. I do wonder."

"A link," said Palliser. "It could be a link—the very first we've had a smell of. But what the hell could it tell us? Even if it is—"

"A step further on," said Mendoza, "maybe?" Adam had set the shot glass of rye in front of him without being told; he picked it up and sniffed it. "I've fallen out of love with your theory of the puritanical nut with different motives, Art. I'm thinking now about some way all these people could have been involved in some incident in the past—somehow, whatever. And if this *is* a link—problematical as it is—let's try to find out one way or the other. If it is, if it was the same little bar on Spring Street—"

"A *bar*," said Palliser. "Edith Varick? Millway up in Glendale?"

"He didn't always live there, I suppose."

"But, Lieutenant—"

"It just could be a link," said Hackett luxuriously. He sat

128

back and drank. "I don't know what it says, but if it is a link, even between two of them—"

"And the *unlikeliest* two," said Palliser. "Bremmer and Atwood, for God's sake!"

"We'll look at it," said Mendoza. "Maybe you've borrowed my crystal ball, Art."

Before they had a chance to look at it, as the possible first link (whatever it meant), they got—in a left-handed kind of way—a possible confirmation. At least something rather suggestive.

They got, at three-forty Saturday afternoon, number six.

Who was a bartender at a cocktail lounge out on Hoover Avenue, by the name of Harry Rodzinsky.

Ten

Homicide got the call at three-forty-one, from an address on Constance Street just this side of Hoover. Mendoza and Hackett were the only men in the office, Landers typing up a report on the elderly man who'd dropped dead in front of the Biltmore. It was a squad-car man calling in, and when he said "strangled," they got on it. They shot over to Constance Street in the Ferrari, the ambulance and the mobile lab following them, and looked at another depressing setup.

It was an old apartment house, and the man who'd called the police was one Fred Pitman. He was excited and upset, and he was doing a lot of talking; they'd sort that out later. One of the uniformed men was guarding the open door of the apartment, which was on the second floor. They went in. It was what used to be called a bachelor apartment—living room with pull-down wall bed, bathroom, kitchenette. Obviously Harry Rodzinsky had lived here alone, but it was all very tidy and clean, except of course for Harry Rodzinsky himself, sprawled out on the double bed, eyes horribly bulging, tongue protruding. And the little file card left on his chest. *The vengeance is just.* He was a big heavy man about fifty, nominally clean-shaven but with a heavy growth of beard, tousled dark hair, and he was wearing white silk pajamas.

130

They looked at him, and at the room, and they swore because they felt helpless, and that was an unusual experience for the men at Homicide. Usually, there was a lot to do: there were ways of finding out things. On every one of these damned garrotings, there was just nothing. You couldn't go chasing a ghost with a lab kit; without physical evidence, and on what was not in the usual sense a personal kill, there was very little the men at Homicide could do.

They turned the body and the apartment over to the ambulance men and the lab crew, aware that neither would be able to tell them anything very useful, and they went out to the narrow old hall and talked to Fred Pitman. No crowd had gathered; probably most people living here were at work.

They heard this and that from Pitman. He was calming down a little, but still excited, grieved, and incredulous. "Harry!" he said. "Old Harry! I can't believe it! A real good guy, you took him as he was. I couldn't believe it, when I walked in and saw—what? What? Well, it was like this—" he eyed Mendoza doubtfully, as if expecting to be disbelieved. "He had trouble waking up, see. Now he's a good guy, I don't want to go giving you guys any wrong impressions, see, but he's a gambler. I got to say so. A drinker, no, that he never was—but gambling, yes. Anything—poker, the ivories, anything, see? He was on nights the last year or so, he was fed up with the hours too, and looking around for a better job, see, but meanwhile he was on nights. Tending bar. He was a bartender, see. He'd been in the Navy—regular Navy man for twenty years, Harry was"—that explained the neatness of the apartment—"and when he got out, he took to bartending. Went to school for it, see. I've known Harry eight, nine years, all the time he's been living here. We been here fifteen. I'm a cabbie, I drive for Yellow. Well, so Harry gets off at one A.M. when the place shuts down, he goes down to Gardena or someplace, for the poker, the ivories, see?" He eyed them a little nervously; nothing but draw poker was legal in the state, and that only in a few places like Gardena. "And, well, anyways, likely he'd never get home till maybe six, seven A.M., and then he'd go to sleep, only he had to be at the bar at five, take over, see, and he liked time to get cleaned up, have a bite to eat and all, and so we had a kind of arrangement—I'm a night worker too, see—that I'd drop in at three-thirty and wake him up if he wasn't. And when I come today—my God, I couldn't believe it, but—"

"How'd you get in?" asked Hackett. "You have a key to his place?"

"What? What? Oh, no, sir, he never locked the door when he was here. It was a thing with him, see. Big guy like him, and he'd done boxing in the Navy, and he kept a gun. He never—"

Hackett looked at Mendoza. Who just shut his eyes. The foolhardy ones. Hadn't Rodzinsky ever taken thought that if he slept so heavily as to need an "arrangement" with a waker-upper, he might not stir when a stranger walked quietly in? And that, considering where he lay dead, was just what had happened. And how had X known that the door would be conveniently open?

"Did anyone beside you know that, Mr. Pitman?" asked Mendoza.

"What? What? Oh, gee, I heard Harry say that lots of times! Kind of boasting. He caught a guy once got into his place, knocked him out. He could take care of himself, Harry. But, my God, when I walked in and saw—I couldn't believe—did they rob him? Sometimes he'd have quite a roll on him when he'd been lucky. Gee, I'll bet that was it! Somebody noticed he had a roll, wherever he'd been, and followed him. And—gee, old Harry!"

"That might be, Mr. Pitman," said Mendoza equably. "Do you know where he worked?"

"Sure, the Elite Lounge on Hoover. He'd been there about a year, but he was looking around for another—"

"Did he change jobs often?"

"Well, I guess you could say so. Sometimes. He never had trouble getting a job, he was a good bartender and he hardly ever took a drink himself, you know—said he'd seen too many lushes, see. He'd get fed up with a place, or the hours, or maybe sometimes when he'd make a killing, he'd just take a vacation awhile, enjoy himself. Bachelor, see, free as air." Pitman looked a little rueful.

"Do you remember," asked Mendoza, "whether he ever once worked at a bar on Spring Street downtown?" Hackett looked at him.

"Gee, I couldn't say, he could have, why? He'd worked around a lot. A good guy, you took him as he was, see? A gambler, sure, up and down, but if he borrowed—he didn't hardly any—you was sure to get it back. An honest guy. I never had such a shock in my life. Just wait till Sue hears. A murder, here! Harry! The only thing I can figure is, somebody spotted he had a roll and followed him home. You find out where he'd been last night and I bet—"

"Could be," said Hackett. He went back into Rodzinsky's apartment. "Give us an approximate time?" he asked the intern.

The intern glanced at his watch. "Four-o-five. Well, call it six to seven hours. Between nine and ten A.M."

Oh, really, thought Hackett. He thought it bitterly. X being canny-clever again—or was it just by chance? Could it be? In a place like this a good many wives would be holding jobs as well as husbands; and of those who didn't, at that hour in the morning the ones who weren't out at market were righteously dusting and doing the breakfast dishes.

Talk about bastardly cases to work . . . Drift in and up the stairs, most people gone at that hour or busy in their own places. Quietly open the unlocked door, and there was the big man heavily sleeping—just into his first sleep, probably. No trouble at all to garrot him. And out just as quietly.

Hell.

He went back to Mendoza and Pitman and asked where Pitman had been at nine A.M. "Asleep, o' course," said Pitman promptly. "I'm on till four A.M., where else'd I be?" The Pitman apartment was cater-corner down from Rodzinsky's on the other side of the hall. "My wife? She works at The Broadway, she's gone by eight-thirty, wouldn't know—say, is that when he was killed? He wasn't *shot*, was he? I'd have heard —I didn't see any marks—"

They told him they'd like a statement, and he agreed docilely; he left a note for his wife, put on a tie and jacket, and rode back to headquarters with them, and made the statement. "Gee, I never expected to be inside of this place. You got quite a setup here. I'm only sorry it's on account of this. Old Harry! Well, he had his faults, don't we all, but a real good guy, Harry was. And only fifty-one."

Maybe last week they'd have pricked up their ears at that: a little thing, but so had Edith Varick been fifty-one. Now they knew it didn't mean anything. Pitman answered more questions, and nothing emerged—nothing useful. Sure, Harry liked the dames all right—once in a while—but nothing permanent, see. He'd never heard of any trouble along that line, and he likely would have, Harry not being exactly secretive. He didn't think Harry'd had any relations, anyway he never talked about any. And so on. Nothing.

Nothing but the little fact that Harry had been a bartender. When he'd signed the statement and they'd sent him home in a car, they sat down and lit cigarettes, and Mendoza said, "*¿Cómo?* Does this unravel at all? Before we go and ask, can we imagine Harry tending bar at that place on Spring where Bremmer liked to go after he closed shop—and Ray Atwood dropped in for a beer after work?"

"I suppose we can find out. How long ago, for God's sake?

And what would it say, Luis? Three of them. Just three, a very possible link. But where does it take us? Nowhere."

"It's a step further on—it's got to be," said Mendoza almost angrily. "Don't drag your heels. My God, if we can't make some sense of this soon—"

Palliser came in looking disgusted and tired. "Jase says he's thinking of resigning. Damn smog again today. We've been poking around down there, and nothing—exactly nothing—shows on Atwood. A great big fat nothing. There were hundreds of cars going by on Beverly, there were hundreds of people all around, but they were all minding their own business and nobody saw anything. We got just one little thing which only confirms the time. One of the clerks at the delicatessen noticed a car pull into Atwood's station about a quarter past three, and sit there a while, and then when no attendant came it pulled out again. Says she didn't give it a thought at the time, assumed Atwood was in the rest room or something."

"Yes," said Mendoza inattentively. He got up and straightened his tie, pulled down his shirt cuffs. "Art, you can fill him in on number six. I'm going to—"

"What?" said Palliser. "For God's—!"

"—go and ask," said Mendoza. "Keep your fingers crossed." He took up his hat and went out.

"You aren't going to tell me—?" began Palliser.

"I am. But on this one we may have a little something, though I don't see that it takes us anywhere," said Hackett gloomily.

"God, if the *press*—"

Mendoza shut the corridor door behind him.

In the block on Spring Street where William Bremmer had had his exclusive little shop, there weren't many other such small businesses. This was brokerage row, office buildings for the most part, and only a few of them had business premises on the ground floor. There was a bank at one corner, and no street-floor shops for half that side of the block—a half-block of tall office buildings, then a half-block of one building with the lobby entrance round on the side street down there, and shops facing on Spring. A drugstore on the corner, a men's clothing shop, a stationers', a bookstore—and, if not exactly a bar, the only place which could be so described on the whole block. The Gray Goose. Its front was discreet and respectable-looking. A small neon sign announced, Restaurant and Cocktail Lounge.

On this side of the street, where Bremmer's shop stood with closed door, there was nothing comparable—only another drugstore on the corner, and four small shop fronts, a tailor, a leather-goods shop, a jeweler, and Bremmer's; and in the middle of the block the public parking lot where Mendoza left the Ferrari.

And down at the other corner there, a gas station. A Shell station. Where—just maybe—Ray Atwood had once held a job?

The Gray Goose had to be it, if that priest was right.

Mendoza walked up to the corner to cross with the light. He thought, God, this thing. Just the grace of God it wasn't making headlines. All they needed, the unsolvable murders in a series, more irresponsible talk about the dumb cops. He'd been sending memorandums up to the chief; he could imagine that the chief was tearing his hair, but knowing Mendoza was keeping hands off. What could be done, they'd do; but on one like this, when there wasn't one damn thing to use as a handle—

It was a bastard. The offbeat thing, the real mystery.

If they could just get a glimmering of how all these people were connected—*if* they were connected (maybe only in the avenger's mind?)—

The light changed and he started across Spring. And he thought, if they did catch up with him—when, by God, they caught up with him—as was so often the case on the multiple killings, the chances were he'd be tried on only one or two of them, and they might still keep the rest out of the headlines. And being caught up with, he might crack up, so there'd just be the nice quiet hearing. Guilty by reason of insanity, and not much publicity at all . . .

Which was putting the cart before the horse with a vengeance. *With a vengeance,* he thought wryly; and then for a quarter-block before he came to the entrance of The Gray Goose, his mind switched to the other thing Hackett had been talking about before they got the call on Rodzinsky. The Orvidez thing. He thought about it shrewdly and gratefully, because it probably wouldn't take much untangling, and after trying to make bricks without straw on the vengeance bit, find some possible loose end which would show them *anywhere* to look on this damned thing, the prospect of a piece of ordinary routine was refreshing . . . The ones like that, Luis Mendoza knew. He'd grown up down here, rubbing shoulders with the Orvidezes and Ruizes and Aradoreses. He wasn't having any guesses as to what was behind this particular thing until he'd seen the people involved, but he knew that kind, and from what Art said about Mama and Margarita—bring them in and lean on them a little, all polite but sounding as if you knew more than you actually did, and ten to one they'd come apart and tell you the whole story . . .

He took off his hat and went into The Gray Goose. As he had expected, a very discreet and even elegant little place. Low octagonal tables, leather chairs, a small bar at the end of the room. About twenty people here, prosperous-looking business types. It was getting on for six o'clock. A good many of the brokers, brokerage clerks, and professional men in offices roundabout would regularly come here for lunch, for a little drink after office hours.

He went up to the bar and told the bartender he'd like to see the owner; produced the badge. He was exclaimed at: this was a nice quiet place, never any trouble here, what did he—

"No trouble," said Mendoza. "I just want to talk to him, that's all. Is he here?"

Grudgingly the bartender admitted he was there, and went away. He came back in five minutes with a tall, well-tailored, dark, and good-looking young man about thirty. "This is the cop," he said. "For all he don't look like one. Wants to talk to you. We never have any trouble here—nice clientele. What the *cops* are doing here—"

"I'm Jack Mayfield," said the young man pleasantly. "What can I do for you—ah—"

"Lieutenant Mendoza." Surveying him, Mendoza swore mentally and at length. If this thing traced back over any period of time—Mayfield couldn't be more than thirty. He hadn't been thinking; it was in the cards the place had changed hands, yes, and just how long had it *been* here? "You're the owner?"

"Well, part owner," said Mayfield. "Why? I can't imagine any complaint—"

"Nothing like that," said Mendoza. "All I wanted to ask you was, have you ever employed a bartender by the name of Harry Rodzinsky? At any time?"

Mayfield frowned. "Well, I can tell you right off, Lieutenant, not in my time here." Hell, thought Mendoza. "Charlie and I here took over together about the same time, and our relief barkeep is Endicott—Jim Endicott . . . Offer you a drink?"

Mendoza felt he needed one. "Straight rye. And how long have you owned this place and can you tell me who owned it before?"

"I'll have a sherry, Charlie," said Mayfield, hopping up on the stool beside Mendoza. "Sure. Whatever it is you're after, maybe—I took over here about five years ago. It's a family business, Lieutenant—not the only one. My father opened this place first, you can believe it or not, forty years back. Wasn't quite the same décor—*or* clientele!" He grinned and sipped sherry. "Eventually the old man acquired a little string of 'em—we've got eight now, all going strong—one place on the Strip. But Pop always felt kind of sentimental about this place, where he got his first start, you know, and as long as he was well he managed it. Hired managers for the rest of 'em—until my brothers and I were old enough to take over." He cast Mendoza an oblique side glance. "Mayfield, it sounds nice and Anglo-Saxon, doesn't it? Papa landed here in nineteen-o-four as Giovanni Giorgione with fifty bucks in his pocket and about a hundred words of American."

"*¡Pues hombre!*" said Mendoza. "And more power to him."

"Yeah. Well, anyway, as I say, he puttered around here up until five years back, about, and my God," said Mayfield humorously, "would he listen to us about redecorating the place? Little coat of paint fix the old place up just fine— that's Pop! But—" He finished his sherry and grimaced. "The arthritis finally caught up to him, Papa. He doesn't get around so much any more. Still sharp as nails, I do assure you, and we have to fetch the books for him to look at!" He laughed. "First thing I did when I took over here—I'm the youngest, and doesn't the old boy keep an eye on me!—was do the whole place over. Turned out pretty effective?"

"Very nice," said Mendoza. "Oh, yes."

"We get a lot of the professional types from the high-class bond houses on the street," said Mayfield cynically. "Carriage trade. But about what you're after—a bartender, you said—?"

"Harry Rodzinsky."

Mayfield shook his head. "Rings no bells, and I do all the

hiring and firing. But if it was any further back than five years—"

"It could have been," said Mendoza. This was a very wild, wild goose he was chasing.

"—well, then, I'd lay you any money Papa could tell you. He may be slowed down from getting around physically, but his brain's still working overtime, I do assure you," said Mayfield. "You should have heard the argument I got last month about a gross of new cocktail glasses. I'm an idiot, I am, spending that much money when I could have beat the wholesaler down ten per cent—*he'd* have beat the robber down *twenty* per cent—" Mayfield grinned affectionately. "Tell him times have changed? You don't, with Papa. But you want to know anything that went on around here when he was managing, lay any money he could tell you. What's it all about, anyway?" he added curiously.

"Just a little thing that came up," said Mendoza.

"Which tells me a lot. Ask no questions, you get told no lies. But I suppose we've got to cooperate with our upstanding peace officers. You want to go see Papa? Brighten up his day."

"Where?"

"Beverly Hills, where else? You think Papa'd be satisfied with second best? Roxbury Drive," and Mayfield added the address. "He'll like you, Lieutenant. Only he'll tell you you ought to've changed your name to Mandeville or Churchill and gone into business."

Mendoza laughed. "What, serving Mammon?"

"Oh, Papa thinks of everything. Just as insurance, he sees Mother Church gets her share. You never can tell," said Mayfield seriously, "it might all be true, about purgatory and all that."

"Mr. Mayfield," said Mendoza, "you've brightened *my* day. I'm feeling the hell of a lot more optimistic than I was

140

when I walked in here. I'll go see your Papa. With fingers crossed. And thanks for the drink."

"Glad to've obliged. But I'm curious *as* hell about what you're after here. We've never even had a holdup. Can't you give me a hint?"

Mendoza slid off the bar stool. "Well," he said, "just to whet your curiosity some more, Mr. Mayfield—it's Lieutenant Mendoza of Homicide."

He called Alison from a public booth near the parking lot and by seven-thirty was pulling up before an imposing colonial house on Roxbury Drive. Papa had done himself well, all right: call it about a thousand a year in property taxes. Triple garage, outsize pool in back, the works.

And maybe Luis Mendoza was going sentimental as he got older, God forbid, but he liked Papa and was pleased to remember the affection in the youngest Mayfield's eyes when he spoke of him. Papa all alone in the big house, but for an honest-to-God butler and a male nurse: Papa in his wheelchair, casting a shrewd look at Mendoza.

"I don't get so many visitors no more," he said, "except of course the family. Good boys I got, four good boys, if they got only nine kids, the three married ones—only nine, imagine!—don't know what gets into people these days—and I still got to keep an eye on them, you know. But you say you a policeman? A detective like? So what could I be doing for you?"

"I understand," said Mendoza, "that up to about five years ago you were managing The Gray Goose down on Spring Street?"

Papa snorted. "Goose! Such a name—crazy, I said, but Jackie, he thinks he knows it all. It was always Mayfield's Inn—nice, dignified, sounds like a place maybe in nice part of London England, don't it? Classy. Goose, it's crazy. But

141

that Jackie. So I was. And so what about it, Mr. Mendoza you say is the name?"

"Yes. Do you—?"

"So. That's a Basque name, Mendoza," said Papa. "A queer people."

"What?" said Mendoza.

"Sure. Basque. Nobody knows where they come from, them. The language even, it don't trace with any other at all. Didn't you know? That's funny too, you a smart policeman. I can see you're a smart one, all right. And that suit you didn't buy for eighty dollars at Brooks's," said Papa acutely. "I had the idea these policemen here, they're all honest, good boys."

"Well, we try to be," said Mendoza, suppressing a grin. "It was my grandfather, the old sinner. A lucky gambler, he was." And crooked.

"Ah," said Papa. "So. You look like an honest fella. So what can I do, Jackie sending you see me?"

"Answer a question. When you were at The—down there, did you ever employ a bartender named Harry Rodzinsky?"

"Sure," said Papa calmly. "Sure, I remember Harry good. Not a bad man, but a gambler. This is to be a fool, unless you get born lucky which it don't happen to one man in a million. Harry I remember. He was there maybe two years. A reliable man, I'm sorry when he quit."

Mendoza expelled a long breath. "When?"

"Oh, good ten, eleven years back. No more."

"And"—Mendoza leaned forward eagerly—"while he was there, can you remember anything happening at The—the restaurant, anything at all—such as a holdup, or—someone taken ill—an accident of any sort—a fight maybe, or just any incident at all out of the ordinary?"

Slowly Papa shook his head in negation.

"Think!" said Mendoza urgently. "Anything, anything at all—"

"I don't need to think on that. Was nothing. It's nice, dignified part of town. Stockbrokers, lawyers, big smart people like that. Not even a holdup we ever had. My other places, yes—trouble, drunks, and fights when foolish people get drunk—a couple times, holdups. Not there, my good quiet nice dignified place. No trouble," said Papa. "All the time I'm there, no trouble. Oh, well, early days, sure, fights, like that. Not ten, twelve years back. Well, sure, I'm not there all the time, I go on vacations, but anything about trouble, I hear when I'm back, don't I? Sure. Harry Rodzinsky I remember. Reliable man, yes. He says he wants more money, he gets a better offer. I'm sorry see him go. That was maybe—I'm sure—about the summer in 1956." He looked at Mendoza placidly.

And Mendoza looked back at him, baffled.

Eleven

MENDOZA went home and blew off steam at Alison. "This is the damndest thing—it looked as if it could be starting to make sense, and then—damnation!"

"And why doesn't it still?" asked Alison. She put her book down; she'd finished Landseer and was reading the new Agatha Christie.

Mendoza looked at her.

"A link," she said, "of a *kind*, Luis. Didn't I say it went back into the past? Vengeance, for some reason, because of—of something that happened when, maybe just momentarily, all those people were together. All right. You know when three of them *could* have been together, don't you? At least ten years ago, at that cocktail place. This bartender Rodzinsky, and Brommer, and Ray Atwood. What are you dithering about, *amador?* It seems to me you're making progress."

"Progress hell. If anything, any incident out of the ordinary happened at that bar when Rodzinsky worked there, the good Papa would have—"

"What tells you it was anything that happened at the bar?" asked Alison.

Mendoza, who was pacing up and down the living room, turned to stare at her. And very elegant she looked, his Alison, in a jade-green silk houserobe, Bast a topaz circle of warmth on her lap. He approved of her letting her hair grow; its warm copper glowed in lamplight. "What—?" he said, and swore as Sheba landed on his shoulder from behind without warning, digging all her claws in. "¡Monstruoso! Just what do you mean—?"

"Why at the bar?" said Alison. "This is pure imagination, of course, but as long as you *are* imagining, why limit yourself? Because there are the others to think about too—the Varick woman, and Millway, and the ex-con. Aren't there?"

"There are. So what are you talking about?"

"Well, the bar," said Alison thoughtfully. "It could be a starting point, Luis, but—what are we imagining? Some incident, goodness knows what, anything from an accident to—well, heaven knows—in the past. If you're right, and that bar connects Rodzinsky to Bremmer and Atwood, it has to be at least ten years ago. *¿Conforme?*"

"*Sí.* So?"

"Nothing tells you yet whatever it was connected with the bar," said Alison. "Look, some people have literal minds. It could have been something that happened on the street outside, while—well, while all three of them were there. Or—"

"That's very thin, *amada.*" Mendoza stood staring into space for a while, and then went over and put Sheba down on top of Nefertite at the other end of the sectional, and went out to the hall. Alison heard him on the phone there for quite a while . . . "But everything! Everything we can possibly dredge up about him. He's very much the unknown quantity so far . . . What? Well, you said this Kettler was the friendly type. A friend of Millway's, sure, and Millway not friendly with anybody else in the place, but Kettler probably was. How long since Kettler moved? . . . Oh. Well, from what George told me, I gather it's the kind of place where tenants tend to stay. Let's ask, anyway—not that I want to tell you your business, Lieutenant, but we've had

145

two more since—that's right . . . How right you are. Let's ask whether anybody still living there knew Kettler, knows where he moved. Because if we can locate him, he can probably tell us a good deal more about Millway . . . Yes. All right. And—yes. O.K., you get on that and we'll keep our fingers crossed." Phone in cradle and immediately picked up again . . . "O'Connor there? Good . . . Because if we can find out more—you can see that. Sure. If you'd see what Varick—I don't suppose you'll get much, but we'll be looking around down here too, where she worked . . . O.K., thanks." The phone put down again; he dialed. "Rory? Did Nick find that note Art left? Go out on it? The Orvidez thing? O.K., just checking . . ."

When he came back to the living room, he said abstractedly, "Damn it, it's got to mean something. One coincidence I will accept, but not more. That Shell station. We'll have to check there. And if Mrs. Atwood or maybe the station manager remembers—if we can tie those three up—it's *got* to mean something!"

"I had one thought," said Alison a little sleepily. "You know what, Luis? Maybe the avenger has read that John Masters novel too—about the Thugs."

"*¡Bastante—ya lo creo!*" said Mendoza sarcastically.

He hadn't still, in the three and a half years they'd been married, wholly accepted the fact that Alison's female intuition was apt to be absolutely right.

But when he got into the office on Sunday morning, if they were no further ahead on the vengeance bit overnight, they had—by the two pages of scrawled notes Galeano had left for him—ferreted out the gist of another case.

Mendoza read over Galeano's terse report—what he and Piggott had got out of four separate neighboring families who knew the Orvidezes and the Aradoreses—and he said softly to himself, "*¿Quién tiene la culpa?*" And he grimaced

146

at the page. People, people. Very laudable idea, see everybody got educated and made a useful productive member of society, sure: given all their rights and liberties, fine. But when you came down to it, they did come all sorts—rich or poor, smart or dumb or in-between: sooner or later you came up against that great common denominator, human nature.

Granted that Hackett and Higgins hadn't been woolgathering about the funniness they smelled there, which he really didn't think they had been—neither of them was much given to woolgathering—he rather thought he could spell this one out without a dictionary. Always provided that Jim Aradores was the type he suspected.

Report in hand, he went out to the anteroom. Hackett had just come in, big and broad and sandy, just taking off his hat. Higgins and Landers were in the sergeants' room, and as Mendoza opened his mouth to say Hackett's name Jason Grace came in and said, "Morning. What's on the agenda today?"

"I had jobs marked out for us," said Mendoza, "but they'll keep half a day. We'll get one thing cleared up at least, with any luck, get that off the agenda. Carlos Orvidez." He handed the report to Hackett. Grace came up and cocked his head to read it past Hackett's arm. "Sound suggestive?"

"Oh, my God," said Hackett suddenly. He went on reading, passed the first page over to Grace, who stood absently smoothing his mustache as he read.

"A little lower than the angels," he said. "Yes indeedy . . . So you think, this Aradores, Lieutenant? Yes."

"Hot-tempered Latin," said Mendoza with a sardonic grin. "Don't you?"

"I am not," said Grace, "a hot-tempered Latin, Lieutenant. I'd have called the Vice Squad."

Mendoza laughed. "But how the hell did he—they—hope to get away with it?" asked Hackett, looking up.

147

"I rather think," said Mendoza dryly, "that friend Ruiz threw the monkey wrench into the works there."

"Oh?" said Hackett. "Oh! Oh, yes, I see."

"Anyway, let's find out. Let's fetch 'em all in—leave the kids out for the time being—and have a little session here. I think maybe we'll hear some pretty singing."

"Not so pretty," said Grace. "Not to philosophize, Lieutenant, but—well, some of us are still one hell of a lot lower than the angels . . ."

They went out and fetched them all in, Jim Aradores and Margarita and Mama Orvidez and Salvador Ruiz, and they had a session. When he first laid eyes on Aradores, Mendoza felt that small warm glow of satisfaction that tells a detective he has guessed true—and, especially after trying to cope with the handful of nothing their avenger was handing them, he felt gratified.

Jim Aradores was about thirty-two, a good-looking fellow but with the slightly flared nostrils and under-the-eyebrows glance that said maybe a temper. The women were scared to death.

And it wasn't, of course, necessary to pretend they knew; if it was only a guess, it was a shrewd guess. The neighbors had seen this and that, and Margarita had talked to one of them.

"So all right," said Mendoza gently, after the four of them had sat down on direction and he'd stared at them meditatively for a full minute. "You stabbed him, didn't you, Jim? Grandpa."

Aradores jumped. "What the hell you talkin' about? Me? The old fella got rolled for what he had on him. Down on Temple. He went roamin' off like that, my wife, she told you. We didn't know nothin' had happened to him." It didn't sound very convincing, and he cast a very baleful look at Ruiz, who was a little fellow and who seemed to be trying to sink into his chair and stay invisible.

148

"Now come on," said Hackett. "We're not exactly fools, Jim. After we'd talked to the neighbors—"

"Why'd you have to—? Just a lot of gossip!" burst out Margarita wildly. "Oh, my God, why'd you—?"

"You just shut up," said Aradores coldly. "There ain't nothin' they can—"

"Don't drag your heels, Jim," said Higgins kindly. "We can piece it all together just dandy. Grandpa Orvidez had been a little nuisance, hadn't he? In one way and another— starting to get a little senile maybe, coming home drunk— and other ways. Yes. We heard about that too. You should have remembered that females will talk. Margarita had talked to her friend Carlotta next door, and—"

"*Friend!*" said Margarita, and started to cry.

"Well, few people care to get involved in a murder," said Hackett.

"Listen," said Aradores, "listen, for the Lord Jesus' sake, you guys—what am I gonna—?"

"You could," said Mendoza a little tiredly, "have called us and laid the complaint, friend."

"Listen, you—I'm gonna just see the old bastard maybe locked up awhile? Maybe stashed away at Camarillo? When he done *that*? You just tell me somethin', mister—you just tell me—" He was out of his chair, shaking one big fist under Mendoza's nose, shaking all over. "You—"

"Jim! No! Don't you say, don't—he *don't* know, he's just bluffing—" Margarita flung herself on him.

"I just ask you, mister, *you* got a daughter? You got—?"

"Yes, I've got a daughter," said Mendoza.

"Then I just ask you—"

"*Jim!*"

"Sit down and let's take it step by step," said Mendoza. "Sit down!" Hackett pushed Aradores back into his chair. "You found out that—"

"And you *bastard!*" said Aradores, rounding on Ruiz.

149

"Why the hell *you* have to go and tell the cops right off who he was? For the Lord Jesus' sake! Anybody have better sense—"

"You found out," said Mendoza, "that Grandpa, going a little senile maybe, had raped your daughter. And you—"

Margarita began to sob. "Old *bastard!*" said Aradores between his teeth; he was still shaking. "Dirty old bastard—she's twelve years old, mister! Twelve years old! Scared to death—scared to tell, until her mother—what the hell, a family's got to live, kids got to have things! The old bastard's got the pension, but Mama, she's got to work at a job, don't she, two kids still at home, she's got the job at the grocery, she's away most o' the day, can't keep an eye—and Margarita, she can't be at home all the time, out to market, to—what the *hell*, mister? Find out he done *that*—dirty old wino he was turnin' into—*why wouldn't I kill him?* I killed him. I did. He deserved it."

The vengeance is just, thought Mendoza. He asked economically, "How?"

"All right," said Aradores, breathing heavily. "I was wild, all right, why wouldn't I be? Hearing *that*—from Margarita. Seeing the kid—*my* kid, mister—like she was. Scared. Hurt. That old—I go lookin' for him, all right. By the Lord Jesus I do! I know some places he goes, all his wino pals—Temple, Alameda—places down there. I go lookin'. I find him wanderin' around down on Temple that night, the dirty old man, minute I see him it comes over me what he *done*, my kid, my Dolores—good, sweet kid, we bring her up right, she's just got confirmed, first communion—I don't know what I'm doin', all I see is the dirty old man. I don't carry no gun or knife, I'm an honest man, but I got a pocketknife, who hasn't? and I just want to hurt him like he hurt my Dolores—" Aradores stopped suddenly. After a minute he said in a different voice, "So you do what you got to do to me for it. I'm not sorry, hurt the old bastard. I'm not. For what he done."

150

"And then you thought," said Mendoza expressionlessly, "maybe if you just left him there, nobody would ever know. Tell the neighbors he'd gone away somewhere."

"I thought—he was no loss," said Aradores dully. "A nuisance to Mama, the last year or so, way he was drinking and all—a nuisance. Dirty old man. I thought—leave him. When I—when I come to myself again. It was an alley down there, nobody'd seen. Nobody knew. The city'd bury him. I knew he carried a billfold. I took it, so you wouldn't find his name in it. And Mama and Margarita never knew till—"

"Until you told them. You had to. So they'd help cover up."

"What are we gonna *do?*" Margarita flashed out at him. "I'm gonna come down here, say my man's done a murder? What are we—?"

Mama just sobbed, her shoulders heaving.

Mendoza turned to Ruiz. "And where do you come in? Just by chance? Recognizing the description, and thinking that might be Uncle Carlos, and trotting down here all officious?"

Ruiz was a little man, a not-very-bright little man. He looked at Mendoza, at the sullen Aradores; at the two weeping women, with piteous eyes; and he said in a very small voice, "I—I hear it from my wife. Good friend Margarita's, and family got to help keep it all quiet—no questions, they say, sir. Sensible. Terrible thing, I think—the Grandpa—thing like that—I don't blame Jim. Jim, I don't blame you—maybe I do same thing, it's my María. Only I get to thinking, was a good man once, God just take away his wits when he get old—or the devil—I just think, deserves Christian burying under his right name. I don't stop to think what—I just—" He shrank under Aradores' glare.

It took a little while to get the statements down and signed. To get the warrants.

"What a business," said Hackett, as they went out to a

belated lunch. "God." They had, of course, to arrest the two women—and Ruiz' wife—and Ruiz—on accessory-after-the-fact. There it was in black and white—they'd known, and tried to cover up. (As Margarita said, what else could they do?) And the kids, all under age, would be incarcerated in Juvenile Hall pending the outcome of the case. Mendoza thought in all probability a tenderhearted jury would acquit Mama and Margarita and the Ruizes, and maybe put Aradores away on a five-to-ten on a second-degree charge, which meant he'd be out in three. Which was all right with Mendoza. The dirty old man no loss.

One thing cleared up, at least.

They ran into Glasser at Federico's, staring into a Scotch and soda, and Mendoza beckoned him over. "Where've you been the last two days? You were on that corpse over on Second, and all I've had is your preliminary report."

"I've been chasing around from Dan to Beersheba, sorry," said Glasser. "That guy had more contacts—whole address book full, Lieutenant, and all female. If you want a considered opinion, he was either running a string of call girls or trying to set one up."

"*¡Parece mentira!* Any pedigree? Who was he? I've been so damn busy I just saw the first report—"

"Gave the landlady the name of Reginald Hope. Fancy," said Glasser. "No record with us, by his prints. I sent 'em back to Washington, of course, should hear sometime today if they know him. There's really not much to get hold of. Just, there he was in the living room, shot. In the head. With an S. and W. .32. It's one of those big old houses cut up into four apartments, and the owner—a Mrs. Breen—lives in one, rents the others. All she can tell us is, he rented the apartment the first of last month, and he told her he'd just hit town."

"Well—" Mendoza shrugged. "Another one no loss. Wait

152

and see what turns up." The waiter came up and they all ordered.

"How are you fellows doing on the avenger?" asked Glasser. Hackett groaned.

"Don't ask. The very damndest—"

"Just what I was coming to," said Mendoza energetically, sampling his drink. "Now listen to this," and he told them about the link with The Gray Goose. They listened interestedly. "First we're going to try to confirm that that was the place Atwood used to stop for a beer, ten years ago. Then it *is* a link. Don't ask me what it says because I haven't the remotest idea, but it's something. We—"

"But if this former owner says nothing ever happened in the place—" said Hackett.

"None of us infallible, Arturo. We don't know." Mendoza thought about what Alison had suggested and dismissed it as too nebulous. "The next thing we're going to do is really dig back into all these people. For the moment, forget about Bremmer and Atwood and Rodzinsky. Let's try to find something that brings in Varick and Jamison and Millway. I've got that Glendale lieutenant on Millway—if we can locate somebody who knew something about the man—Art, I want you to take Varick. At least, if I'm not just seeing ghosts here, we can guess the period, call it ten years back when Rodzinsky was still at that place—"

"I might argue that," said Hackett, "but I'll let it pass. I can think of *possible* circumstances—well, let it go."

"Let's not make things complicated," said Mendoza. "We can only look at probabilities, for God's sake. Take Varick. Was she ever in that place? Did she, maybe, have lunch there every day then? And Jamison—" he paused to finish his drink. "It's not a very likely place for one like Jamison," he said dubiously. "I will admit that. But damn it, it's got to mean something, hasn't it? Three of them connected to—"

"We're not sure of that yet," said Hackett flatly. "Who in hell could say about Atwood, after all this time?—if you're right about *that*. And why? The coincidences do happen."

"Not three times in a row, damn it," said Mendoza. "Let's go and look. If there's anything at all about this damnable thing I am fairly certain about, it's that the victims aren't picked at random. And the more we can find out about them —I want to know every last little thing we *can* find out about them! Something may show—"

They all agreed to that somewhat dispiritedly. If the will-o'-the-wisp they were chasing was ten years old, that just made it more difficult.

Mendoza got a little satisfaction that afternoon from the manager of that Shell station on Spring Street. His name was Frank Ring and he'd had that station for fifteen years, and he remembered Ray Atwood right away.

"A nice young fella," he said. "Good, reliable. You don't run into guys like Ray every day. Responsible, you know? I often thought, I shoulda kept up with him—send him a Christmas card, like that. Ambitious, Ray was—I'd bet he'd get places. Saving to get a station of his own then. And so darn crazy about his wife—what you want to know about Ray?" Evidently Mr. Ring hadn't seen the two-paragraph story in the press about Atwood's murder, presumably triggered by an attempted holdup. (In a way, praise be for the rise in crime; reason it hadn't rated more, no nosy reporter yet making connections.)

Ring didn't recall Atwood ever mentioning any bar he went to; he didn't drink much. "They was saving . . . On Spring, here, next block? Oh, that place, sure. I couldn't say. And why in time you should be asking—? Ray'd know, him-self. It could be, I couldn't say. What's a beer? Fifteen cents, them days. It could be, because he didn't have a car then,

154

see? He'd walk down to get the bus at the corner. And he could've stopped in that place, handy. But why you're asking —what's this all about, anyways? All this time after? I wouldn't know, you better just ask Ray . . . A very nice young fella, I often thought I shoulda kept up with him— you know where he is, what doin', now?"

Mendoza wasted a little time telling him.

Even when they could talk to her, would Sandra Atwood know or remember?

But it was something. A strong probability.

Something, thought Hackett. Something?

Even smart cops have moments of stupidity. He'd gone to the trouble of looking up Fred Harkness' home address, to ask him more questions about Edith Varick. Completely over-looking the fact that, if Luis was right in his wild guess about something ten years ago having anything to do with all this rigmarole, Edith Varick hadn't been working for Harkness then. But something, he had got.

Harkness had a very handsome French provincial house in Brentwood Heights, and he was home. He said, anything he could do, only too happy—such a terrible thing, Edith — whatever the sergeant—

And he was staring at Hackett now, a little surprised. "A *bar?*" he said. "A *bar?* Oh, didn't you know? She was a very strict teetotaler, Sergeant. Really—well, we all have our faults—really rather fanatical about it. I—er—believe her father had been an alcoholic. Very sad." He coughed dis-creetly. "These things—but she never would have—she'd never even go into a restaurant with a liquor license. Matter of—er—principle. Why did you think—?"

Hackett felt even more annoyed and frustrated than he'd been feeling before. So much for Luis' brain wave. Damn coincidence, that was all, on those other three. Where the *hell* was any logic in this—? And right then he suddenly thought, ten years ago; and he said, "But she wasn't working for you then, was she—in 1956?"

"What?" said Harkness. "1956? Why should—well, no, she was with Wendell Mays then. Fine man. Fine lawyer. Profession lost a great lawyer with him." He coughed. "Edith was with him for years—twenty years at least. Often heard him say he didn't know how he'd manage without her. Such an efficient woman. Just a terrible thing, only fifty-one, and nicely settled down with Earl—another fine man, Sergeant—these irresponsible hoods! Makes you stop and think."

Hackett agreed, and asked—just occasionally even a cop was inspired by something beyond logic—"Where was Mr. Mays's office, do you know?"

"Mays's *office?* Well, he's three years dead, Sergeant, after all—oh, certainly, certainly," said Harkness. "Spring Street. Though I scarcely see why—eight hundred and something, it was—we occasionally had reason to consult each other—one of the office buildings along there—"

The same block, thought Hackett, along which was Bremmer's little shop—and The Gray Goose.

Ten years ago.

Coincidence? With Edith Varick the fanatic teetotaler? And just what made any sense?

Mendoza had just asked Lake to get him the number of Glendale Police Headquarters when Sergeant Lake broke in and said the F.B.I. was on the line.

It was the local director. L.A.P.D. had, he said dispassionately, sent some prints back to Washington. "Yes?" said Mendoza. The mysterious fellow who had possibly been getting together a string of call girls. Mysteriously shot.

They were, said the Fed politely, the prints of one Ronald Jerome Hopper who was on the Ten Most Wanted list, and they'd be obliged if Lieutenant Mendoza would afford them chapter and verse as to where picked up, and—

"You don't tell me," said Mendoza. "You can take him off the list. Somebody's obliged you. Unfortunately the rest of it is our business."

Twelve

THE Fed went on to say this and that, however, which made Mendoza sit up and then start issuing orders. Hopper had been mixed up with the organized pros back East; they hadn't, said the Fed, known he was here, and . . . Mendoza promised cooperation, hung up on him, and went out to see who was in the office. Alone of all the big cities in this country, L.A. had never let the organized pros—the Syndicate and the rest—get a toehold here. The simple reason being that the L.A.P.D. subscribed to the maxim that eternal vigilance was the price of liberty—from the organized czars.

Hackett was just coming in, with Higgins behind him, and he started to tell Mendoza about Edith Varick. "A teetotaler of all things, wouldn't even set foot in a place that had a liquor license. So what price your brain wave about connections?" He sounded disgusted.

"Forget about it for a while and go talk to some Feds," said Mendoza tersely. "Better find Glasser and take him along, he's got the details on that." He told them about Hopper, and their expressions hardened. They both knew, any hint of the Organization landing in town, they wanted to get on it fast.

"Hank said he was going back to see that landlady again," said Higgins. "Pick him up there? O.K., we're on it." They

158

went out again, and Mendoza, forgetting about his call to Glendale temporarily, sat down at his desk and put Hopper out of his mind—he didn't really think Hopper was too important, though he could be wrong—and ruminated.

Since lunch at Federico's, Mendoza had been having the same experience Hackett had had the other day. His subconscious mind was trying to tell him something, he heard the faint bell ringing somewhere, but he couldn't come up with anything definite. Something trying to get through to him, but it wouldn't jell.

He opened the top drawer of the desk, took out the pack of cards, and began to shuffle automatically. He had put the Orvidez business aside: finished as far as they were concerned. He didn't think there'd be much to Hopper. (Was that a valid hunch?) He thought it was a kind of miracle they'd managed to keep the vengeance bit—*six* murders (so far!)—out of the headlines, and he thought if they were ever going to get anywhere on that, somebody had better do some serious, in-depth thinking about it.

Edith Varick the teetotaler, he thought. Sad. Awkward. (What the devil *was* the thing at the back of his mind?) So, no possible connection with The Gray Goose. *But,* ten years ago she had worked at an office on Spring Street in that very block. Did that say anything? Hundreds of people also had—teetotalers and otherwise. All those office buildings, hundreds of offices, secretaries, stenos, file clerks, tax accountants, lawyers, brokers. God. What could it say? Up in the air. Only she had been one of the victims.

Camarillo, taking its own time, had finally reported on Richard Warren, Edith's first husband, yesterday, and so that very nebulous little notion had been disposed of, because he was dead. He had died, still in Camarillo, in 1963.

Something—something—what the hell was it? Like trying to remember a name—almost on the tip of his mind as it were, and yet he couldn't put a finger—

Very methodically Mendoza set up the stacked deck and dealt poker hands around the desk. Just in the event that everything crashed and all the money went, so he'd be able to provide for his hostages to fortune, better keep his hand in. He kept a mental count of what he hoped he was dealing himself, and was mildly gratified to have it check out. Royal flush. He could surely as hell use a royal flush on this one. *The vengeance is just.* Bremmer, Jamison, Varick, Millway, Atwood, Rodzinsky. Any link that meant anything?

Suddenly he put the cards down. A little stray thought had suddenly come to him—or was coming: wait for it: yes. Of those six people, Jamison was the odd man out. They were all different, yes, but Jamison was more than just different: he was the only one of the bunch who was a bad one, had a pedigree.

Jamison the rapist.

Jamison the one really due the vengeance. The one somebody could plausibly have wanted due vengeance on. The others, no. Not visibly.

Mendoza looked at the cards meditatively. He also had the fleeting thought—irrelevant or was it?—that the victims could not have known the avenger by sight: he'd been able to get close to them, unrecognized, with no trouble. But the idea about Jamison loomed larger.

But Bremmer was the first killed, he thought. If Jamison—

Only those two counts, on Jamison. But that kind, as with his pal Valdez, they always pulled off a lot they didn't get dropped on for. If the rapist got away, at the time, so seldom any real evidence; and so often a woman in a state of shock uncertain about identification. And, down here: the reason Jamison had hung around down here. Women leery of yelling cop. Women caught on dark streets, ashamed to say so; embarrassed to say so. Afraid to say so. Mrs. Rose Anderson caught not exactly down here—on her way to get a bus home, up on Seventh Street near Spring.

His subconscious mind gave a little twinge.

Really, and disregarding all the rest of the rigmarole for the time-being—simple first causes—if you were looking for a reason for vengeance, Jamison was the most likely to have triggered that off, wasn't he?

Mendoza swept the cards together, put them tidily back into the drawer, and got up. "I'll be down in Records if anything urgent comes up, Jimmy."

"O.K.," said Sergeant Lake.

Down in Records, he told O'Brien he wanted to look at some ancient history.

"How ancient and on what?" asked O'Brien.

"Reported rapes and assaults-with-intent-of we never got anybody for. Out of the Pending files. Mmh—" Mendoza considered. "Eight to ten years back."

"Jesus," said O'Brien. "Ancient history all right. Well, we'll try to oblige you, dig out what's here. I sometimes think they ought to rotate us to different departments, we all get the same disease here—I swear to God we get to be nothing but magpies, if somebody finds a lost button on the floor it gets filed away . . ."

It took some time to dig it all out, that far back, of course, and Mendoza borrowed a desk and at five to six had just finished copying all the details down for private rumination, when his own office called him.

"What are you doing down there all day?" asked Sergeant Lake. "I've got Art on the phone.He wants to talk to you."

Mendoza brought his mind back to the current year. "Ask him if it's anything urgent, Jimmy. If it can wait half an hour" —he looked at his watch in vague surprise—"tell him to call me at home then. O.K.?"

"Sitting around swapping stories with O'Brien," said Lake.

"I am not. I've been doing some research. Which probably means damn all," said Mendoza ruefully.

"O.K., hang on a minute . . . He says he'll call you at home. He says Hopper looks funny."

"Oh? Well, he can wait awhile. Thanks, Jimmy—see you." Mendoza folded his copious notes away in his breast pocket, thanked O'Brien, and on the way to the elevator realized that he had to go upstairs again for his hat.

He found Sergeant Farrell already on the desk, Lake gone. "What," asked Farrell, "is a six-letter word meaning mystery, with an *A* in it? It's on the tip of my tongue, but I can't—"

"Enigma," said Mendoza absently. "It's a mystery, all right. Good night, Rory."

"Hell, of *course!*" said Farrell, scribbling.

On the way home, Mendoza thought some more about all this. Forget, for God's sake, the enigma Millway and the tee-totaling Edith Varick—you started with first principles, damn Brémmer being first in line. Jamison was a very likely target for the avenger. All right. Could there be, among these old unsolved cases, one in which the victim had been sure it was Jamison but there'd been no evidence? It was a thin and unpromising premise, but he wanted to think about it. So if that could have been the motive on Jamison, what about the other five? Different motives? It almost had to be—

His subconscious twinged again. He told himself to forget it, and it would come to him—whatever it was—when he least expected it. He braked for a light and an immense city bus wheezed and belched behind the Ferrari, and traffic stalled as a siren screamed close.

There hadn't been, of cases filed away in Pending from eight to ten years ago, as many as he'd expected. This was a damn good police force. Only eighteen altogether, and only six of them completed, real rapes. It wouldn't do any *harm*, he reflected, to look at them: maybe even talk to the women involved: maybe even find out who'd handled the investigation, talk to them for what stray details they might remember.

162

He battled traffic through Hollywood and came at last to Rayo Grande Avenue in the Hollywood hills. It had been smoggy again today. Not for the first time, he wondered by what aberration of human nature the biggest city in the world—in area if not quite in population—had grown up in this climate. And almost smack on top of one of the most serious earth faults on the globe, where at any time the buildings could come crashing down and half the population get killed.

He thought, the seismologists saying now they were overdue for a big one—worse than 1906 or 1933.

Cheerful thought.

He crept up the drive, alert for cats, though they were all usually in by this hour. Alison met him at the door; the twin monsters were being noisy somewhere.

"You look tired to death, *amante.*"

He kissed her. "I'm not really. Just been poring over a lot of musty old records, and my eyes are tired."

"You probably ought to be wearing glasses," said Alison, "at your age. You can't go on—"

"Don't be silly. I've never—"

"Well, you can't expect," said Alison reasonably, "to go on forever being just as good as you were at twenty-five, Luis. Every way. Though I *will* say—still, you can't. You're all bloodshot, your eyes I mean. Don't you think—?"

"No, I don't think," said Mendoza. "Damn it, I'm not about to go senile yet—"

"Who said you were? Three out of five people," said Alison, "do wear glasses, and all I'm saying is, at least an *examination—*"

"*¡Por Dios!* Stop nagging me, woman."

"Trust a McCann," said Mrs. MacTaggart briskly, appearing down the hall with a drink for him in one hand and a saucer of rye for El Señor in the other. "Leave the man alone, *achara.* You come and sit down, relax before dinner, man."

163

"Thanks, Máiri." Mendoza took off his jacket. El Señor, scenting rye whisky, came in four bounds from the window seat. Alison followed Mendoza down to the bedroom where he hung his jacket away, stripped off his tie and folded that away, and sipped rye.

"Have you got anything new on it at all, Luis? It's really the queerest thing—"

"On—oh," said Mendoza. "Well, I don't know, *cara.*" He was vaguely surprised to realize that it was still Sunday— quite a lot seemed to have gone on today. "Edith Varick," he said, "was a rabid teetotaler."

"*¡Dios me libre!*" said Alison. "But how annoying."

"But there's something, damn it," said Mendoza, "trying to get through to me—no, I don't know that it's on that exactly—it's right on the tip of my—no, it's gone, I can't—"

"It'll come to you," said Alison, and the phone rang.

"That's Art." Mendoza went to answer it. The twins, belatedly discovering he was home, erupted down the hall and flung themselves at him, and he staggered before the onslaught. Alison and Mrs. MacTaggart hurried to the rescue.

"You can talk to Daddy later, not now—"

"Now don't go bothering the man, Johnny, Terry, come away now—"

"Art?" Mendoza finished the rye.

"Luis, this Hopper thing looks a little funny," said Hackett. "We sat in with the Feds and hashed over all they've got, and then Glasser gave us all he's turned up, and it looks a little bit mysterious."

"How?"

"Well, by all the Feds have got—and you know how good they are on all the documentation—this Hopper's an old pro from away back. Never done any time, but he's been in the rackets all his adult life. The vice rackets. Tied up for a long time to one of the big bosses back East—Trenton, New Jersey —but the Feds have got it on pretty good authority, from an-

other one like that who sang them a very pretty song before New York burned him, that about six months back Hopper and his boss had a falling-out as they say, with the result
—it seems to have been quite a fight—that Hopper's kicked
out pronto and warned never to show his face east of the
Mississippi again—words to that effect."

"Oh, really?"

"Yeah. And since then he's dropped out of sight to the
Feds. They want him on an old assault charge, but all this
they know for sure. And they are also pretty sure that he was
spotted in Tulsa, Oklahoma, a couple of months ago. So he's
new here, all right. We kind of pieced it out with what Hank
had got the couple of days he's been on it."

"I'll train Glasser to write prompt reports yet. Which is?"

"Well, it looks as if," said Hackett, "Hopper's been trying
to start up the same deal on his own here. It is also pretty
clear he's got no henchmen, so to speak. Which figures, him
getting kicked out of home territory. He had a notebook with
all sorts of details about local females, where they work and
so on, it looks as if he'd been discreetly soliciting—personally—local department stores and so on. And Hank even
turned up one girl from the neighborhood—near this apartment he'd rented—who said he'd sounded her out. She
turned him down, incidentally. But you see what it looks—"

"Um," said Mendoza. He lit a cigarette one-handed.
"Natural. Old-time rackets boy all of a sudden on his own,
turning to what he knows."

"But, Luis—so how come he gets shot? Nobody here knows
him. The pro racketeers he was mixed up with never had any
connections here, and evidently as long as he stays away
they're leaving him alone. He's only been here six weeks or
so. He doesn't know anybody here. How come—?"

"Hot-tempered boyfriend or husband of some girl he so-
licited," said Mendoza.

"Well, I suppose it *could* be. I can't say," said Hackett,

165

"that I'm so very damn concerned about Hopper, you understand. The Hoppers we can do without. But it's a funny thing."

Mendoza agreed that it was a funny thing. "And," said Hackett, sounding aggrieved, "I've got up to a hundred and ninety-eight and Angel says I can't have a baked potato. Just the steak."

Mendoza grinned at the phone. "Your cross in life, Arturo."

He went into the living room and suffered the second onslaught of the twins. "*Caray,*" he said to Alison over their heads, "and you're saying I'm going senile? These two living proof—"

"I never said anything of the sort," said Alison. The twins presently took themselves off to pester Mrs. MacTaggart in the kitchen, and Mendoza tried again to think what the devil it was, just a faint something there at the back of his—ringing just a faint bell—

"What did you do with yourself all day?"

"Oh, that exhibition of medieval art at the County Museum," said Alison. "Some of it interesting. I picked up Pat—she wanted to see it too—she's just got a commission for something rather along that line, quite a good commission, local publicity outfit—"

"Mmh," said Mendoza. He rather liked dumpy, cheerful Miss Moore.

"I gather," said Alison, "it could develop into something for her, if they like her work. I do hope it does, poor Pat, she's had bad luck. She deserves a little break, some money for a change."

"Mmh," said Mendoza, thinking about Jamison. Odd man out, all right—among those six—when you thought about it.

Alison laughed. "Poor Pat. She said if it *did*—turn out to mean some money, you know—the first thing she'd buy was a car. She does admire the Facel-Vega. It's terribly awkward,

166

here, being stuck without a car, dependent on those awful—"

"*¡Santa María y Jesus y José!*" exclaimed Mendoza, leaping up.

"What? Luis—"

"*Buses!*" said Mendoza. "My God, my God—" His subconscious mind had got through to his conscious at last. "My God, yes, *that* was it! That Shell station manager saying it to me—Atwood with no car, he'd go up and catch the bus along Spring there—the bus stop on that corner, a *bus stop!* So, *así, así,* count Atwood in on either of two counts—at the bar, whatever the hell *that* connection is, or waiting there on the corner for the bus—*and*—"

"Luis, what on earth—?"

He looked at her raptly. "My God, we never thought of that—how many people in this place *don't* have cars? Few. But some, naturally. Dependent on the—" He flung down his cigarette in the nearest ashtray and dashed for the phone and dialed . . . "Art? Did Edith Varick have a driver's license?"

"What—Luis? A—I don't know," said Hackett. "Why? I expect she did, most people do. We can find out."

"So let's find out," said Mendoza. "First thing in the morning, *amigo* . . . And even if she did," he added, coming back to the living room, "it could be that ten years ago she didn't have a car—or, of course, even having a car, preferred not to drive in downtown L.A. Spring Street," he said, lighting another cigarette. "The office where she worked right on Spring. Handy to the bus."

"Oh!" said Alison. "I see. Didn't I say so, *amante*—not a thing necessarily happening *at* that bar. Something nearby —on the street?"

"No guesses," said Mendoza. "But just possibly. Just possibly. And possibly, in that case—though it's thin ice, all right, I see that, but just possibly, another connection, can we say? Three of them linked to The Gray Goose—"

"And maybe," said Alison, "the rest of them waiting for a bus at the corner!"

"Leaping," said Mendoza. "Leaping from *A* to *Z, cara.* But I had overlooked the buses . . . It's a thing to think about."

Monday was a quiet humdrum day. Nothing much happened, nothing much showed up. Hackett was inclined to take the inspiration about the buses with a grain of salt, but he contacted Earl Varick at his office and asked him . . . A little time had been wasted, of course, on all the inquests (Homicide firmly requesting that the barest minimum evidence be taken and the open verdict returned) and on the funerals, but nothing unusual had showed at the latter. Why, no, said Varick, sounding surprised, as a matter of fact Edith hadn't been a driver. For all her efficiency otherwise, traffic made her nervous, and she'd never—

"Well, don't tell me you could be on the right track," said Hackett.

"I don't know. Just an idea," said Mendoza. What about Millway, on this? Damn it, Millway was still an unknown quantity . . . And on second thought, maybe his little idea on those unsolved rapes wasn't so hot. Very nebulous. Look first at the real completed rapes (which would constitute more plausible reason for the vengeance)—well, what the hell? Eight to ten years back. Not all those women and their families would still be living here, probably.

Well, look at them. Marjorie Lejeune, Ninth Street, April, 1956. Edna Richards, Boyle Heights, 1957. Rita Garcia, Vernon, 1957. Ruth Shrum, View Park, 1958. Linda Shaw, Commerce, 1960. Wilda Polawsky, Hollywood, 1963.

Not as many as you might expect, filed away under Pending. But how many not even reported in the first place? That they never heard about? The ones like Jamison—

Hackett, Higgins, and Glasser were out with the Feds on

168

Hopper. A funny little thing. Palliser went out on a traffic fatality—mere formality. It was Jason Grace's day off . . . Grace maybe reading the contemporary literature his wife brought home . . .

Jamison—

The phone rang. "It's Wheelwright in Glendale," said Sergeant Lake.

"Oh, I was going to call you. Have you got anything?"

"We have," said the Glendale lieutenant pleasedly. "I must be ready to retire, it never occurred to me until you suggested it—chasing that Kettler up. Other people there maybe knowing him. It's true enough, what you said about it's being the kind of place tenants do stay. We've checked. We found Kettler."

"*Bueno*. What does he say?" asked Mendoza eagerly. Millway, the unknown quantity, he could bear to know more about.

"Well, we haven't got that far yet," said Wheelwright apologetically. "When I say found, I mean we've located him. One of the old-time tenants on the ground floor knows him well. I told you he'd been in an accident and in the hospital. Now we learn that after that—after he came out of the hospital—he went to live with his nephew and his wife up in Fresno. We got the name—this fellow at the Salem Arms still sends him Christmas cards—and address. Mr. and Mrs. Fred Lamson."

"Have you—?"

"Sure," said Wheelwright. "I sent off a teletype just now to the Fresno boys, asking them to go see him, get everything he knew about Millway, and shoot it right down."

"*Bueno*," said Mendoza again. "I'm getting damn curious about Mr. Millway. You'll be in touch then, thanks."

"No trouble. I'm damn curious too," said Wheelwright. "At least you've kept it from hitting headlines, Lieutenant."

By the grace of God, thought Mendoza. The press liked

the sensational, the offbeat, which came along so seldom; and, never knowing (until a while later) what juicy news it was missing, the press had seized joyously, today, on Carlos Orvidez and his raped granddaughter and the righteously outraged Jim Aradores. Some enterprising reporter on the headquarters beat had cornered John Palliser yesterday afternoon, and Palliser, thought Mendoza, was a very shrewd young man. He'd given them Orvidez in garrulous detail, with this result.

So the press was still off their necks on this damned, offbeat, incredible, and all too mysterious vengeance bit.

And just where else had they to go on it? Guess about connections!—the bar, the buses.

And just who else, maybe—they couldn't even guess— had he marked down for vengeance? The just vengeance? And why?

Mendoza was still brooding over those rape cases filed away in Pending; and Hackett was telling him he was really reaching. All right, Jamison the odd man out—but he hadn't been the first one taken off.

So what? thought Mendoza.

But Hackett was fond of saying, when all the chips were down on the board, Providence had a way of stepping in on the right side. To see justice done.

On Monday night at eight-forty-nine, Sergeant Farrell dialed the house on Rayo Grande Avenue. "Lieutenant, we just got a call—it looks as if it could be the garroter—and this time he missed! Guy fought him off and got away, by what the squad-car man says—and he left his garrote—*and* one of those damn file cards."

"*What's the—?*"

"Douglas Street," said Farrell. "Three-forty—"

"I'm on the way!" snapped Mendoza.

Thirteen

Douglas Street was just on the downtown side of Glendale Boulevard. It was a typical street for that section of town, the kind of street which is repeated many times over through many parts of most big cities, but perhaps also unique to L.A. It was a narrowish street, black-topped, lined with old—for Southern California—single houses, mostly frame California bungalows, a few stucco crackerboxes. It wasn't a classy street, it wasn't a slum street. Some of the narrow lawns would be kept up better than others, and some of the houses would need paint—seen by day.

When Mendoza got there, the scene was better lighted than it would have been ordinarily, two squad cars and an ambulance with their flashing lights in front of the house and in the drive. As he slammed the door of the Ferrari, a stocky figure detached itself from the crowd in front of the house.

"Lieutenant? What do you know about this one!" said Galeano. "It's our boy all right. And this one he missed but good."

"How and why?"

"He isn't even much hurt. I heard the intern say they won't take him in, he's O.K. Come over here." Galeano led the way to his old Ford down in front of the next house. "I grabbed these the minute I hit here. I don't think anybody's handled 'em—Sears's wife was too excited to notice them, probably, and one of the squad-car boys spotted 'em and stood guard till I got here. The wife's the one called in." He opened the door and showed Mendoza a Pliofilm lab bag. In it were the avenger's garrote and the little card.

"*¡Por Dios!*" said Mendoza softly. "That is a nasty little thing, isn't it, Nick?" He prodded it with one finger through the Pliofilm. It was a diabolically simple little thing too; and he suddenly thought of those Thugs.

The twine was the very thin and very tough twine used by professional packers and sometimes by gardeners: light brown and wire-thin, but very strong. It was about a yard long; and each end of it was fastened very securely, with picture wire, to the double wooden handle from a child's jumping rope. The handles were painted bright red.

"Something," said Galeano.

"Something indeed. What happened?"

"I don't know any details yet—the ambulance boys were still looking him over when I got here."

"So let's go ask." Mendoza cast another slightly incredulous look at the homemade garrote, and Galeano relocked the Ford, and they started up to the house. It was just another California bungalow, with a deep front porch all across the front, twin strips of cement with grass between for a driveway. But there was quite a little crowd in front of it by now, all the neighbors for some way around attracted by the squad cars and ambulance. Mendoza stopped at the perimeter of the crowd, which was talking to itself excitedly, and said, "Let's save a little time for ourselves and ask these people if anybody saw anything." He handed Galeano his car keys; there was a telephone in the Ferrari. "Go call up somebody else from the office to help, and then you start to ask around."

"Will do."

Mendoza pushed through the crowd and gained the front

porch. There was a uniformed man there who let him in. All the lights in the house seemed to be on.

In the long narrow living room, a couple of interns were closing their bags, lighting cigarettes. "You'll be O.K., sir," said one of them.

"Damn right I'm O.K.," grunted the subject of their ministrations. "Such a thing! Jump a man in his own backyard, never heard o' such a thing! I want to talk to the cops—you, Millie, you stop fussin' and tell the cops I want to see 'em! Not that I got any *look* at the bastard, but I *felt* of him, and—"

"It was that Ed Lundy," said the woman indignantly. "You know how he acted when you complained about that dog of his—"

"Now don't you be more of a fool than you can help, Millie. Ed Lundy wouldn't go to try and strangle me. It was a nut, that's what it was. Trying to strangle people!"

Mendoza could see in a way why their boy had failed to get his man this time. Joe Sears was easily six-feet-two and weighed in the neighborhood of three hundred pounds. He was about sixty, completely bald, with little shrewd light-blue eyes in a fat face with several chins, and he was looking slightly disheveled, but his tan work shirt and pants were clean. He was sitting on an ancient sofa; this living room was furnished with nondescript odds and ends of old furniture.

"Oh, Joe!" said the woman. "Who on earth'd try to *strangle* you, for goodness' sake?"

"I know what happened, don't I?" He peered at Mendoza. "Are you a cop? I want to—"

"Lieutenant Mendoza, Homicide. Mr. Sears, if—"

"Hah!" said Sears. He beamed at Mendoza, immensely gratified. "Homicide, now that's better—those squad-car men don't know nothin'. You got here nice and quick, Lieutenant. *Homicide.* Now that's just what it was, too—or was goin' to *be*—I can tell you! And it must have been a nut of

173

some kind, and you better find him quick or he really will kill somebody. Jumpin' a man in his own—"

"We'll certainly try, Mr. Sears. I've got some men out looking now. I'd like you to tell me just exactly what happened, sir."

"I'll do that," said Sears with great dignity. "Millie, you go get me a beer, will you? I can sure use one."

"*Strangle* you," she muttered, turning away. "Crazy!" She was nearly as big and fat as her husband.

"Offer you one, Lieutenant?"

"No, thanks. What—?"

"Well, I'd just got home," said Sears. "The hell of a thing. I take the bus home, see, naturally, and I'd got off down on Glendale Boulevard and walked up . . . What? Well, from my business downtown. I got a nice little business, hamburgers, sandwiches all kinds, best frozen pies and doughnuts, snacks all sorts, you know—good business. I been there for fifteen years, got tired o' workin' for somebody else and started up for myself, and I do all right. I was—what? Well, it's on Hill Street, you got to know everything, up near Pico. I got off the bus and I walked up here, just a couple blocks it is, like always. And I went down the drive to go in the back door like I always do. It was then it happened, he jumped me."

Millie came back with an open foaming can of beer. Sears took it with a nod, threw his head back and poured half the contents down his throat. The interns had gone, with the ambulance. "Ahhh!" said Sears gratefully. "And just as I come to the back steps, I hear just a little kind of sound behind me, and I started to turn around, see what it was—I guess it was that saved me, all right. In my own yard! And you can laugh all you want, Millie, I know what I saw and felt, don't I? Great big long wire sort o' thing come jumpin' right around my neck, there was light from the kitchen window and I saw *that,* all right—I give a kind of yell, to tell

174

you the truth I thought at first 'twas a snake jumpin' at me, and I don't like snakes—" Sears looked at Mendoza sternly, as if daring him to laugh. "And I sort of instinctive threw up my hand, like this, and *felt* it. It was a piece o' rope. And I turned around, and there's somebody there—a man—and I guess I cussed him, anyway I made a grab at him and we had a tussle, but he got away. Ran like a hare." Sears threw his head back and swallowed the rest of the beer. "*Hell* of a thing. Try to strangle *me*. In my own backyard."

"Did you get any sort of look at him, Mr. Sears? If the kitchen light was on—"

"He was too far back for that to reach him. And he was already startin' to run away when I got turned around and went after him. Seein' he'd missed *gettin'* me. But it sure must have been a lunatic—crazy thing to do—you figure he meant to rob me, or what?"

"Didn't you get any impression about him? Size, weight—"

"Oh, *impressions*," said Sears. "Well, I felt of him. Sort of. Just a couple seconds while we tussled. Sure. He wasn't as tall as me, and I'd say he was sort of thin. And," said Sears brightly, "he'd been eatin' peppermint, his breath—"

Mendoza swore mentally, and not just for the paucity of Sears's description. Joe Sears might be a successful small businessman, a perfectly upright and respectable fellow, but he obviously wasn't overburdened with imagination. It wouldn't be easy to convince him (if at all possible) that some small incident long in the past had possibly triggered this attempt at murder—if Mendoza wasn't just woolgathering about that —or to get him to search his memory.

Joe Sears. Another different one—another funny one. Victim-wise, you could put it. Sears running a little hamburger stand on Hill Street. *But,* thought Mendoza, Sears taking the bus. Bus stops. Sears's hamburger stand on Hill, near Pico. Look up the bus routes, but Mendoza had a vague idea that it could be that Sears would get the nearest bus at that

175

bus stop at Ninth and Spring: Or would he? Cater-corner across from The Gray Goose.

And what the hell could it mean? All the bits and pieces, it looked suggestive in a way, but it all fell apart when you looked at it closer.

"And if you're goin' to ask me, have I got any enemies," said Sears, "well, that's just plain ridiculous. I guess there are folks don't like me, just as they're plenty o' folks I don't like so good, like f'rinstance all those Goddamn idiots back in Washington, but there ain't nobody doesn't like me enough to want to *strangle* me, God's sake. I never heard o' such a thing. I'm an honest man. I'm a peaceable man."

"And," said Millie, suddenly getting in on the act, "I heard the scuffling outside, and I opened the door, and there's Joe just getting up off the grass yelling I should call the police."

"Did you see the man running away?"

She shook her head. "Joe told me what'd happened. Fella got clean away by then."

"I'd have chased him," said Sears apologetically, "but I'm not too speedy any more, and way he was going, I knew I'd never catch him. He was prob'ly a lot younger 'n me, way he made off. A lunatic. Trying to strangle people. Did you find his piece o' rope?"

"Yes," said Mendoza. He considered the Sears, male and female. Both still worked up. Understandable. And even in his normal state of mind, Joe Sears wasn't going to believe in the years-old vengeance bit, maybe triggered by something very slight ten years, my God, back. *If* that was so at all. It would take some convincing persuasion, and probably the partial revelation of at least a couple of the other cases, before Sears would be convinced at all, enough to bestir his memory. And that would take a little time. And it couldn't be done right now, tonight.

176

And even if Sears did search his memory, would there be anything there at all? That idea might be just another wild idea. And—Joe Sears. Of all people. The man with the little hamburger stand. Why in God's name should their boy include Sears in his vengeance?

"Mr. Sears," he said, automatically producing his best charming smile for them, "you may not believe me, but you're not the only—mmh—recent victim of this lunatic, you know. We know this and that about him, and guess some more—and there's a very peculiar angle to it, too, that I want to talk over with you. But that can wait until tomorrow. It's getting late, and you've had a little shock, and we want to ask around the crowd out there—all your neighbors—to see if anyone saw anything—"

"Wouldn't think so," said Sears. "Most everybody watchin' TV that time o' the evenin'. You mean this nut's tried to strangle other people?"

"That's right. Now suppose I come to see you sometime tomorrow, and we'll have a nice long talk about it in private. Tomorrow afternoon?" Mendoza's voice was persuasive.

"I'm open nine to eight," said Sears. "Business don't run itself, and I'm not hurt any, this thing. O' course, Lieutenant —you *don't* say, nut like that runnin' around—I would surely be interested, hear about that—what you say—but I got my business to think about. I don't have nobody workin' for me, I do it all myself. So if you were to come by, say when I'm home tomorrow evenin'—and expense or no expense, Millie, you'll turn on the back-porch light as soon as it's dark, you hear?"

"I will," said Millie. "Did he really try to *strangle* you, Joe? And he's tried on other people? For the Lord's sake. I'll see the door's locked too. Might try to get in at *me*."

"Well, all right," said Mendoza. You couldn't hurry Sears, and it was going to be hard enough to get the story (what little shreds of it they thought they guessed) over to him, as

177

it was. And if they got lucky tomorrow, he might have a few more bits of fact to convince Sears to search his memory.

Because Sears, of course, might be worth his weight in gold to them. If. If Mendoza was right and this whole incredible thing dated from years in the past—and if Sears could come up with anything at all, a victim the avenger had missed. Looking at Sears, Mendoza felt depressed. This stolid stodgy fellow, had he any imagination at all, to look into the past and say it might be this or this or this? Something possibly very slight, an incident nearly forgotten.

Don't rush him, thought Mendoza. Kid gloves, handle with care. Lead him step by step.

He said very politely he'd see Sears then, hoped he wouldn't feel any aftereffects of the attack, said good night. Outside, the crowd had shrunk a good deal, and Galeano and Piggott were standing on the front walk with three people. Galeano hailed him.

"A little something, Lieutenant."

It was. It said a few things. Mrs. Miriam Berry, who was an elderly widow and lived next door to the Sears', had seen him running away. She always listened for Mr. Sears to come home because it was a comfort to know he was there in case *anything happened*—big strong man like that—and she heard him come up the drive, nice warm summer night, windows open, and she heard him yell, so she looked out her dining-room window and saw this fellow haring down the drive.

And she said he was a young man. Youngish, anyway. He just moved like that, she said. He'd run down toward Angelina Avenue.

And the teen-age couple in the next block, Linda Smith and Ronnie Wyman, they'd been "just fooling around" on Linda's front porch, when they saw the man come running fast down the street and jump into this car and drive off fast. They were both sixteen. They didn't know how long the

178

car had been parked there. But it was, said Ronnie, a 1963 Olds. He knew cars, that's what it was.

He could be right. No hint of its color or plate number, of course.

But this one might give them some big answers. Always provided that there was any halfway logical motive for the avenger—even a lunatic one—Sears's memory could hold the one clue.

"Statements?" said Galeano.

"Statements," said Mendoza, lighting a cigarette. "If these good people don't mind riding back to headquarters with you." They didn't mind at all; quite an adventure. "And send those things to the lab marked Urgent."

"I'd already thought of that," said Galeano.

"We'll just see," said Mendoza.

He lay awake planning how to handle Joe Sears. Backbone of the country maybe, but stubborn, unimaginative, very unpersuadable. Try to get through to him, somebody with an obsession about (maybe) something happening all that time ago. What?—well, that they didn't know.

Those old rapes. Jamison the odd man out. Yes, and for all they *knew* about this damned thing, Hackett's little idea could still be quite right—different motives for the sinners deserving vengeance.

No, by God, there had to be some meaning, to The Gray Goose, and just possibly the bus stop there—only what? For God's sake.

People waiting for a bus. Bremmer at the little bar for his nip of good whisky. Atwood—

He'd done some tortuous reasoning on it, and nothing he'd dreamed up had to mean anything.

And if they didn't catch up to the avenger, and if he went on—

But, missing his target tonight. Why? Sears a big, heavy

179

fellow, but Millway had been a big man too. But the attempt on Sears had been made from a little farther off, and in the open, and—well, so had the attack on Edith Varick. Yes, but a woman. Did it cancel out? Still, it was just a little funny, wasn't it, that Sears hadn't been taken so easy and quick as the others? When their boy had had so much practice at it, had managed the others so very damned slick?

That homemade garrote—Thugs, thought Mendoza sleepily. Very efficient way to do murder. Like a fish on a line, anybody caught like that—

Joe Sears had been very lucky. Why?

He came into the office on Tuesday morning to find Hackett talking bitterly about another mystery.

"The damn Feds on my neck, aren't we getting anywhere on it, and I ask you! Where is anywhere to get? Two other men living there, in the other two rented apartments, and the landlady out to market at eight in the morning, and one tenant at work, the other coming home to find the body. Naturally. One neighbor heard the shot, naturally thought it was a backfire. Nothing taken—he had quite a roll on him, and a diamond ring—and—"

"Well, he's no loss," said Jason Grace mildly. He'd been typing up a report on that suicide, which had turned out to be a straightforward business. "You're sure it wasn't any of the organization boys. I don't like to leave things open either, but Hopper, does he matter?"

"He seems to matter to the Feds," said Hackett gloomily.

"Don't sweat blood over it," said Mendoza, hanging up his hat.

"I just wish you'd take a look at it, Luis. You might have an inspiration . . . Yes, I saw about your overnight excitement," said Hackett, massaging his jaw. "Why did he miss? When he's been such a slick operator up to now? And does it get us any further on?"

180

"It could—it damn well could." Mendoza started explaining about Sears, and Palliser wandered in and sat down to listen. "You know the type—needs handling, but if we can get it across to him that—"

"That it dates back. But does it?" said Palliser. "We don't know, really."

"Tell me a better guess, John," said Mendoza impatiently.

"Art had one. It could still be."

"Oh, for God's sake! The different motives. Hasn't it got to mean something that Jamison—?"

"Was odd man out? I," said Jason Grace, "haven't been working this as close as you, Lieutenant, but I had a kind of funny little thought there, if you're interested." He smoothed his mustache. "Whatever motive you want to imagine, for whoever, suppose there's this bunch of people you think is due the vengeance. You're out to get Jamison, and Bremmer, and the rest of 'em. You've done a little elementary casing, you know some of Jamison's habits and haunts, hah, and how Bremmer's got a regular routine, and so on. Well—I thought about what you said about Jamison, and sure enough, he's the one of the whole bunch somebody might have a legitimate reason for vengeance on. If you were starting out taking the vengeance, you might surely want to start with Jamison first."

"Yes." Mendoza lit a cigarette. "You're doing some imagining."

"I like that little maxim of yours, Lieutenant. About the first rule of detection being like that story about the idiot boy and the lost horse. If you were a horse—so, all right, you decide to start taking the vengeance. You pick up Jamison at the Pasadena house, and you trail him where—possibly—you've trailed him before, to that Al's downtown. You see him settled down there. It's still light, and in June it's going to be for some time yet. You know Jamison's probably set there for an hour or more. And anyway," said Grace thoughtfully, "you also probably know some other favorite spots of his, where you can pick him up if he does wander away from Al's sooner."

"Are you heading anywhere?" asked Palliser.

Grace grinned and stabbed out his cigarette. "In a way, I just thought, suppose you're sort of keyed-up and impatient. You're going to take the vengeance on all these people at last, you want to get it started, and here's Jamison—the one you picked to do first—settled down in that bar, you can't get at him for a while—and even if you did mean to take him first, as maybe deserving the most vengeance, you get to thinking about Bremmer over there in his shop. Not so far away, and it's roundabout his closing time, a good time to get at him, easy and safe—just hang around to be his last customer. And the chances are you'll get back to Al's in half an hour or so to find Jamison still there to stalk."

"That," said Mendoza, "is some imagining, Jase."

"And that," said Grace, "could be why Bremmer was technically number one. Granting the way the avenger's mind might work. Even though you could also be right that Jamison was the first, prime target."

"Um," said Mendoza. "Those old rapes . . . I don't know, Jase. That's a very pretty fairy story, but—"

Sergeant Lake looked in the door. "I've got a Catholic priest on the line," he said. "Asking for John."

"Oh?" Palliser picked up the outside phone on Mendoza's desk. He said a lot of yesses, and finally said, "All right, I'll come right up . . . That priest from Bremmer's church. I told you he'd been there only five years. He's got the other one—Father Stephen—there now, visiting him. Who knew Bremmer a lot longer. Says the old man—he's retired, I didn't know a priest *could* retire, but apparently he's got arthritis, bad—remembers a little something about Bremmer that maybe we should hear, and as he is also pretty deaf maybe I'd better go up."

182

"Go, go," said Mendoza sardonically. "Even a priest may tell us something useful." Hackett looked at him sideways. Luis Mendoza very voluble on his vaunted agnosticism, but Art Hackett had ridden with him that death-haunted night when the rapist-killer had Alison, and listened to Luis Mendoza incoherently calling on the saints. When all the chips were down on the board—

"That," said Mendoza, "is quite a story, Jase . . ." Palliser went out unhurriedly. "Is there anything in it?"

"I couldn't say," said Grace, shrugging. "I was just practicing being the idiot boy."

"If it could have been like that, does it suggest to us that Jamison—if he was the intended first victim—" Mendoza paused. "Those old rapes? But nothing links him to any of them. He may have been questioned on some of them, but there wasn't any evidence or—"

"It's wild," said Hackett disapprovingly. "You," he added to Grace, "should be concocting all the way-out fiction—contemporary literature, my God—instead of pretending to be a detective."

"It's wild all right," agreed Grace amiably. "Just trying to cultivate what they call empathy. Though it's kind of hard to imagine how a lunatic *might* think."

"And do we even know he's a lunatic?" asked Mendoza bitterly.

"Well, after all, Luis—the vengeance bit, and the people he's—"

"Excuse me," said Sergeant Lake. "You've got a caller." And Lieutenant Wheelwright of Glendale walked in, big and broad and his plentiful gray hair curlier than ever, beaming at them.

Mendoza got up to shake hands and make introductions. "Have you—?"

"Well, I have," said Wheelwright. "I've got something we might call suggestive, Lieutenant Mendoza. Very nice to meet you fellows. This is quite a place you've got here. I understand your lab men get consulted by Scotland Yard." He drew up a chair and planted himself in it deliberately. "Still, we do try to run a nice tight little force up on my beat, not that I can take any credit for this—" he grinned around at them. "But I figured you'd want to know about it pronto, so I came right down."

"What?" demanded Mendoza.

"That Millway. I told you we'd located Kettler, this fellow who knew him, up in Fresno, and I'd sent a teletype off to the Fresno chief to have somebody talk to him. I don't know," said Wheelwright, "what physical shape Kettler may be in, that accident and all, but his mind's working just fine . . . I asked Fresno for every detail they could get." He reached into his breast pocket and brought out two folded pages of teletype. "I got this forty minutes ago. It set me doing a little wondering. I kind of think it'll do the same for you."

Mendoza reached for the pages eagerly, and Hackett and Grace came up behind him to read over his shoulder.

"As per request Glndle Pol H.Q. Wheelwright: W. J. Kettler contacted June 13 P.M. here, questioned re Frederick Millway deceased. Kettler very upset shocked learn of death, but rational eager be helpful. States knew Millway from earliest residence at apartment Glndle. Millway minus relations since death of sister Mrs. Gertrude Hoff 1959. Millway lost wife four children apartment fire Chicago approximately 1936 never remarried. Came Calif. 1937-8. Accredited social-welfare worker Chicago. Attached State Rehabilitation and Welfare Bureau approximately 1940-46, later to app 1958 occupied staff position P.A. commission S.Q. facility until retirement. Retired pension also savings, Kettler states will deposited with attorney Wm. Casey Glndle

184

to his knowledge all left to Red Cross. Kettler states Millway never kept large sums cash, very cautious about locking doors etc. No known enemies at time Kettler knew. Has not heard from Millway since Christmas card. Anxious help investigation will come Glndle if necessary. If further info desired contact back. Kelso, Chief of Police Fresno."

Mendoza said blankly, "*¡Y qué es esto?* He was on the *parole commission!* He was—"

Fourteen

"I'm afraid it's not much of anything at all," said the old priest to Palliser apologetically. "But Father O'Ryan said you were interested to know everything about poor Bremmer, and I did suddenly remember this, and I thought possibly you would be interested. Dear me, what a dreadful thing, that poor man murdered, and in his own shop! But dreadful things do happen, just as they have always happened, and often indeed to the best-living people."

"Yes, sir," said Palliser. The priest was a very old one, a thin and wrinkled man who moved painfully and whose hands were gnarled and stiffened with arthritis. The comfortably plump and benign Father O'Ryan sat behind his desk, old Father Stephen in a chair beside Palliser's.

"But I mustn't waste your time indeed. And I don't know that it is anything at all you'll be interested in—er—"

"Sergeant Palliser," said Father O'Ryan in a loud and distinct voice.

"Ah, yes, indeed, Sergeant Palace." The old priest smiled at him a little anxiously. "Poor William. Such a good man, but inclined to be—hum!—just a *leetle* too preoccupied with himself, *in* the sense of picking and worrying about his own little imagined sins. Not that any of us should *not* be concerned with our own wrongdoings, but in my humble opin-

186

ion, Sergeant Palace, if all of us concerned ourselves more with the *positive* efforts for good, and thought more for our neighbors than for ourselves in every way—" he lost the thread of his sentence and smiled and nodded gently.

"Yes, sir," said Palliser. "It was something you remembered about Bremmer?"

"Ah, yes. And I'm afraid I don't recall any details. It was just that the poor fellow was so terribly concerned and worried about the matter, you see. It was a crime of some sort, I don't recall—a police matter, certainly, for I do remember he said something about being questioned by a police officer, and"—Father Stephen beamed gently and vaguely on Palliser—"how kind and courteous the officer was. I'm afraid my memory's not what it was. But poor Bremmer was most upset. He had got it into his head—this was what I meant, and I'm sure Father O'Ryan will agree with me, by this narrow concentration upon one's own selfish interests in the progress of one's soul, as it were—he had got it into his head, *which* would be quite typical of William, as I remember thinking at the time, that he had been partly responsible for the thing. I told him—"

"Excuse me, for what?" asked Palliser.

"Eh? Oh, *that* I have no recollection of, I'm sorry. It was a police business of some sort—something, I think, he had seen—a criminal running away, perhaps, or—at any rate he was questioned as a witness by the police, and—"

"Excuse me, do you remember whether he had to testify at a trial, or—?"

"Oh, I don't think so," said the old priest vaguely. "No. I don't recall the details at all, only William being so upset about it personally. Because of his getting the silly notion in his head—he worried over every little thing, you know—that he could somehow have prevented it. It *was* a silly notion—criminals—poor Bremmer never a man of action, as they say."

"Don't you remember what *sort* of crime it—?"

"Eh? Oh, no, I'm afraid not, Sergeant. I'm afraid not. It was a long time ago. I couldn't be sure—but when Father O'Ryan mentioned your visit to him, the thing came into my mind. It was police business, and I thought possibly it—er—might mean something to you."

It didn't mean much to Palliser. If Bremmer had just been questioned, about a street robbery or a holdup or something, it wouldn't have got into records anywhere. From what they knew about Bremmer, a fussy, pedantic little man, he had probably (even as Father Stephen said) magnified his importance in it. But if Mendoza was right about this fantastic avenger thing having its roots in the past somehow—Palliser sighed.

"Do you remember exactly when? Or where this—whatever it was—happened?"

"Eh?" And when Father O'Ryan had repeated that distinctly, "Oh, dear me, I'm afraid not. It was years ago, I couldn't tell you exactly when. I only remember the poor dear man's distress, and his foolish notion that he bore any responsibility merely as a witness. I seem to remember that he made a special novena for it—some favor he was asking."

And that was about it. Obviously Palliser wasn't going to get any more here by prodding. And what the hell it meant he wasn't guessing. A crime (at least "police business") of some sort: if this vague recollection had anything at all to do with the vengeance bit, well, you thought about Jamison, the one with the pedigree: but if Bremmer had been a witness to a crime, it could hardly be the counts Jamison had been picked up on. Bremmer living by routine, downtown, the bus, and Hollywood about the only places he ever was.

And if this was at all interesting, it was also useless, because on what the old priest gave them, they hadn't anywhere to look up any more possible facts on it.

Palliser thanked them both, said that was all very interesting, and came out of the church with an idea. He drove down to Cole Avenue and asked Miss Alice Bremmer if she remembered her brother ever writing her about such a matter.

She didn't. He hadn't, she said, been anything of a letter writer. Just a note now and then. She didn't recall anything like that at all. Once in a while, she said, he'd mention being disturbed or worried and making a novena or special prayers about something, without going into detail—that was when she was still back East, just getting the short notes from him. He'd been a man, she said, to worry over little things.

Palliser started back downtown with the annoying feeling that he'd been on the verge of finding out something important—if only various people had taken more notice, or remembered more details. Whatever it was, whatever had bothered Bremmer those years ago, it was past praying for now.

"—a Fed," said Sergeant Lake. "One Robert R. Willis, and he—"

"The hell with him," said Mendoza, who was still staring at the yellow teletype. "He was on the parole commission at San Quentin, for God's sake! The parole—Jimmy, get me Quentin on the line, *pronto!*"

"Well, interesting all right," said Hackett, "but what does it say?"

"It might say this and that," said Grace. "To give us a link."

"Because we've now got a man with a little pedigree and a member of the parole board? We have also got," said Hackett, "five other people, with absolutely no smell of connection with crime or criminals in general, and I can't see—"

189

Wheelwright said diffidently he couldn't see how it tied up either, but it was interesting.

Sergeant Lake buzzed the inside phone and said the line was busy, he'd keep trying, and this Fed was insisting on seeing Mendoza, and after all—

"Are you trying, for God's sake, to tie up Millway with Jamison?" asked Hackett. "Talk about—"

"That was the first connection my simple mind made, Arturo."

"—about crystal balls! The chance is about one in ten thousand, and even if there *is* some connection, what would —? What about the rest of them? Look, Luis, just look. The count Jamison got put away on, if you're thinking, as I suspect you are, of the vengeance bit starting with Jamison —well, you saw that woman and her husband, you said yourself, perfectly ordinary people, they're not harboring any ideas of revenge. At this late date, my God. The one he got acquitted on, ditto. I don't see how you can—"

Mendoza got out a cigarette and looked at it meditatively. "I wasn't thinking about them, Art. The vague notion did cross my mind that—maybe—oh, hell, I don't know —maybe the lunatic once had a daughter raped, and coming across Jamison—hell. It's still all up in the air, I know, but if—"

"Look," said Hackett, "I'll only say this. Even if Millway, on his job back then, did have something to do with Jamison, how the hell would any ordinary citizen *know* about it?"

"That is a point," said Grace. The door opened and a tall, thin, impeccably clad youngish man came in and apologized for intruding.

"Right on our necks, I told you, Luis," muttered Hackett.

"It's this Hopper, Lieutenant," said the Fed. "We're a little disturbed over it, we'd like to have the matter definitely cleared up, to be sure one way or the other, you see—even though we got the word he was out of the organized stuff back East, still with birds like that—there could have been a hired dropper—"

Mendoza said, "Sergeant Hackett is doing all that can—" and snatched up the phone as it buzzed at him.

"Got Quentin for you, Lieutenant."

Mendoza introduced himself and began to explain to authority at San Quentin what he was after, please. Yes, a Frederick C. Millway, once on the parole commission—well, some while back, but it was rather urgent and if their records could be checked—

"Well, my God, Sergeant," said the Fed just a little heatedly, "if we've got hired organization boys in our territory, we do want to find out about it. I realize it's your case, but we've got a finger in this pie too, and while I've got no intention of saying you're not handling the investigation properly —after all, we do realize the quality of this police force, Sergeant, but when a man like Hopper—"

"But there's just nowhere to go on it," said Hackett. "We've given you all we've—"

"That's right," said Mendoza. "Nelson Edward Jamison. A one-to-three. First count. He got out in 1955. Yes . . . Well, about Millway—how long was he on the commission, and, oh, anything else you can dig up on his record . . . Yes, I know. I appreciate that . . . But I'd like the information as soon as you can possibly—"

The inside phone rang on his desk and he jerked his head at Hackett.

"They do keep you boys busy," commented Wheelwright to Grace interestedly.

"Art? I've got a call from a squad car," said Sergeant Lake, "at Eleventh and Figueroa. Traffic fatality, they're holding a drunken driver. Asking for help. There's a little crowd, and the subject's belligerent. I've sent another car, two men."

"O.K.," said Hackett. "Jase, chase down to Eleventh and

Figueroa—corpse, drunken driver, a little trouble. Call in if you need more help."

"Makes my beat," said Wheelwright, "seem pretty damn tame. I guess I'd better be getting back to it and let you fellows get to work." He stood up.

"I'm just saying, Sergeant," said the Fed, "that we're carrying a work-load too, you do realize that, and in any case we haven't any jurisdiction over a homicide on your beat, but this Hopper—well, when we know it could be a—"

"That's right," said Mendoza, nodding and grinning at Wheelwright as the big lieutenant lifted a hand and made for the door. Grace went out ahead of him, thoughtfully feeling his shoulder holster. "I'd be much obliged . . . As soon as you can dig it up. Thanks very much." He put the phone down.

"Who ever heard of a hired dropper using a .32?" asked Hackett reasonably.

"Well, all I'm saying is, we're concerned about Hopper," said the Fed.

"You may be," said Hackett, "but I'm not, so damn much. I've looked at it and Hank Glasser has looked at it, and neither of us is exactly an inexperienced detective, Mr. Willis, and by all we've got—which we passed on to your office— about Hopper's recent activities, known and apparent, we both think that some relative or boyfriend or whoever connected with one of the women Hopper tried to solicit, is the likeliest X for the job. And sure, as we have the time we're continuing to check all those women he'd listed—Hank's out somewhere on it right now, with Landers, I think—but we don't feel it's so very damn urgent, and there's no guarantee at all that the girl in question got listed in Hopper's little book, so—"

"I must say, Sergeant—" began the Fed stiffly.

"*¡De lo lindo—bastante!*" said Mendoza. "You're supposed to be on the same side, boys. Calm down. Why the hell are you dithering about Hopper, Willis? You just heard what our view is."

"I'm afraid we can't altogether agree, Lieutenant. By our information, there could be a gun out for Hopper from the organization back East, and—"

"And he didn't know it? All innocently occupied trying to set up his own business here? Word gets round."

"He needn't have. And if you're not concerned, Lieutenant—the organization's never got a foothold in this burg and I kind of had the idea you boys don't intend it should—"

"I'm concerned, I'm concerned," said Mendoza. He had lit up, Hackett thought amusedly, like a Christmas tree, all for that damn teletype that might mean nothing at all; he was cracking along on all cylinders, convinced they might at last be getting somewhere (where? for God's sake, thought Hackett) on this fantastic vengeance thing, and he lit a cigarette and pointed it at Willis sharply. "The trouble with you Feds is," he said, "you just hate to delegate authority. You just hate to admit there's any force as good as you are."

"Pot calling the kettle black," said Hackett.

Willis grinned unwillingly. "Well, I guess I'll take that, Lieutenant. But we'd like very much to see this thing cleared up—"

"All right, all right," said Mendoza. "I'll see to it." He grinned back at Willis. "Art's been saying he wishes I'd have a look at it—I haven't. I will, and take a look in my crystal ball and come up with an answer on it. Satisfied?"

Willis laughed. "I've got to be, I guess. We don't go in much for crystal balls." He looked at Mendoza a little curiously; he was a new transfer to the local office and hadn't run into L.A.P.D. Homicide—or Mendoza—more than once or twice in the six months he'd been here. "Er—now? You mind if I tag along? The chief said—"

"Cooperation, cooperation!" said Mendoza. "¿Qué más?" He looked at his watch. "I suppose we can't expect Quentin to dig through all those records and call back before noon at least. All right, why not now? Art, you can brief me on the way, we'll go have a look at the terrain."

"I've *told* you about it, and—"

"Not many details." Mendoza picked up his hat.

"— and there wasn't any physical evidence, the lab went all through the place. Just, there he was, dead. An S. and W. Masterpiece .32, an old one. He wasn't robbed, he had a roll of nearly eleven hundred bucks, a diamond ring, a Hamilton watch. The only prints in the place were his and the landlady's, Mrs. Stella Breen. Ordinary sort of woman, lives in one of the ground-floor apartments."

"What time was he shot?" They all got into the elevator.

"About eight in the morning. It's a working-class neighborhood—he was evidently conserving his money—didn't I give you all this? The report I—"

"We've been busy," Mendoza reminded him. "And?"

"Not many people home in other places around there, that time. Working people. One woman heard the shot—we think —thought it was a backfire. Nobody who was home saw any stranger coming to or from the house, but nobody was looking. Why should they be? No strange cars noticed."

"Mmh. Take my car," said Mendoza. "Did we search the place? All the other apartments?"

"We're trained to be thorough. Hank did that. Nothing."

"Mmh." Mendoza rattled his keys, and the Fed looked slightly stunned at the long black Ferrari, but said nothing and meekly climbed into the jump seat in back. "Where?" asked Mendoza.

Hackett told him. He always rather got a kick out of this Mendoza, the hot-as-a-firecracker boy sharp enough to cut himself, cracking along with metaphorical sparks shooting out from him—and all because (today) of that silly damn teletype, thinking it *meant* anything. God, that vengeance bit. All up in the air. After some doubt and rumination, Hack-

194

ett was again back to thinking that his first little idea could be the right one—different motives on all of them. The so-unlikely people. There *appeared* to be a link, tenuous as it was, and it could be entirely coincidental, among Bremmer, Rodzinsky, The Gray Goose and—very doubtfully—Atwood, but it didn't seem to mean anything: point in any direction. And what about Edith Varick the teetotaler? And where did Joe Sears come in? And nothing whatever linked either Jamison or Millway to the bar or all the other people. By now their pictures had been shown there, and unrecognized—neither known.

He wondered what that priest had had to tell John.

And in the years he'd worked with Luis Mendoza, he'd seen him pull off this and that, and sometimes he'd thought a little superstitiously that Mendoza had second sight or something, though it wasn't infallible; but occasionally he startled even Hackett. I'll take a look and clear it up, he'd said: and that was just exactly what he did. And even while Hackett realized commonsensibly that it wasn't ESP exactly, but a faculty for catching the nuances from people—well, he was startled.

They got out of the Ferrari and walked up the short, shabby front walk, and Mendoza stepped onto the porch almost audibly sniffing, bloodhound on a trail. He looked up and down the street: narrow lots here, old part of town, houses close to each side. He said, "Kind of neighborhood where people know each other." Hackett agreed. Maybe Mendoza was regretting his insouciant boast to Willis, who was watching him curiously, but if so it wasn't apparent. "You can usually be trusted at the routine, Arturo—I expect you're right about this, but I'll just have a look . . . Seem to remember you said something about Hopper trying to rope in a girl from the neighborhood around here? Yes. Bad judgment . . . He'd depended on the henchmen too long."

"Well, she turned him down," said Hackett impatiently. "We *looked* here, Luis. And so did the lab."

"Mmh. Other tenants?"

"Ronald Wagner, sixty-three, widower, lived here four years, works as a night watchman, some building downtown. No record. Same like Bremmer, lives by routine."

"Who's Bremmer?" asked Willis.

"And Sam Clinton, forty-two, divorced, lived here three years, has a part-time job clerking in a men's store and an Army disability pension. No record. Nonentities, Luis. Neither of 'em had anything to do with it—Clinton was at work, accounted for, and Wagner had just come home and found him. Take my word."

"All right," said Mendoza, looking at the front doors. There were three. Two to the ground-floor apartments—the big old frame house, circa 1900, cut up in a makeshift way —one to the upper floor. "There's a landing up there," said Hackett, "and two more doors."

"*Naturalmente*," said Mendoza, and pushed the doorbell under the inked card saying *Mrs. Stella Breen*.

"We've talked to her," said Hackett. "She was out at the market when it probably—"

"But I haven't seen her," said Mendoza mildly.

She was a very thin woman with a haggard face and lackluster eyes, and she was dressed in a fresh cotton housedress and sensible shoes. She was polite, if unenthusiastic about police on her doorstep; she asked them in politely. It was a neat, clean, entirely characterless apartment living-room.

She answered Mendoza's questions in a dull voice. Yes, she lived here alone. She was a widow. Her tenants had always been respectable men—she preferred men tenants, yes. Some of the types of women who came wanting to—no, she'd known nothing about Mr. Hopper, he'd looked all right, he'd paid promptly, and she'd been terribly shocked when that police officer had said—it was an awful thing, and in her house. She'd been out to market that morning. No, it had been Mr. Wagner found him, seeing him there, door left open, when he came home—she eyed Mendoza a trifle uneasily. He was wandering around the room, almost audibly sniffing the air. He stopped in front of the old-fashioned upright golden-oak piano.

"Pretty girl," he said genially. Mrs. Breen was silent. "Your daughter, Mrs. Breen? She has a look of you somehow." He turned and smiled at her.

"Yes," she said. "Yes, my daughter Sylvia."

Mendoza said, "A very pretty girl." The silver-framed portrait showed a wide-eyed young girl, probably just out of her teens, soft dark hair to her shoulders, pearls at her young throat. There was a dime-store vase with one fresh American Beauty rose in it in front of the portrait. Mendoza cocked his head at the piano. A very old piece of sheet music was propped on the music rack—"My Ain Countree."

"Has she been dead for a long time, Mrs. Breen?" asked Mendoza softly; and Hackett nearly jumped.

"She—what do you mean?" Her voice rose an octave. She leaped up.

"She is dead, isn't she?"

"Yes, she's dead," said Mrs. Breen.

"I wonder how," said Mendoza.

She looked at him from across the room. "You haven't been here before. Going straight to—oh, you are a devil to see things, aren't you?"

"When they're there to be seen," said Mendoza. "Not until I came here just now. But I had heard that Mr. Hopper had—mmh—attempted to solicit a young woman in the immediate neighborhood, and it just occurred to me—neighbors are sometimes neighborly—that somebody who knew about it might have told you just how unrespectable your

197

new tenant was. In fact, that was very likely. When I thought about it. And it seemed a little odd you claimed not to know. And now—just how did you lose your daughter, Mrs. Breen?"

"You are a devil," she said dully. She moved toward him slowly. "To come here and in five minutes—but I don't mind it. I expect it was wrong. It's said, vengeance belongs to the Lord. I don't know, but I don't mind. Only how you could come, and straightaway—she was murdered by another one like him. They called it suicide but it was murder. A man—like that—who seduced her, just to put her—to put her—a place like that—a—a—brothel. So she—they said suicide but it was murder. The man never even went to jail, they said there wasn't—*you knew!*"

"No," said Mendoza. "I didn't know, until you told me. I only wondered why you hadn't found out what he was. And there could have been innocent reasons."

"Innocent!" she said with a half-sob. "Innocent! That man murdered her—twenty she was. Eleven years ago. And Brenda Kling comes to me—nice girl down the street—and tells me what this Hopper says to her—another one. Like that. Dirty old man. Like that one—only he was young—the murderer. I didn't let on anything to her, but it was like I went a little crazy. Maybe I did. Nobody here knew a thing about my Sylvia, I moved here after." She looked at him blindly. "You are a *devil*. Coming. Seeing. But I don't mind, after all. I thought about it all night, and next morning when I knew Mr. Clinton had gone to work—I knew he was in, that Hopper. I went upstairs with the gun my husband had, I'd kept it against prowlers and such, and there wasn't nobody else in the house—he was there, that devil, worse than devil, another murderer, and he never suspected at all and I walked up to him and shot him dead. And afterward I just kept the gun in my brassière so you wouldn't find it. I'm not sorry, and I don't mind whatever you do to me," said Mrs. Breen.

198

They took her back to the office; there'd be paperwork on it; and they started to arrange for the warrant.

"My good God in heaven," said Willis to Hackett. "Just like that." He looked at Mendoza with awe. "You don't tell me you have any problems with crime here, with that one in operation even six days a week?"

Hackett laughed. "Whatever it is—ESP or just brains—it doesn't always function, friend. Sometimes, like now, he almost scares you. But I've known him stymied too."

"My God," said Willis. "My God."

"Maybe next time," said Hackett, "you'll be readier to delegate the authority."

"You don't suppose," said Willis, "he'd be interested in switching over to us?"

"Brother, he's dedicated. Took the oath at twenty-one."

It was getting on for twelve-thirty. Landers and Lake were starting to get Mrs. Breen's confession down; she was sitting there docilely talking in a dull, slow voice. Palliser had just come back and was arguing about something with Landers in the anteroom. "For the love of God!" Mendoza was saying irritably, "hasn't Quentin called back *yet?* I swear to God that's got to say something—and now I think of it, damn it, all those old rapes and assaults out of Pending—my God, that far back, I suppose half the original investigating officers are dead or retired, but wouldn't do any *harm* to—"

Fifteen

T<small>HE</small> F.B.I. man went away to report the successful clearing up of the Hopper thing, and Mendoza had just decided to put in another call to San Quentin when Sergeant Lake thrust his head in the door and said tersely, "Quite a Donnybrook going on down on Figueroa—pint-size riot, Grace's yelling for help. Everybody, and Traffic's got five cars rerouted to hit it—"

Mendoza remembered to tell him to send for a female officer to baby-sit with Mrs. Breen before they took off. There was a car waiting downstairs. Mendoza, Hackett, Palliser, and Landers piled into it and the siren started.

When they got there, it was being quite a little thing. The drunken driver who'd rammed a motorcycle and killed its rider happened to be joy-riding around with four other cars full of his juvenile-gang pals; and most unfortunately the motorcycle rider had been in similar company. None of the motorcyclists happened to be drunk, but of the other juvenile crowd a couple were and the rest were just high enough to be minus any inhibitions, not that they had many sober. The trouble twenty-six big strong kids can cause under such circumstances is surprising. By the time Grace and the first two extra squad cars had got there, a pitched battle was going on between the two gangs, and somebody had felled the lone officer in the first squad car to answer the call, and taken his gun, so there was another corpse lying in the street—one of the motorcyclists—and the officer bleeding and unconscious. A sizable crowd had collected, and traffic was absolutely stalled because the kids were fighting all over the intersection.

The men from Homicide and four two-man squad cars landed there about the same time, and waded into it. Mendoza, scrambling out of the squad car last as the smallest man, spotted Jason Grace, gun in hand, in the middle of the mêlée out there, heard him shouting, "Now just hold it! Get away—get back, or we'll fire!" A uniformed man beside him, gun upraised, caught one big lout by the shoulder, swung him around, sent him stumbling toward the first squad car and brought out the handcuffs. A joyous sudden yell went up from several of the kids—"Cops! Hey, more cops!"—and then there was chaos.

Naturally. The irrational, no-occupation-but-amusing-themselves, undisciplined roving juveniles, they'd forget a few personal differences any day to gang up on the cops.

That they did. Another patrolman went down before the onslaught, and there was another gun gone. Two more squad cars roared up. The police didn't want to fire on them (COPS SHOOT TO KILL ON JUVENILE GROUP) but the kids didn't mind at all. A gang of them happily descended on a squad car, rocked it back and forth until they turned it over, and proceeded systematically to destroy it as far as possible. (Cost of squad car to taxpayers approximately five grand.)

Grace was caught out in the middle of the intersection, the nearest uniformed man unconscious at his feet. Hackett and Palliser made for him, hitting the yelling, fighting crowd as one man, Hackett wishing absently for George Higgins' bulk and weight beside him; by the time they got there Grace was face down in the street. Another squad car came up and men poured out of it—Traffic was on the job.

It was quite a thing, but they got on it, and got enough men on the scene, and an hour or so later the violent part of it was all over. All the young louts were rounded up and taken in, and two ambulances had taken away the corpses and wounded, and only the really tedious part remained to be done: all the paperwork, the legal processing, and much later, when everybody was busy on something else, the time off to testify in court.

There were two uniformed men shot, one critical, and one innocent bystander. Grace, loaded into the ambulance, was still unconscious. Hackett, nursing a badly skinned knuckle and an incipient black eye, went down to the General to find out how bad Grace was, and the rest of them went back to the office, Mendoza in a savage temper with a brand-new suit jacket ripped halfway apart, and a painful bruise on one cheek; Landers had a black eye too, and Palliser was still making occasional crowing sounds, having sustained a low kick.

Nobody had had lunch, of course. Mendoza said he wanted a drink instead and Palliser didn't want anything. Sergeant Lake regarded them sympathetically, said at least thank God they were all reasonably intact and wasn't it the truth that Satan found work for idle hands—these God-damned j.d.'s—and he was sorry but there was an attempted homicide, a stabbing, just reported by a beat car.

"*¡Diez millón demonios!*" said Mendoza violently. "I'm going nowhere until we hear from Art." He planted himself at his desk.

Landers said with a sigh, "No rest for the wicked. I'll take it, Lieutenant. Go have a look, anyway. What's the address, Jimmy?" He took the memo slip and went out, limping slightly.

About ten minutes later, with Palliser sipping black coffee and gradually regaining his color, Hackett called from the General and said Jase would be O.K.—just a little concussion, they said, they'd keep him overnight, and Jase had come to and asked him to go tell Virginia, so he'd be about an hour on that, and how was John?

"Alive," said Mendoza. "Just. And to think he's planning on getting married on Saturday! The risks we do run. All right, boy, we'll see you." He put the phone down. "And isn't life strange, John? When all those irresponsible, trouble-making, anarchistic louts come up in front of a judge a while from now, they'll have changed into just an innocent bunch of mischief-making youngsters."

Palliser sat up straighter and finished his coffee. "God be thanked," he said, "the judges are being some tougher these days. The citizenry has been getting the message, so many of 'em running up against it themselves. I feel better. How's Jase?"

The Graces lived in Leimert Park, which was a very nice section of town at the present, roughly half-and-half as to population, black and white. Hackett had never met Grace's wife; she was a pretty young woman with a nice figure, but the minute she looked at him there on the doorstep of her little colonial house behind the manicured green lawn, instant alarm sprang into her eyes. Hackett had "cop" written all over his bulk, and Virginia Grace was married to a cop.

"He's O.K.," said Hackett, and told her about it.

"Well!" said Virginia. "You'd better come in, Sergeant, you look as if you could use a cup of coffee, and as long as I needn't go tearing down there to catch his last words— I'd have a guess his father is there by now."

"Was when I left, sure." Grace's father was one of the doctors on the staff at the General. "He was saying, kind of resigned, that he'd tried to talk him into going in for medicine."

Virginia smiled, her eyes a little anxious still. "Oh, so did I, Sergeant."

"He really will be O.K.," said Hackett.

She looked at him, turning around with the coffee pot in one slim brown hand. She said, "This time, Sergeant. Yes."

And there wasn't anything Hackett could say to that at all.

He sometimes did wonder—especially at times like this—why he, or Jason Grace, or anybody else, had gone to such trouble to get to be a cop, of all things. On this force, which had such high requirements for recruits that it turned down ninety per cent of the men who applied. He did wonder.

He said to Virginia Grace, "It's just some kind of satisfaction, Mrs. Grace, to know you're on the right side. Law and order."

She smiled. "Which is what Jase says. I suppose so, Sergeant. Would you like sugar or cream with that?"

And of course there was still the mountain of paperwork they were trying to catch up on; reports, lab reports, statements, on all of the avenger's victims. All the details to be garnered, and typed up in triplicate, and filed away, because you never knew when this or that would help the D.A. make a case, or help you in solving one.

The warrant came through on Mrs. Breen, and she'd been formally charged and taken down to the new facility on Alameda.

Mendoza for the second time had just placed another long-distance call to San Quentin, and when the phone buzzed at him, he picked it up eagerly, but Lake said, "It's Tom."

"Lieutenant?" said Landers. "Are you sitting down?"

"Yes, I—why, ¿por Dios?"

"You'd better chase down here. It's our boy again."

"Not—?"

"That's what," said Landers. "The avenger. And—take a deep breath—it's Sears."

"Sears?"

"That's right. Only he didn't get him again. I mean—well, looking at it with all the rest of 'em, it's funny, but it looks as if this joker, after he missed getting Sears last night, made up his mind to get him any old way. He tried with a knife this time. And left his little card."

"For God's sake—where? I thought that call—"

"Yeah. At his hamburger stand. On Hill just down from Pico."

"Hell *and* damnation!" said Mendoza. "He didn't get him?"

"Nope. The ambulance had come and gone by the time I got here, but the squad-car man said the intern said it was anybody's guess how long Sears had been lying here bleeding—danger was loss of blood—but he might have a fifty-fifty chance to make it. It's a hole-in-the-wall joint, it looks as if the joker waited until he was alone there and Sears went into the back, and—"

"I'll come and see." Mendoza hung up the phone and looked at Palliser. "Now will you have a guess, John, why it is so important to our avenger to get Joe Sears? To deliver the vengeance on him?"

"Sears? Has he—?"

"Yes. Tell you as we go, if you're feeling all right to—"

"I'm all right. What about—?"

"*Sears,*" said Mendoza. He got up and looked down at himself in dissatisfaction. It simply wasn't normal for dapper Lieutenant Mendoza, in the middle of the working day, to appear tieless—his tie had been shredded before the jacket —and minus his jacket. "For God's sake, Sears! Absolutely no possible connection to *any* of the rest of them—damn it, except that he hasn't got a pedigree, he's as much odd man out as Jamison! A little hamburger stand on Hill—I ask you, what possible—? It just makes no sense!"

And this time, having missed Joe Sears once, the avenger so determined that he abandoned his garrote—which had

205

been so successful up to then—and used a knife. It was, you could say, getting more offbeat all the time.

It was, when they got there, a very small hole-in-the-wall place, in the block on Hill down from Pico Boulevard. It was about ten feet wide, fronting the street, no door at all but one of those steel grilles to be pulled across and locked at night, and it ran back perhaps thirty-five feet, with a long counter and a row of about eighteen stools. But it was a very clean and burnished little place, with a big coffee maker still perking energetically away behind the counter, an electric grill, a Coke-dispensing machine, a big white refrigerator at the far end of the counter, and a big sign listing the menu—sandwiches, hamburgers, hot dogs, hot soups, sodas and malts and sundaes, all the short-order snacks.

It could be that Sears did very well out of this place, in a modest way; it wasn't a greasy spoon, it looked attractive, and there was a good deal of business around on all sides, a gas station at the corner, small shops, whose personnel might habitually drop in here for the coffee break or lunch. A sign over the entrance said *Joe's Place*.

And that was Sears all right: unimaginative, stolid, honest, stubborn as hell. What had he ever done, in the eyes of the avenger, to deserve the vengeance?

Landers was waiting there in front with the uniformed squad-car man and another patrolman. "Harrison," he said. "And Mr. William Golonowsky. Lieutenant Mendoza and Sergeant Palliser."

"Pleasure," said Golonowsky gloomily. "These God-damned hoods. Even go for a little place like Joe's. A caution, these days, I swear to God. I'm the one found him and called you."

"When I saw what it was," said the uniformed Harrison, "I was careful, sir. I hope I did right. I asked the intern first. But I'm taking that course in Police Science at L.A.C.C., sir, and I thought—I was *careful*."

"He may make rank young," said Tom Landers genially. "He was careful."

They went into Joe's Place, and Landers led them down to the rear of the public part. This was a little slot of business frontage, and there was a partition at its rear, where the counter ended in a flap that lifted up, between the front and, they found, a much smaller room where there was a second, much older refrigerator, a tiny partitioned-off lavatory, and open storage shelves; a rear door led out to an alley where refuse cans were stacked.

"They said God knows how long he was there," said Golonowsky. "I hope the poor guy makes it. Nice guy, Joe."

"They took him right off," said Harrison, "he was still alive, of course, and they wanted to—and I hadn't any chalk on me, Lieutenant. But he was right here, right in the middle next to the refrigerator, see, his head toward the back door. And I didn't know but what those damn interns—well, I asked, and they said sure, and I did have a piece of string on me at least, and I just tied it around the hilt; and places like this generally use some of that foil or wax paper, and I looked around—"

He had the knife all neatly packed up for them, in waxed paper. Mendoza said, "Good man," and Harrison looked gratified; but Mendoza didn't think there'd be any prints on the knife.

"I couldn't make head or tail of the card, sir—it was lying on top of him—but I put it in a sandwich bag for you."

It was, of course, just like all the rest. *The vengeance is just.*

"I," said Golonowsky, "have got ulcers. I'm a tax accountant—the ulcers, it figures—up the street. Golonowsky and O'Neill, tax accountants, notary public, outside bookkeeping service. On the weekends I moonlight. Keep body and soul together. Not to mention a wife and four kids. So, ulcers I got. And so a few times a day I come down here, drink a glass of milk. For the ulcers. Joe was obliging. He got in special my favorite, that Jersey Golden Creme kind. So I come in about half an hour, forty minutes back, no Joe. Well, I know he's got to be here, always is, I give him a couple minutes to come out of the lavatory, I sing out to him, no answer, so I think, Joe, he's not a young man, things happen, heart attack, stroke, I know he's here because the place is open, I go looking. My God. There he is. Here. With a knife in his back, my God. But breathing. So first I phone for an ambulance and then I phone you."

There was a great spreading stain across the worn linoleum floor in the little back room—dried and still-drying blood, turning rust-color. "You can spell it out," said Landers. "It's what, getting on for three now. He'd have his biggest crowd around lunchtime, I'd think, up to two o'clock or so. The joker'd have to be alone with him, so do we say it was after two? He'd hang around, over coffee or something, until Sears started for the back room—"

"Or," said Palliser, "being alone with him, maybe on the end stool there, just lifted up that counter flap and went through and showed the knife to him—"

"I don't think so," said Mendoza. "No. Not Sears. Sears would have showed fight—and there'd be people on the street not far off to hear. No, he waited until Sears went through to the back room, and followed him. *Sears.*"

"Very nice fellow," said Golonowsky. "Till empty, I suppose. I didn't look. These hoods."

It wouldn't be, of course. The avenger, after last night, uncertain of his garrote—after so much success? Or hadn't he had time to make a new one? And Mendoza had a further depressing thought suddenly . . . Buses, he thought. Sears with no connection whatever to the other victims, and even if you counted in that nebulous notion about the bus stop, you couldn't figure him in. Because there would be a closer bus stop, here, where Sears would have waited for his bus home, than the one at Ninth and Spring. Hell. What did anything mean?

"I suppose you put in a call for the lab truck," said Landers. "Not that they'll pick up anything. Is there a head or tail to this thing? Damndest thing I ever—"

Mendoza swore absently and looked at Golonowsky. "We'll want a statement from you, sir."

"Sure. Supposed so. Public duty," said Golonowsky. "I suppose I can't get my glass of milk first?"

"At headquarters," said Palliser. "We'll oblige you, sir."

"Hell of a thing," said Golonowsky. "Poor Joe. A very nice guy. We agree on politics. Will somebody be telling his wife? I hope he makes it."

Mendoza turned the lab team loose in Joe's Place, went back to his office and called the General.

San Quentin hadn't called back yet.

The General said that Mr. Sears had suffered the loss of a lot of blood, he was considered to be in critical condition, but had a chance of making it. Neither the heart nor any vital organ had been touched. He could not, of course, be questioned for some time.

Naturalmente. Hackett came in and said Grace's wife was a nice woman, and Mendoza fired the news about Sears at him. "For God's sake!" said Hackett. "A knife? A—how the hell, Luis, does Sears link up to the rest of them?"

"*¿Qué tiene de particular*—what's so odd about it?" said Mendoza sardonically. "They're all different, Arturo. Night from day. I was thinking I had a glimpse of a very much maybe idea, at least—"

"Those old assaults out of Pending. Really reaching," said Hackett. "I don't know, Luis, I was back to thinking my original bright little idea was the likeliest answer—the different motives. But Sears really stymies me. One like that. One of the little people, the ordinary people in any city, any time. Little quiet business. He probably goes from home to work, vice versa, sits in front of the TV with beer, his set ideas you couldn't change till kingdom come, he—"

"Backbone of the country. And he wouldn't even—if we are talking about my left-field ideas," said Mendoza, "he wouldn't even have used that same bus stop."

"What? Oh, *that* notion," said Hackett. "No, he wouldn't, would he? And this has been a day, hasn't it? D'you suppose that fancy tailor of yours can fix up your jacket?"

Mendoza said probably, for a price. And he didn't suppose Palliser was getting anything at all useful out of Mrs. Sears.

Palliser wasn't. He'd gone to break the news to her, and taken her to the General, but of course she was shocked and concerned for her husband and in common humanity he couldn't press her with questions.

"I didn't *believe* him," she said. "I didn't *believe* him, he said about somebody trying to strangle him last night. And now—you think it was the same *one*? Could've been? But nobody's got any reason to—Joe!"

He couldn't ask her searching questions, even if he'd known the right ones to ask. It had been quite a day, and his stomach still ached slightly. As far as Palliser was concerned, the vengeance bit, *six* murders, was just jumble and confusion; he couldn't see any pattern in it at all. And the boss sometimes had brain waves, but he was really reaching if he thought any possible ancient-history connection between Jamison and that Millway was going to turn out to mean anything where the rest of them were concerned.

He phoned a report in to the office and went home.

Mendoza went home carrying his ruined jacket and was pounced on by the twins in the backyard as he left the garage. Alison was wandering around cutting fresh roses; she stared at him over a mixed bunch of Talismans and Condesa de Sástagos and said, *"¿Quién salió ganando*—who won the fight? For heaven's sake, Luis—a brand-new suit, and is that a black eye? *Amante—"*

"Not quite," said Mendoza. "We have had quite a day, my darling. I need soothing. I need my hand held. And I *thought* I'd had a brain storm on this vengeance seeker, but now I don't think so. Sears, my God. A knife. And—"

"You're dithering," said Alison. "Come and be soothed. What on earth—?"

"Well," said Mendoza, adjusting a twin in each arm and nearly choked with four small arms entwined about his neck, "it was quite a day, *cara.*"

"You and El Señor. That stray tom showed up again and we had to rescue El Señor from him. Only a long drink of rye restored him."

"That cat. Alcoholics Anonymous. Maybe," said Mendoza, "it'll do the same for me."

Hackett went home and told Angel morosely it was another Jack the Ripper case. "And only by the grace of God the press isn't making headlines. We've been able to—but they may be, if he keeps it up. And what's to stop him? We said, a lunatic. All right, so was Jack the Ripper, probably. They never caught *him.* Not a smell. There's just not one single thing to get hold—oh, but, my God, Angel, you'll never believe what Luis pulled off this morning! Sometimes he almost scares you—second sight or whatever—" He started to tell her about Mrs. Breen.

Angel was frosting a cake. One of her special cakes. Almond-mocha frosting, he noticed. She listened interestedly; the baby was asleep, and Mark absorbed with his crayons, sprawled on the kitchen floor. "Really," said Angel. "I

211

thought second sight was reserved for Scots. That Mendoza . . . Well, maybe you can have a *small* piece, Art. If you don't have any potato. After all, you have to think of the physical exam . . . Have you weighed today?"

Hackett went dutifully off to the bathroom, and the scale stopped depressingly at a hundred and ninety-nine.

"That doctor is nuts!" he muttered to himself. "After all, I am six three-and-a-half—"

Higgins had had a nice leisurely day off. Get back to the rat race tomorrow. He was invited to dinner at the Dwyers', but he went up there at noon and took Bruce the Scottie for a walk, and watered the backyard. Save Mary a little work.

He wondered if anything more tangible had showed up on that avenger thing. Very offbeat—a bastard to work. Thank God the press hadn't—

And at seven o'clock Mary had one of his favorites, Swiss steak and mushrooms and creamed potatoes, and she smiled at him, and the kids chattered, calling him by his first name. Higgins was reasonably content.

Palliser took a shower while a TV dinner was warming in the oven, and ate it with the pleasurable reflection that presently he wouldn't be eating TV dinners alone—or at all, it was to be hoped. He was still somewhat in debt, the doctor bills and all, but not really bad. He could make it. They could make it.

At eight o'clock he called Roberta.

"It's all set?" she asked. "Have you—?"

"Well, hell *and* damnation," said Palliser, "this thing— this series thing, the avenger—not a smell yet, and if he pulls another one—I just hope to God we can make it, darling. Saturday at least I can ask for, I've got sick leave piled up, and it's only about forty minutes' flying time to Vegas, and we've already got the ring—listen, Robin, we'll make it. And the proper honeymoon on my vacation—"

"What I'm letting myself in for," she said with a smile in her voice. "Marrying a cop. I must be out of my mind . . ."

Sixteen

But Providence appeared to have decided to see that Homicide got a little break for once. It wasn't until the inquest on Rodzinsky that an enterprising reporter had been present and pricked up his ears at the murder method, which was sufficiently unusual to encourage him to poke around a little. There was a story about Rodzinsky on the second page of the *Times* on Wednesday morning; and of course—although Homicide had suggested that they'd prefer people didn't talk about it—too many people knew about the little file cards, and the garroting, for the series thing to be covered up forever. Sooner or later the press would ferret it out; it was the kind of offbeat thing the press loved. As a matter of fact, all unknown to Homicide at the moment, a reporter on the *Times*, that Wednesday morning, collecting material for a human-interest story at the General, had spotted Mrs. Sears, and talked with her, and later would talk to the reporter who'd been at the Rodzinsky inquest, and heads would be put together and all recent inquests looked at, and the thing would break with a loud roar in Friday morning's *Times*—AVENGER ON MURDER SPREE: WHO WILL BE NEXT? But that, as it turned out, would be a day after the fair.

And even if the press had been shouting about it all along,

and the populace alarmed, the full story wouldn't have been told—it never was, it never could be, for it would make damned dull reading. The populace never knew, even on an important case, the full story: which was a pity. If they had, they might give a little more thought to the cops they hired with their taxes. For the full story would have given all the tedious routine. The search of the Plaza; the patient hunt for some trace of Jamison around there, his pals. The laboratory examination of Bremmer's shop, all the questions asked of all the people; the questions asked about Varick, and the search of the Varick yard, and the Glendale lab's search of Millway's apartment, and the minute hunt all round that gas station Atwood had managed, and of Rodzinsky's place, and Sears's hamburger stand. The time spent, the probing questions, the thought and effort and teamwork that had to go into it, the technical skill and experience.

Thousands of citizens drove past the big rectangular building looming on the L.A. skyline there every day, without thinking at all about what went on there, or reflecting that they drove back and forth to work and play without the necessary gun on the front seat handy because that place was there, and the men who worked there—and at all the precinct houses—keeping the wild animals in the jungle at bay on behalf of the citizenry.

On the following Friday and Saturday the citizens would read the story in the press, and marvel, and comment, and on Sunday most of them would have forgotten about it.

And Homicide would be just as happy to have them do so.

When Mendoza got to the office on Wednesday morning the first thing he did was call the General. He got some good news. Mr. Sears was much improved; they were now certain he would recover, and it was possible he might be able to answer a few questions sometime today.

Mendoza dispatched Palliser and Landers to do tiresome

legwork in the area around Sears's hamburger stand, in an effort to pin down the time of attack and turn up anything else there might be obtainable. It was probable that there were other regular customers among people who worked nearby.

There was a stack of reports on his desk—routine stuff, not all on this case: the regular routine went on regardless of whatever big thing was in the works, of course; and Hackett was typing up a report on Sears.

Higgins had come in early and been immediately sent out on the first call the day crew had had—burglary and homicide out on San Pedro. Hackett said when he heard about that, "Speaking of contemporary literature, I wish real life was more like the mystery stories, Luis. The villains in the mystery stories are so damn considerate, usually—they only hand the cops one mysterious case at a time to solve."

Mendoza laughed and said he understood some of the better ones were a little more realistic.

Palliser and Landers spent most of the morning, singly, covering a two-block area around Sears's hamburger stand. They met at eleven-thirty at the drugstore on the corner and compared notes, and they'd come up with this and that, but it didn't take them much further; however, if this thing ever got as far as an arrest and trial, it might make another point in the prosecution's case.

There were about twenty-five people roundabout who frequently dropped into Sears's place for lunch or a coffee break. Clerks male and female from the shops and stores, and the men at the gas station. They said it was a nice little place, clean, and Sears a nice old fellow. Made good coffee. And what Palliser and Landers had collected between them narrowed the time down considerably. Quite a few people had been in for lunch yesterday, between about eleven-thirty and one o'clock. The latest time they had for anybody being waited on by Sears was "between a quarter and half past one" from a girl who was a salesclerk at the linen shop up the block. She'd just had coffee, wasn't there ten minutes. She thought there'd been a couple of other customers there, one anyway, yes, a man, but couldn't describe anyone, hadn't noticed particularly. Then, at "about two o'clock, five, ten minutes one way or the other" they had another girl who'd come in for a late lunch—she was a typist for a lawyer in the next block and some extra work had kept her from lunch until then. And Sears wasn't there then. She'd waited, and when nobody came, she'd finally gone up to the drugstore. Hadn't thought of investigating; she only went to the place now and then, didn't know Sears personally.

There was no telling, of course, what passing strangers had perhaps dropped in like that and left, before Golonowsky had come. But it was near enough.

"Too early for lunch?" said Palliser.

Landers looked around the drugstore and said definitely yes. It was a good deal hotter today: and still only June. If they were going to have a hot summer, and things went as usual, they'd be kept busy next month. They redeemed Palliser's Rambler from the public lot and went back to the office with what they'd got.

"Well, that's as near as we could expect," said Mendoza. "Call it between one-thirty and two. You know, I've had a rather belated thought about our boy. Has he got what the lady novelists used to call Independent Means, do you suppose?"

"Why, what do you—?" Hackett stared at him.

"Well, his time seems to be his own, doesn't it? I don't see how he can be working a regular job and doing all this too. He had to case these people, find out about their routines and so on. Maybe he didn't have to know much, but something. He probably trailed Jamison here and there—possibly all the rest of them. He must at least have a lot of free time at his disposal."

They thought that over.

"I'll tell you," said Palliser, lighting a cigarette, "just thinking it over logically, I think one thing does seem significant—anyway to me—and that's what you said about Jamison being odd man out. I don't see what it could mean, unless it goes back to an assault he pulled, and *that* just can't be because—"

"Because, obviously," said Landers, "neither of the women we know he actually assaulted is bent on vengeance—or any male connected with them—and while he was probably questioned in other rape and assault cases, there wasn't any evidence on him or he'd have been charged, so nobody could definitely pick him for one of those. And that seems to be that. And while we've got this very slight suggested link with that bar—Atwood and Bremmer and Rodzinsky—that could be entirely coincidental. Because there's no link at all with Millway or Varick. Edith the teetotaler." He sniffed.

"Well," said Palliser, "what that priest said. How Bremmer was once—however slightly—involved in 'police business.' No guess as to what. And if, as seemed to be the case, he was just questioned about an accident or something, no record on it. I just wonder, though, if any of the rest of 'em ever were too."

"Were—oh," said Hackett. "Well, today's great thought."

"Now it just could be," said Mendoza softly. "It's a line anyway, and God knows we've got nothing else."

"Because if there is any link at all—"

"I don't see it," said Hackett, shaking his head. "You're taking it back to your 'years ago?' Just one little objection, John. If all these people had once been, say, witnesses to a crime of some sort, an accident, God knows what, well, wouldn't they have remembered each other? Talked about it, so we'd have heard? A thing like that is an event to the ordinary citizen."

218

"Not if it was a while back, necessarily. Oh, hell, I know—it sounds wild. But we might just ask and see."

"We might," agreed Mendoza. "Having a reasonably logical mind, I've now fallen out of love with my idea on those old assaults. Nobody could be sure Jamison was on any of them. If it wasn't for all we've got on the upright characters of the rest of these people, I'd be back to considering Art's notion of different motives. As it is"—he got up and stretched—"I am fresh out of ideas. So it won't do any harm, and it'll give us something to do, to go back and ask, Were they ever questioned by the police as witnesses to anything? Accident, shoplifting, assault, holdup—anything."

"It's nothing," said Hackett. "We know Bremmer's type. And what the priest said about him. Magnifying things."

"I know, I know, Arturo. But there's nowhere else to go on it, and we can't just sit here talking about what a bastard it is. You never know where something might point a new line. And one thing, if I know Joe Sears's type we'll be getting a description from him, and that's something to look forward to."

"But I had a belated little thought myself," said Hackett, "which is that, funny as it seems, they don't know him, you know. By sight, at least. He was able—the way we read it's got to have been—to approach at least three of them, Bremmer, Atwood and Millway, openly. He pitched some tale to Millway so he was let into the apartment, and Atwood apparently didn't recognize him, or Bremmer. As, for God's sake, an old enemy."

"*De veras,*" said Mendoza. "Funny isn't the word for it. And I suppose you saw the story about Rodzinsky in the *Times.* I have the foreboding that the press is closing in."

"Well, it's just an idea," said Palliser. "About the police-business thing. Because the average citizen doesn't once in a lifetime run into a crime, you know. Cops—aside from traffic tickets. And if we find that a couple more of them ever did—"

"You're imagining fairy stories," said Landers flatly. "In a place this size? Six citizens—well, on that score count out Jamison and Millway, both professionals in a way—as a coincidence, out of seven and a half million people, three or four of them very well could have been witnesses to an accident, a mugging, something like that."

"Well, it can't do any harm," said Palliser.

"Let's go have lunch," said Mendoza.

Before they left the office, Grace called to say he was home, and feeling O.K., except that he still had a little headache, and he'd be back to work tomorrow.

San Quentin remained remotely silent on Millway.

Higgins was contemplating the new one with a little satisfaction, and when he thought about it the satisfaction surprised him until he realized it was because this was the very ordinary thing, with all sorts of routine work to do on it. It was an old tan-brick apartment house out on San Pedro, and the manager had called in. This old tenant, a Frank White, found dead by another tenant, sprawled in his open doorway. Place ransacked. White wouldn't have had much— he'd been a janitor at some building—it was a cheap, sordid little crime. Lock forced on the door, and Marx and Horder had already picked up some dandy latent prints on the door and a steel cashbox and the bureau. Which might say nothing, of course.

It wasn't certain that the burglar had caused White's death. White was an elderly man, and shock and fright might have caused a heart attack or a stroke. The autopsy would tell them. Meanwhile, Higgins had got a few leads, an ex-tenant with a record, and another tenant who'd noticed a stranger in the lobby late last night, and this and that.

On a thing like this, the routine usually turned up the answer sooner or later. You knew where you were, on a thing like this.

Before they got out of the office, the lab report came up; those boys could be quick.

The knife used on Sears had no prints on it at all; it was an ordinary kitchen knife, nine-inch blade, with a plastic handle, and it was new, and its counterpart could be purchased at any of thousands of stores for about two-seventy-five. The lab had, of course, picked up a lot of prints, good to bad, in Sears's place, but none of those identifiable had showed up in Records and some, of course, belonged to Sears.

They went out to lunch and kicked it around some more without having any ideas brighter than Palliser's rather lame one; so after lunch Mendoza went up to Douglas Street to see Millie Sears. Sears off the danger list, she wouldn't be allowed to hang around the General at all hours; he found her home, all right.

"We're very glad your husband's going to be all right, Mrs. Sears."

"So am I!" she beamed at him. "But Joe's not one to let things beat him. Come in and sit down. You found out who did it yet?"

"I'm afraid not. I—"

"If it don't beat all," she said. "Somebody going after Joe with a *knife*. And that other business—" she shook her head. "Peaceable honest man like Joe. No sense to it."

"No. What I'd like to ask you," began Mendoza, and neatly outlined the idea of the grudge killing, maybe something that had happened quite a while ago, they couldn't guess what—but had Joe Sears ever been, not in police trouble, but involved in something where he'd been questioned by the police, had to make a statement, something like that?

She stared at him, the fat old woman, her fat baby-face (that had once been pretty) well powdered and rouged.

221

"For the Lord's sake!" she said. "I never heard of such a thing! A person harboring some feeling for years—well, that don't make much more sense! No, I never heard Joe had to do anything—wait a minute. There *was* a thing, but it wouldn't be what you mean."

"What, Mrs. Sears?" *Por Dios*, he thought, was this far-out bit going to pay off?

"Oh, it was an automobile accident," she said. "On Hill, right in front of Joe's place there. But it was just a little accident, nobody was killed or anything like that, and he just had to tell the cop what he saw. Like whose fault it maybe was. He didn't have to go to court or anything . . . What? Well, it was about nine years back, I remember because we hadn't been married long . . . What? Oh, no, Joe's my second husband, and I'm his second wife. Lost my first fourteen years back, and by the time I met Joe—he'd just lost his wife then—both my boys was grown and married, off my hands, and Joe and I hit it off fine, so—"

"I beg your pardon?" said Sandra Atwood politely to Hackett.

Sometimes—in fact, rather often—it wasn't much fun being a cop. Hackett and Palliser were not enjoying themselves. They were trying to handle Sandra Atwood gently, but it was hard not to feel they were bullying her. Her mother, Mrs. Muriel Dover, sat beside her daughter on the couch protectively and exuded silent disapproval of them.

Hackett felt all the more awkward because he thought this whole idea was wild. Far out. He repeated quietly, "Anything—maybe quite a while ago, Mrs. Atwood—as long as eight or ten years—when your husband was a witness to a crime, or an accident, and talked to police officers about it? Do you remember anything like that?"

She turned dull eyes on him. He thought irrelevantly, she'd be all right eventually; she was a game one (like his

Angel), and she'd pull herself together for the sake of the kids. He thought that because she was making the effort now —her hair was combed neatly and she had makeup on and a clean cotton dress. But her eyes still looked blank and empty, and her voice was slow.

"Police?" she said. "Ray never—no, I don't think I remember—anything—"

"Certainly not," said her mother sharply. "Why on earth should you ask—?"

Hackett wondered himself. "We're still thinking," he lied —as far as he was concerned—"it could have been a grudge killing, and we just wondered—"

"Police?" said Sandra. "There was—it was something— do you think it could be something to do with *whoever*—" She leaned forward, and suddenly her eyes burned on Hackett and Palliser. "I don't see *how*. I don't know much *about* it."

"What, Mrs. Atwood?" asked Palliser in an unintentionally loud voice.

"About *police*. It just came to me, when you said—but how could it have anything to do—? *Did it*? All that while ago? I—I know," she said painfully, "you're supposed to be —a good force. But how—? And I don't know much about it. I never did. I didn't ask. But he was late home one night—"

"Sandra, don't get excited now," said her mother.

"I'm—not. They asked, and all of a sudden I thought of that. But I don't see how it could have—he was late. It was just before Glenn was born, and I hadn't been very well—I was worried. But when he came, he—he apologized, and he said—he said he couldn't help it, he'd been—the way he said it—a 'sort of' witness to something, he'd had to stay and answer all the cops' questions about it, and he wasn't going to tell me about what it was because it'd just upset me and I mustn't get upset, the doctor had said—that was all I knew

223

about it. I—it was about two days before Glenn was born. Yes. I remember, because I *was* worried when Ray was late, and then—the next afternoon it was when I started labor, and Glenn was born very early the next morning, and—"

"Well, I never heard about that," said her mother.

"No, I—with Glenn coming and all—it was just a little thing. But—all that time ago!" said Sandra Atwood. "I don't understand. How could a little thing like—I don't understand!"

Hackett looked at Palliser, who was looking a little excited. "Mrs. Atwood, do you remember if your husband had to testify at a trial later, or did he ever say anything else about—?"

She shook her head. "No. Nothing like that. I'd remember, I guess. He never said anything about it again. I was in the hospital, I don't know if he had to talk to any police again, but—I—you see, it was our first baby, it was Glenn, after more than six years, and I—I don't remember that he ever said any more about that. But how could—?"

"You mustn't get upset, dear." Her mother looked at them darkly.

"Something?" said Palliser. "By God, Art, something! Just a wild idea, but—"

"I'm ringing no bells yet," said Hackett.

They went to see Earl Varick and sounded him out. He looked bewildered and said he couldn't recall Edith ever mentioning such a thing as being questioned by the police about something. But, he said, she had seldom talked about the past—anything in the past. Edith thought that that was one way to stay youthful—not to dwell in the past. She'd sometimes referred to her old long-time employer, Mr. Mays, she'd been so happy in his office, but she'd always gone on to say that she shouldn't hark back, what was gone was gone, one should live in the present.

Which told them nothing, so they went down to Constance Street to see Fred Pitman who'd known Harry Rodzinsky, but he had already left for his cab-driving stint. Check him later: though the idea didn't seem to be panning out, except —maybe?—on Ray Atwood.

They went back to the office. They found Higgins busy typing a report, and Mendoza contemplating a long yellow teletype sheet and smiling dreamily at it.

"Something new?" said Hackett. "We've got a very small something—John thinks it's worth more than I do."

"*¿Cómo dice?* What?"

Palliser told him about Sandra Atwood. "Something," he said. "If we can track it down—it gives us a definite date, you can see—"

"You," said Hackett, "are looking like the Cheshire cat. Smug. What's the teletype?"

Mendoza slid down in his desk chair, lit a cigarette, and shut his eyes. "From Quentin," he said. "At last. The mills of the gods—or is that the quotation I want? Mr. Frederick C. Millway, *amigos*, was the parole-board commissioner who backed the parole appeal of Nelson Edward Jamison in 1955 and got him out. And signed the papers which turned him loose. *Va aclarando.*"

"Oh, you think that helps to clear up the mystery?" said Hackett. "So what?"

"It's a link, Art."

"A link! For the love of God, Luis—I don't know how long Millway was on the commission—"

"Seven years."

"—but, so how many other paroles would he have recommended, how many other releases would he have—?"

"And besides," said Palliser, "what possible connection could the rest—?"

The outside phone buzzed and Mendoza picked it up. "Mendoza . . . Oh? Yes, thanks very much. We'll be right over." He stood up. "Sears is conscious and eager to talk . . . You don't think this says anything? I think it could say quite a lot."

"Pictures in your crystal ball?" said Hackett.

"A couple of rather cloudy little pictures," said Mendoza absently.

Sears looked up at them from the hospital bed, and he looked wanly indignant. He was still a big fat man, but somewhat shrunken, and they'd taken away his false teeth so his round triple-chinned face had fallen in grotesquely. There'd been, of course, a uniformed man beside him since he'd been brought in, in case he came to suddenly and volunteered some information; the uniformed man sat now at the other side of the bed, pencil poised over his notebook.

"Don't tire yourself or get upset now, Mr. Sears," said Mendoza, leaning over the bed. There was a starched-white nurse standing by. "Just tell us, if you can—"

"Tell you!" said Sears huskily, breathily. He wheezed and coughed. "I tell you, all right! Help you get—the bas'ard. Hell of a thing." He mumbled his words slightly, without the teeth. "*Hell* of a—tried to kill me! No reason. Ordered—a cup o' coffee—and I give it him—an' no other cus'omers, I go out in back—lavatory—"

"Just take it easy," said Mendoza. "What did he look like?"

"Knife," said Sears. "Think—'twas a knife." He glared up at Mendoza with righteous anger. "The bas'ard! Man about forty-five—tall, thin—blondy-like hair he had—Roman kind o' nose an' blue eyes—high forehead—light-gray sports jacket an'—a perfec' stranger. A *perfec'* stranger t' me—I never saw him before in my *entire* life!" said Sears, and fell back on the pillow, and the starched nurse said that was all, they'd better go.

Seventeen

MENDOZA was silent all the way back to the police building and up to the office, and Hackett didn't interrupt his thinking processes. He was thinking himself, the fact that at least four, they now knew, of the victims had not known the avenger by sight, made him think that it could be indeed just the random lunatic. A cheerful thought.

They came into the office and Hackett told Palliser and Landers what Sears had said. "A description, so all right. But a stranger to Sears. I'm thinking now—"

Mendoza said nothing and didn't sit down at his desk, but stood in front of the window smoking furiously and staring out at the smog-hazed line of the Hollywood hills. Higgins came in, hung up his hat, and said, "Oh, Luis. Got a minute to hear about this new one?"

Mendoza turned a vague gaze on him. "Burglary to start with," said Higgins. "I think myself White had a heart attack or something—the autopsy'll say. Anyway, I got a line on this ex-con who used to live there. The front door of the place is locked at night, see, and it wasn't forced—or the back door —and unless it was somebody living in the apartment house now, it could be somebody who'd had the front-door key copied while he was living there. So I thought—are you listening to me?"

"Yes," said Mendoza in a reasonable tone, "but why just *now?* If it does date back. And if it was on that account that Millway—well, of course the Atwood thing says nothing for sure. *Nada absolutamente.* No. On the other hand, of course, it could, and in *that* case—but it needn't. It could be Art was half-right. One reason on Jamison and Millway, and the others different. *¿Pues qué?*"

"What?" said Higgins.

"He is," said Hackett, "having some kind of brain wave, George. Don't bother him. He's operating the invisible crystal ball."

"You think he's getting anywhere for real?"

"I don't know," said Hackett. "If he's reasoning along the line I suspect, I think it's just his damned orderly mind wanting to see logic where it just ain't."

"You can both go to hell," said Mendoza, but still absently. "If anything comes up you can't handle before the night crew comes on, I'll be down in Vice." He stood up.

"You still lonesome for that place?" asked Hackett; but after Mendoza had gone out, he added seriously to Higgins, "He does get the inspirations. As witness Hopper. Second sight or whatever. Let's keep our fingers crossed."

"Yeah," said Higgins, looking after Mendoza thoughtfully. "Yeah . . ."

"Well, well," said Sergeant Eddy Decker down in Vice. "You still getting lonesome now and then for your old stamping ground, Lieutenant?" He was getting on toward retirement age, Decker, and had sat at this desk for twenty years, manning the switchboard.

"*¡Cómo no!* Homicide's just a bit more refined. Eddy," said Mendoza abruptly, "what's Sergeant Harding doing these days, and Prince?"

"Oh, Harding went on the retirement list five years or so back. Still get a Christmas card from him, like that. He's not

228

doing anything but trying to get his golf score down, I guess."

"Stayed around here? Where?"

"Sure—over in West Hollywood. Why?"

"Prince," said Mendoza, "got invalided out, I remember."

"He did," said Decker, sobering. "Good man, but he couldn't make the physical after he got shot up that time. He was all *right*, you know, but our damn high standards—he went into a private-eye outfit, where I think he's doing O.K. Greenman and Branscome, Ace Investigators in L.A."

"Oh," said Mendoza. "Thanks."

"You want 'em for something?" asked Decker curiously.

"Pick their brains," said Mendoza vaguely. He was silent, and then said to himself, "Of course, if it *does*, if it *could*, then the one old case—but it really needn't. Not at all. Vice versa. Same reason for those two, others on the rest. And in any case, if it was one case in *particular*—not the two in Records—how could anybody *know*? For sure?"

"What?" said Decker.

"What?" said Mendoza. "Oh, thanks very much, Eddy."

Decker grinned and sighed after his slim dapper departing back. "That guy," he said.

It was six o'clock. Mendoza collected the Ferrari and started home. It was just as well the freeway and the surface streets were familiar to him, or he might never have got there. At the turnoff from the Hollywood freeway he was muttering, "But how could anybody know about Millway?" —and as he turned onto Rayo Grande Avenue, "And even if all of them—which does seem impossible—but people get around. It could have been—" He pulled himself together to watch for twins and/or cats, but as it turned out all of them were safely inside.

He greeted his household very absently, even when Sheba jumped him from behind and the twins from in front. He looked at Alison over the twins' heads and said abstractedly,

"You know, *cara,* I did very nearly kill that bastard that night. I did."

"*Who,* for heaven's—? Oh," said Alison. "Oh. You mean—"

"Yes. But that was *then,* when I thought you'd been— damn it," said Mendoza, "I've just got a hunch there's something *there* to look at, that's all. And something Jase said about Jamison—mmh."

"You're getting somewhere on it?" asked Alison excitedly. "The Thug?"

"Thug hell. I don't," said Mendoza, "need that," as Mrs. MacTaggart came up briskly with a shot glass in her hand, "but it may further stimulate the brain wave. Thanks, Máiri." He put the twins down, handed over Sheba to Alison, and El Señor arrived loudly demanding his preprandial drink too.

"That cat," said Mrs. MacTaggart, and went off to get it. Mendoza took his drink down the hall to the telephone, and Alison trailed after him, interestedly.

He looked in the book and tried Prince first, but he wasn't home; his wife said he was out on a job. "You know the hours, Lieutenant. It's just as bad as when he was on the force," she said resignedly. "I don't know when he'll be home, but you can probably catch him at the office in the morning."

"All right, thanks. Hell," said Mendoza, and tried Harding. Here he was luckier . . .

"You're being secretive on purpose," said Alison. "Who are they and what new have you found out about the avenger?"

"Two ex-colleagues," said Mendoza, sipping rye, "and nothing. Which adds up to a fact. I don't think. It's just a little something ringing a faint bell in my head . . . I did indeed come damn close to murdering that bastard. *Then.* Does it make any sense to imagine that—just possibly—? All right. All right. Jamison and Millway, the link. But if that absolutely left-field bit of John's means anything at *all,* which

230

I don't see how it can, you know—how did anyone *know?* Any private person? When there wasn't a trial, or even a charge? So the old cases couldn't have—but *also*," he said suddenly, "*also*, it could have been one we never heard about? One some woman never reported? Yes. And so, possibly, Jamison picked just because he was *a* rapist, not necessarily because—but that's wild. It all comes back to that— how did anyone *know?*"

Alison did not say he was dithering, or ask him any questions. Perceiving that he was in the throes of labor pains —which might or might not produce something tangible— she went away and left him staring into space, and told the twins to play something quiet instead of the race-the-circle-round-the-house, because Daddy was thinking. She reflected not for the first time that with Luis it wasn't so much thinking as a procession of jumps from here to there.

The twins had already been fed, and Mrs. MacTaggart corralled them into the bathroom for their bath-before-bed while Alison and Mendoza had dinner. Alison didn't get much sensible conversation out of him. As he finished the pot roast and browned potatoes, he suddenly asked her, "But how *would* a woman feel who'd got raped? Enough to—?"

"Goodness, Luis, it'd depend on the woman. I couldn't tell you. I expect," said Alison, "that any stable, sensible woman would get over it, just realizing it was a thing that *happened*. Why?"

"A very silly idea," said Mendoza. "I think . . . Because I still don't see—well. I'm going out to see Harding."

"So I gathered. Whatever the inspiration is," said Alison, "good luck on it. I suppose I'll hear all about it some time."

"I don't believe in unnecessary compliments to wives," said Mendoza. "Give you ideas about your station. But you are one in a million, *amante*."

"*¡Qué hombre!*" said Alison.

231

"And Harding's phone number is on the pad in case the office calls."

"Yes. It's about time you had number eight, isn't it?" said Alison.

"Don't say things like—I wonder," said Mendoza. "I do wonder. After Sears . . ."

He got an open-handed welcome from ex-Sergeant Harding in West Hollywood. Harding, now pushing seventy, had spent nearly forty years on the force, and if he'd joined up before they had the present high standards, he was still a shrewd and honest and reliable man. After introducing Mendoza to his wife, he planted himself in an armchair and said, "I don't suppose you've come looking me up to ask about my latest golf score, Luis. What can I do for you?" Mrs. Harding smiled gently at them and took herself off discreetly.

"I don't know, Frank. Maybe something, maybe nothing," said Mendoza. "It's a rigmarole. I've had a couple of peculiar visions about it, and I may just be woolgathering. I am sometimes wrong."

"And sometimes not," said Harding. "On a homicide, I take it."

"Plural. Let me just ask you—" Mendoza hauled out his notes. "These old leftovers. Eighteen of them, because we can't, if we're going to be thorough, take just the actual rapes. The rest, assaults-with-intent-of. And on a couple outside our territory, we were probably just asked for cooperation, and you wouldn't—but the others, either you or Bill Prince handled. I just want to ask you—"

"Hm? Hell, Luis, I retired and put it all out of my mind. The routine—the mess," said Harding, grimacing. "The mud at the bottom of the jungle. I probably can't tell you a damn thing, but let's see . . . Oh, *that* I do sort of recall, the one in Boyle Heights. That was just a kid, poor—who? Don't recall the name. Jamison? No."

"About my size, rabbit face and fancy clothes. A chancy one—unpredictable."

Harding wrinkled his brow. "Rape suspect? Well, if so we probably hauled him in to—wait a minute! Yeah. Yeah, I remember that one all right. He was offbeat, there was money. He'd always tell you you couldn't get *him* for anything, he could pay the smart lawyer."

"That figures. Anything else?"

"I don't remember him on any of these particular cases, but I remember he was one we automatically hauled in to look at. I wouldn't doubt he was responsible for rapes we never got a lead on. A couple of times we even got a tentative identification on him, but nothing to make it stick . . . No, I can't give you any details. Some of these names I remember, sure, but nothing definite, sorry. On *that* one, anyway, I wouldn't know anything because by the date that was just after I got shot up in that raid, I was in the hospital. This one in April of—"

"Oh," said Mendoza. "You don't remember that maybe on one of these, there *was* some evidence on Jamison, you just couldn't make—"

"Nope. Like I say—now you call him to mind I do remember that one, sure, and probably he was questioned on some of these at least. But you know how it is, Luis," said Harding. "A rape, even just an assault, a woman's not thinking or seeing straight. A lot of times you can't even get any kind of description out of her. She either doesn't know or can't say if he was tall or short, fat or thin—sometimes, even black or white. And at the same time, you can't go by *just* the woman's description, because at a time like that—she's emotional at least and a lot of 'em hysterical—she's not a competent judge."

"I know," said Mendoza. "You can't tie up Jamison with any of these you worked on?"

"Uh-uh. Like I say, we probably questioned him. But you

233

know things don't get shelved in Pending unless we've got absolutely nothing on 'em."

"Also true," said Mendoza. Somewhere in the back part of this pleasant old Spanish house the phone rang. "Damnation," he said.

"I'm sorry as hell. Just what did you think tied up, anyway?" asked Harding curiously. "Say, can't I offer you a drink?"

"No, thanks," said Mendoza absently; and plump Mrs. Harding came back and said it was someone asking if Lieutenant Mendoza was there.

"*¡Dios!*" said Mendoza. "Don't tell me, number eight? My God—"

"I'll show you the phone," said Harding, all business and much concerned at Mendoza's concern.

It wasn't number eight. Unexpectedly, it was O'Connor up at Wilcox Street. "Well, I had a little time finding you, Lieutenant. They gave me your home number at your office, and I called there, and your wife gave me this one. I—"

"Don't for God's sake tell me you've got another one in your territory," said Mendoza.

"Another—? Oh, no. I've got something," said O'Connor, "very funny and very thought-provoking, I guess you could say, which I think you ought to hear. So I asked the nice gentleman to stay while I tracked you down so he could tell it all over again, and if I'm not interrupting anything important, can you chase up here to listen? I can guarantee you won't be sorry."

"You arouse my curiosity. Something on this?"

"Oh, but definitely," said O'Connor. He sounded both amused and perplexed. "Something very funny indeed."

"A laugh I need," said Mendoza. "You're at Wilcox Street?"

"That's where. Come right up to my office," said O'Connor. "I'll have a cup of coffee waiting for you. Cream or sugar?"

234

"Black, *por favor*," said Mendoza.

He thanked Harding, who said all over again he was damn sorry he couldn't be any more help, and started back for Hollywood proper. There was a good deal of traffic, and it was nearly ten o'clock before he got to Wilcox Street and the old tan-brick precinct house.

But O'Connor's nice gentleman was waiting for him, drinking coffee with O'Connor, and at first glance Mendoza appreciated the description, sizing him up as a very nice gentleman indeed.

"Mr. Cecil Watson, Lieutenant Mendoza," said O'Connor.

"How do you do, Lieutenant Mendoza," said Mr. Watson, rising correctly to take Mendoza's hand. "For some reason Sergeant O'Connor thought you'd be interested in hearing my rather strange little story, and I was only too happy to—I hesitated to bother the police with it, you know, such a small thing and if it was queer, well, no harm was done. But the more I thought about it, the more it was borne in on me that the man might be a mental case, and it was advisable that someone in authority should know. So I did call."

"And we have," said O'Connor, "a few reasonably intelligent squad-car men in this precinct. So I heard about it. And I went up to hear more from Mr. Watson. And then I thought he'd better make a statement about it, so I fetched him down here."

"Only too happy," murmured Mr. Watson, looking slightly bewildered. He was a tall thin man in his sixties, very well dressed in gray Italian silk, well-polished brogues, with a darker gray and very well-bred Homburg sitting at his elbow on O'Connor's desk. He had regular features, a bristly gray mustache, thin gray hair brushed carefully over the bald spot, and a nicely modulated voice. "I assume it must have some significance for you gentlemen, but I can only say—"

235

"If you'd tell the whole thing to Lieutenant Mendoza just the way you told me, sir," prompted O'Connor.

"Why, surely. I," said Watson, "came home about eight o'clock, Lieutenant. Later than usual, but since losing my dear wife I sometimes stay downtown for dinner. And what with the traffic I find it more convenient to leave my car in a lot up on Glendale Boulevard and take the bus right in to town, so that takes a little extra time too. I should say, I live up on Gower Avenue." Mendoza nodded, placing it: the steep, narrow, darkish street up above Hollywood Boulevard. "My house—I had better explain—is on a corner, and the garage is on the street. Quite close to the street—the side street. And there's a hedge about four feet high round the front yard. Well, I drove into the garage, and came out and shut the door and locked it, and went along the path from the driveway to the little walk into the front yard. I'm not a nervous man, I may say, Lieutenant, and I frequently return home after dark like that, but one does read of the rise in crime lately, and when—just as I stepped into the front yard —I heard a movement behind me and a bit to the right, I confess I was alarmed. And the next moment the strangest thing—really, I had scarcely time to think about it before it was all over—well, a—a—*something* flew at me, the only way I can express it, sir, it was quite dark, of course—and whatever it was fell onto the grass and then I heard a—a rustling sort of sound. And I thought at once of a—what you call a mugger, I think, and I turned round sharp, not to be attacked from behind, and called, 'Who's there?' which was perhaps foolish, but—I have," and he fished it out of his pocket to show Mendoza, "a small flashlight attached to my key chain—very handy at night—and of course I had my keys in my hand, and I pressed the switch. And there, Lieutenant, standing just inside the hedge on the front lawn, was a man . . . Oh, yes, I can describe him to you, after a fashion. But the startling and peculiar thing was that he had a *child's jumping rope* in one hand." Mr. Watson nodded once, emphatically.

"*¡Válgame Dios!*" said Mendoza softly.

"I thought you'd like it," said O'Connor. "Listen. And, Mr. Watson?"

"Well, it looked so *very* odd, you know—when I'd imagined perhaps some lout with a club," and Watson smiled apologetically, "that I just stared at him. And he looked back at me, and then he said—I can give you the exact words, because the whole affair was so very odd, naturally I—he said, very simply and naturally as a child might say it, 'But I can't do it any more. It's no use, I can't.' And then he turned and ran away. He ran down the hill, in the street, not on the sidewalk, and I'm afraid I just gaped after him. Then I went on into the house and made sure nothing had been touched, that he hadn't—but really the more I thought about it—a *jumping rope*, you know—and finally I—"

"*¿Qué es esto?*" said Mendoza. "What the hell?"

"Your boy going all remorseful?" said O'Connor. "It struck me. We can say for pretty sure it *is*, can't we?"

"Can we? I think maybe so," said Mendoza slowly. "One thing, he hasn't been operating so fast and furious as just at first—though on Sears—*still*. Still. My God, and I thought I had a brain wave on this! I'm going senile. Or am I?" He looked at Watson. The nice gentleman. Who didn't, maybe, realize how lucky he'd been. Another one in line for the vengeance? Another one that, just on looks and probably in background, would be very difficult to link up in any way with Bremmer, Jamison, Varick, Millway, Atwood, Rodzinsky—hell! Hadn't he been thinking—even if there was something valid in his brain wave about the Jamison-Millway link (though how the hell anyone had *known*), Art's idea could still be halfway right, and the different motives on the rest of them, if—

Watson had listened to the exchange between Mendoza

and O'Connor, courteously silent, curious and interested. "Mr. Watson," said Mendoza abruptly, "if you wouldn't mind some questions—"

"Whatever I can tell you, sir."

"What's your job, where do you work?"

Watson looked surprised. "My—well, I'm an adviser, Lieutenant, at Sterne, Lawrence, Bunker and Adamson. I've been with them for about fifteen years, since I left Roundtree and Wilkes . . . Well, it's a brokerage house, yes . . . I beg your pardon? Oh, yes, downtown, we're on Spring Street. I beg—well, I catch the bus at the corner of Ninth and—"

"Stakes down and wait for the jackpot!" whispered Mendoza. "Mr. Watson. I want you to take your time and think hard on this one. At any time in your life—it could have been somewhere around ten years ago, but at *any* time—were you ever by chance a witness to some kind of crime—or accident—or anything like that, and subsequently questioned by the police about it? And possibly asked to make a statement, at headquarters—or a precinct station? I'm sure you'll remember, if—"

Watson stared at him. "A—? Well, if it's at all *relevant*, sir—though I'm blessed if I can see how it might be—why, yes, I did. I was. I did. On one occasion. But, really, Lieutenant, how *that* old business could—oh, a very tragic thing, of course, and if I had realized at the time, if any of us had realized, we might have—but really I can't see the relevancy—"

"Just tell me about it, please," said Mendoza gently. "I think it's relevant, Mr. Watson."

"Well—" Watson took a deep breath.

Mendoza got home at midnight, and Alison murmured drowsily as he got into bed, "Your brain wave pay off, darling?"

"*¡Qué bello!*" He pulled her around into his arms. "Like

238

hell. Mysteries still abound, but—if I can only get hold of Prince! . . . *Amante, enamorada—¡Acércate!*"

"*¡Qué tipo!* . . . Well, I did say maybe just one more besides the twins," mumbled Alison.

"*¡Ay de mí!* You haven't inflicted enough on me?"

He landed at the office at ten to eight, and had Sergeant Lake dialing Ace Investigators thirty seconds after he'd taken off his hat. And thirty seconds later was swearing; Prince was out on a tailing job, and God knew when he'd report in.

"Private eyes!" said Mendoza.

He wasn't interested in Higgins' burglary-homicide, and wouldn't discuss it. He barely remembered to ask Grace how he felt when he turned up. He snapped at Landers and paced the office.

"Who the hell is Prince?" asked Higgins. "And what's he got to—?"

"The answers," said Mendoza. "It could be, all the answers, George. It just could be. I'm still in the dark on some—why the hell Varick?—and I don't see—and I still, for the love of God, do not see how anybody connected Millway—God, when I *have* got hold of Bill, have to call Wheelwright in Glendale—" He stabbed out a cigarette, lit another one immediately. "No, by God, I'm saying nothing until I've talked to Bill. And Harding a very nice guy, but Bill Prince—by what I remember of him—the hell of a lot sharper. He'll remember. If there *is* anything to—Jimmy, dial that number again, see if Prince—"

Higgins went out to the sergeants' office and said the boss was still in the grip of the brain storm. And if past experience was anything to go by, he might just have something. Time would tell.

"If it's on the vengeance bit," said Palliser, "fingers crossed. I've been expecting number eight at any minute.

239

Listen, George, even if it is still kicking around, I *can* take Saturday, can't I? Look, we—"

"Ask the boss."

"The way he's creating right now? I wouldn't—"

"He seems to think he's got something," said Grace mildly, "all right. Let's hope so. At least—what with the concussion —I caught up on some reading. One of Virginia's study-group books—"

Higgins said something rude about contemporary literature.

At two o'clock on Thursday afternoon Mendoza, with an incipient headache from too many cigarettes, got hold of Bill Prince at the Hollywood office of Ace Investigators. Prince said sure, anything he could do, Luis, and he hadn't had a chance for lunch, suppose they—

"I'll buy you lunch. I'll even buy you a drink with it. Federico's in twenty minutes?"

"Well, haven't dropped in there since I was invalided out. Sure. Make it half an hour, I've got to report to the boss first."

Mendoza was waiting at an isolated table when Prince—big and bulky as Hackett, with a square bulldog face and thinning gray hair—walked in.

"Good to see you again, Luis . . . Scotch and water, and can I use it! We get so damn much of this skip-trace work, and of all the damn tedious routine—as bad as being back on the force. Hear you're making quite a reputation for yourself these—"

"Bill," said Mendoza urgently, "just look back ten years and tell me every last little thing you remember about this case, if you do remember anything—"

"What case? Anything I can do . . . Oh, *that*," said Prince. He lit a cigarette. The waiter brought his drink and he sampled it thoughtfully. "That one. Sure I remember that,

Luis. Now you recall it to my mind . . . It was kind of tragic—and *also* annoying—because that guy—"

"Everything you remember, *¡por favor!*" begged Mendoza.

Eighteen

"—AND the funny thing about it is, or maybe I should say tragic," said Prince, swallowing the last bite of his steak and picking up his coffee cup, "is that the guy evidently did make it, later. At least, if it's the same one, and it isn't too common a name. I told you he was a writer—claimed to be. Had a couple of things published then, so I guess it *is* the same one. Anyway, if it is, I saw something in the *Herald* just the other day—one of his novels, a best seller, some producer had just bought the movie rights to it for a couple of hundred grand. That Thomas Pickering."

"Oh, really," said Mendoza. "Really. Bill, I think you've given me some answers. I *think*. Still this and that I do not see, but—I really do think—"

"And I'd like," said Prince, lighting a cigarette, "to hear all about it, Luis, how it links up to anything of yours now —you've got me curious—but later, hah? Tomorrow's my day off if I'm lucky, you can call me at home and tell the story. Right now I've got to run, I've got this report to type and—"

"Bill," said Mendoza, "thanks. Yes, I will. I really do think —yes. Thanks very much." He shut his notebook—he'd taken some notes—and got up as Prince did, and dropped a bill on top of the check on the tray.

242

"I'll be curious to hear."

"And I'm still curious about a few things. But I think you've given us the big answer. Thanks." They shook hands and Mendoza went out to the lot for the Ferrari, thinking furiously. It couldn't be otherwise, with all those names— Prince had a good memory for names . . .

And if it was the answer, it was just another little piece of truth—which was maybe the real reason Luis Mendoza (or any of them) stayed cops—another curious and interesting bit of truth about human nature. About people. As he drove back to headquarters, irrelevantly Mendoza was trying to track down a quotation—what was it?— "In all the world there is nothing so curious or interesting or beautiful as the truth." Who? Ask Grace, he'd probably know. And that was true. And another reason why good cops stayed cops, despite all the disadvantages.

It was Hackett's day off, but as Mendoza came into his office he found Sergeant Lake on the phone, and Lake said, "Hang on . . . It's Art. He's interested to know whether your brain wave paid off."

"Brother," said Mendoza. "Tell him we've hit the jackpot, for ninety-nine per cent sure. There are aspects—but it's got to be. And if he wants to make the collar with me, come running."

"For *sure*, Lieutenant? Be damned!" said Lake, and got back on the phone.

Mendoza sat down at his desk and sought the phone book, and then the city directory. Lake had relayed the news and in a minute Higgins and Palliser charged in demanding details, with Grace on their heels. "In a minute. Damn," said Mendoza, "he's not in the book. Hell, am I seeing visions again? Maybe he doesn't live here any—no. No, it's got to be, because by what Bill—" He groped for a cigarette. "And what he said about—I suppose a V.I.P., a best seller, might indeed have an unlisted phone. And in *that* case, how very lucky that—" He flipped open his desk index and picked up the phone. "Jimmy, get me this number *pronto*—"

Some while ago, Mendoza had been in a position to do a little favor for that well-known producer Thomas ('Toby') Pickering. Ordinarily, easier to get the President on the phone than a movie producer of any stature; but the magic repetition, "Lieutenant Mendoza wants to speak with him," to several secretaries, hauled Pickering away from an extremely important conference on costumes to the nearest phone. What could he do for the lieutenant?

"I'm trying," said Mendoza hopefully, "to locate a man by the name of Jacques Lejeune. A writer. Somebody told me you'd bought the rights to one of his books, and I thought—"

"Oh," said Pickering. "Lejeune. Sure. I did. I guess we can make something of it, though—sure, he lives here. Palos Verdes Estates, you want the address?"

"Please."

"Just a minute, I've got it here some—Via Arriba." He added the number.

"Thanks very much. Sorry to have disturbed you."

"Anytime, Lieutenant."

And it was as simple as that.

Grace said, "Lejeune? *That* Lejeune? Can't say I care much for his books, a little bit arty and highbrow, but what's he doing in this?" Mendoza started to tell them, and in the middle of it Hackett arrived demanding to know what was up, and heard most of it, making incredulous noises.

"So," said Mendoza, "let's go and see how much he'd like to tell us. Art and George and me. Scare him a little. Maybe."

"For God's sake—but with all of them showing up in— yes," said Hackett. "Let's. But I still don't see, Luis—all this time after, why—"

"We'll ask," said Mendoza.

They didn't have to do much asking, as it turned out. The

address was that of a very elegant and modern new apartment house of four units only. Rent probably three to four hundred per. The apartment they wanted was on the second floor, and they climbed thickly carpeted stairs in silence and Mendoza pressed the bell.

After a moment the door swung back and they looked at him. He was about forty-five, a man six feet tall, with a pale complexion, a high-bridged Roman nose, sandy-blond hair still thick, a wide and yet somehow weak mouth. He was wearing gray slacks and a blue shirt open at the throat, and he had a cigarette in one hand. He looked at them, and slow understanding entered his pale blue eyes behind the horn-rimmed glasses.

"Mr. Lejeune? I'm Lieutenant Mendoza. Sergeant Hackett. Sergeant Higgins. From Central Homicide."

"Oh," said Lejeune. "Yes." He had a thin, rather high voice. He took off his glasses and rubbed his eyes. "I wasn't —exactly—expecting—but I had thought of going to see you. Because now I—I'm not sure. I don't know. You'd better come in." He walked away across the room and stood with his back turned, staring out the window.

"Mr. Lejeune. Just a little over ten years ago," said Mendoza, "your wife Marjorie was assaulted and raped in an alley on Ninth Street near the corner of Spring. Nobody was ever charged with the crime, but—"

"No," said Lejeune. "It's all right, I'll tell you about it. Now you're here. I haven't been sleeping very well." He turned around slowly. "You'd better sit down," he said. "It may take some time. You see—you don't know, of course, about Marjorie. Could I offer you a drink?"

"No, thanks." This was almost as incredible, in a way, as the man himself—his readiness to talk.

"I'll have one, if you don't mind." Lejeune went over to a built-in corner bar of this handsome and expensive-looking living room, all quiet silver-gray and emerald-green décor.

245

He poured three fingers of Scotch into a tumbler, added soda and ice from a small refrigerator under the bar, and faced them leaning on the Formica-topped counter. "I don't know that I would have come to tell you," he said, "but I'll tell you now. I—think—I'd—like to tell you. Because all the nightmares—I'm no longer sure I was right, you see. You don't know about Marjorie, no. I've got to tell you that first. She was sweet—and shy—and afraid of so many things, I used to laugh at her, I teased her about it—nervous. She was—sweet. And she was younger than I am, perhaps I was flattered—oh, what does that matter? I'm tired, you know. So tired." He drank thirstily. "She was twenty and I was thirty-four. And a writer—a professional writer—success doesn't come early or quick, or maybe not at all. You can't know. You just go on working. Without getting paid. It takes time. I—"

"Mr. Lejeune. Your wife was working as a file clerk for a lawyer named—"

"Yes. I'll tell it," said Lejeune in a dragging voice. "I'm telling it. I was always so confident—I would get somewhere —I would—and make a reputation, and the money. If I could just have the time to write—I felt—no fidgeting routine nine-to-five job—that was why she was *there,* you see. Working. So I could stay home to write. She said she didn't mind. She didn't. And then—and then—" He drank again. "All right. It happened. That—bastard—did that—to her. Down there. You just don't know—how it was *then.* She'd never been—I tried to be, you know, quiet and—and good with her, but she'd—and after *that,* you just don't know. How she was. And it was very damned ironic, you know, but it wasn't six months later that *Sounding Brass* got on the best-seller list. I had a psychiatrist for her then—but he—it was worse, and he said—all the double talk—sanatorium— and you don't *know* how she was. All this time. Three times she came—home. It wasn't any good. She tried to kill herself, you know. She tried—"

Mendoza thought about the sensible young woman who had also got raped, and had learned to live with it as "a thing that happened." Unmarried, yes, but maybe she would have been anyway. He said gently, "Mr. Lejeune—" and stopped, overridden by the man's slow tired voice.

"And all that time, it didn't mean much to me, the money —it'd have meant so much once—but it couldn't help Marjorie. So sweet, my dear little darling, so good—working down there—if it hadn't been for *me*, my colossal vanity, she'd never have been—and the Goddamned police saying— *she told them!* She—"

"Yes," said Mendoza. "I know. I've heard all about it from the officer who was on the case. Who talked to all the people —involved. Innocently involved."

"*Innocently*—my God, I don't know now," said Lejeune. "I don't know. She told them—that officer—"

"I know. The next day, when the hospital released her, she looked at a line-up at headquarters, and she picked out Nelson Jamison," said Mendoza. "But then she went into hysterics, and the next time anybody questioned her, she was ready to identify any man they showed her, from the desk sergeant to John Citizen brought in off the street, and consequently we didn't feel justified in charging Jamison on it. Nobody else identified him, you know. A couple of people saw him running up the street, afterward—when they saw your wife come staggering out of the alley—but nobody got a good look at him."

"*She* did. She was in shock—in such a state—the first time, she knew! She told me. The few times she was—almost herself—again—afterward. Afterward! How could any of the rest of them identify him? They didn't look—they didn't care—they didn't make a move. To help her," said Lejeune, and drank.

Hackett stirred at Higgins' side on the low modern sofa. Mendoza had remained standing, watching their host.

247

"I used to think about them, you know, when I'd go to see her. If *they* could have seen her, would they have been ashamed? I wondered. If it was my fault—my fault she was *there,* it was theirs that he—that he—*they* could have saved her, and they didn't. They didn't. They let that—bastard—do that to her. And she identified him, but the Goddamned police—"

"Those people," said Mendoza, "just—roundabout. By chance. But the couple of them who thought they heard a woman scream, they said it wasn't loud—they weren't sure. You—"

"She did scream. She did. She said so. She would have—they were just afraid to get involved," said Lejeune. "Or cowards some other way—afraid of getting hurt. And some were big strong men too, they could have run down there and gotten her away from that bastard—I used to think about it. About them. When I was with her. The doctors didn't like me to come, to see her, they said it was bad for me—for *me!*" Lejeune laughed a little wildly. "Do you know something?" he said suddenly to Mendoza. "I haven't really written anything for most of these ten years. Since. That's a fact. I haven't *wanted* to. The four books I've published—all written before. And just after, before I realized—realized—and the money not meaning a damn. No. Only for her. And she was—they didn't like me to come, but I did. And I'd sit and watch her—how she was, what that bastard had turned her into—and I'd think about those people. Their fault. As much as mine."

It was no use to tell him that if Marjorie Lejeune hadn't been a little or a lot unstable in some way to begin with, it wouldn't have done that to her. He had needed a scapegoat—other than himself. He had found a number of scapegoats.

"All their fault," he was repeating. "I thought. For ten years. I'm not sure—now." He put a hand across his eyes.

248

"William Bremmer," said Mendoza. "He'd just left the little bar and was waiting for the bus on that corner. Before his sister came to live with him he used to keep his shop open til nine on Saturday nights. It was about nine-thirty then. And Harry Rodzinsky, who'd just come off his shift tending bar, was walking up Ninth toward a parking lot. He thought he heard a woman scream, and he looked around, but he didn't see anything so he went on. And young Ray Atwood, who'd also just got off work at nine and stopped for a beer, was waiting for the bus too."

"Big strong fellows. They could have—she told me she screamed! She—"

But noises, on a busy street. It made little difference now whether she had, or had been too scared.

"And Joe Sears," said Mendoza. "I don't know what he was doing there—"

"He used sometimes to walk up to a United Cigar store a couple of blocks from—his place. And take the bus—at the next corner—instead. Oh, I found out about them," said Lejeune dully. "I hadn't—much else—to do, or think about. And besides—"

"And besides," said Mendoza, "at the time, you came deviling Sergeant Prince about the case. I know. Why wasn't Jamison arrested?—you'd been with her when she identified him. The once she did. And demanding to know what all those not-quite-witnesses, the bystanders just fortuitously there, had said and done—and not done. Very bitter you were about it. And when he wouldn't tell you much—because there really wasn't much to tell—you went so far, a few days later, as to steal the sergeant's notebook from his desk, and he—"

"I gave it back to him. I wanted all their names. There were more that were guilty, you know. More than—the ones I—punished for it. *Punished*," said Lejeune. "But I'm tired. If it hadn't been for all they—didn't do—you don't

know. Yes, those. Bremmer and Rodzinsky and Atwood. Just
—passing by on the other side. Not caring."

"They didn't, Mr. Lejeune. They didn't know what was—"
He wouldn't listen to that.

"—and that officer had let it out to me that—that bastard
—was on parole. For attacking another woman. Like that. As
good as *murder*—and it was some time after—after that, I
saw just a little article in the paper—about the parole commission at San—a man retiring, and somebody else put on
it—and it came to me that man was guilty too. All of them,
but he was the only one whose name I knew." And so that
answer was a very simple one too. "He was guilty for *letting
him out*. To do that."

"I did see that," said Mendoza gently. Halfway, he
thought; and things sometimes simpler than they looked—
that was all Lejeune had known about Millway, and yet that
little connection was largely what had triggered Mendoza's
brain wave. "How did you find out where he was?"

"What? Oh, I wrote a letter and asked for his address. I
forget what I said, it wasn't any trouble. I thought a lot about
them. A lot. The ones who were as guilty as I was. There was
that woman—"

"Edith Warren Varick. How was she guilty, Mr. Lejeune?"

"Marjorie would never have been there that late, you see.
But that woman had asked her to stay overtime. That night.
For some extra work. And I'd never have let her come home
alone," said Lejeune, staring into his glass, "if I'd *known*.
But she called—and she said the other girl in the office
would be walking with her, down to the bus stop—and taking the same bus—and the chapter was going fine, so I—" He
drained the rest of his glass quickly. "Brenda Flagg," he said.
"Her name was Brenda Starling then. She should have been
with Marjorie. But her boyfriend dropped by at about nine
o'clock, and she went off with him instead. That other woman
—had already gone. Thomas Fletcher, the boyfriend. She

married somebody else but she was going with him then. They were guilty too. I meant to punish them. And I used to tease Marjorie about—being afraid of the dark—and she must have thought—to be brave about it, just a block to walk —and then that bastard—and all those cowards, those damn cowards, just stood by and let it happen!" He banged his fist on the bar once, and put both hands to his head. "And the Goddamned police didn't even arrest—there was that broker Watson, such a gentleman—a man, wasn't he? He could have —waiting for the bus not a hundred feet away—" Lejeune turned and poured himself another drink as if automatically. "And Bremmer, and Sears, and Atwood, and that big lout Rodzinsky—and Watson's secretary was with him, you know, waiting for the damn—if the *women* had all ganged up on the bastard, *they* could have— And Margaret Talford, she worked at The Broadway, and that busboy Jack Denny at the bus stop, and another woman, a big colored woman there, Ena Shaw—I was going to punish them *all*, but I'm tired," said Lejeune, and drank.

"You'd—kept track," said Mendoza. Hackett muttered something under his breath.

"I used to think about them so much. If *they* ever thought about it. Her. The cowards. Afraid of getting involved. Oh, yes. Yes. I knew where they all were, what they were doing. That was quite easy. I—kept track of them all. The guilty ones. I used to stop for gas at Atwood's station—where he worked, and then when he got his own. I was a regular customer, he liked me," said Lejeune with a rather wolfish smile. "And Rodzinsky—" he stopped, and a queer taut expression came over his face. "I used to stop in where he worked too. I'd heard him boasting about—not locking doors, I—"

They could, Mendoza reflected, fill in that part of it themselves; and the way Lejeune was acting (competent or not? There'd be an examination; anybody's guess) they'd get a nice signed confession. "Mr.—"

"I told Millway I was inspecting for gas leaks," said Lejeune. "No trouble. And of course I'd shopped at Bremmer's place, he knew—I *meant* to punish that bastard first, you know—when—I'd—decided. But he was in that bar, I couldn't get at him, and I thought—drop in at Bremmer's just as he was closing, and—"

Grace had made a hell of a good guess there. Practicing the detective work. The lost horse and the idiot boy—

"Mr. Lejeune," said Mendoza. "Why just now? Why ten years later?"

Lejeune looked up slowly from his new drink. Not an unhandsome man: but, as writers sometimes were (you couldn't generalize) a shy, retiring man: it could be—let the head doctors sort it out—that his sweet, shy, and patently unstable Marjorie had been the only woman who'd ever looked twice at him. That there had been something a trifle abnormal, some way, about his relationship with her. And first of all he had blamed himself, as that kind of man naturally would; and then, not able to live with that guilt, needing so desperately another scapegoat, he had in the darkest corner of the mind found not one, but many. The guilty ones. The equally guilty ones. In time, probably, the only guilty ones.

"Why?" he said. "Marjorie's dead. Now. It all finished—a month back. I think it was about then, I don't quite remember. I haven't been sleeping very well, even with the tablets. She finally did it, you see. They watched her, but she finally did it. She hanged herself. She's dead. My dear darling. I saw what it did to her—all this while. And when I knew she was dead, I thought about *them*—still alive. Not deserving to be alive, when it was their fault—oh, my God, mine too, mine too, but—I thought, you see, if I punished *them* for it—maybe *I* wouldn't be—quite—as—guilty. I don't know about that, now. I was so sure then. And I'd read a book once—about those Thugs. It sounded—and besides, it would make it like—being—hanged. For murder. It *was* murder. And it was easy—I was surprised how easy it was—until that man Rodzinsky. It was queer, but I *minded* about Rodzinsky. I don't know if you'll understand that," said Lejeune, drinking thoughtfully. "It was walking in like that—and he was asleep. I did it, but I *minded*. It seemed just a little—wrong—somehow, because he was asleep and didn't know. I don't know. Only then—next time—I couldn't do it so easy and quick as I—and that fat man—Sears—and I ran away. I didn't mean to, but I did. Only he had to be punished like the rest of them—the ones guilty—and I tried again, but a knife seemed all wrong—and when I waited for Watson there, and he came, it was strange, it was strange, I *couldn't*. I don't know why." Lejeune finished his second drink and looked at them. "Vengeance—it was *right*. It was easy. And then something turned in my mind. I don't know. I don't know how—you found out. I didn't mean to be found out, because it was—only—just—vengeance. But I think perhaps I am thinking a little more clearly now—and after all—I am the *most* guilty one, you know. In the first instance. And so it's just as well you *have* found out. And that—I—will be—punished too," said Lejeune.

He made no trouble about coming with them at all. He was docile, and after all that, silent; but they'd probably have no trouble getting the signed confession.

And Hackett said, when the routine was all accomplished and the warrant got and Lejeune stashed away in the new facility down on Alameda, "My God. So simple once we knew. Naturally a thing like that not in Records. And if you hadn't had the inspiration to look where you—"

"Not sixth sense," said Mendoza. "Experience, Arturo." He was pleased; the orderly mind relieved to have the off-beat one cleared up. It was getting on to six o'clock and the shifts were changing, but he snuggled deeper in his desk chair and lit a cigarette. "'Nothing so curious or interesting—'" he murmured. "*De veras*. Probably one reason I am still here instead of enjoying the money, going round the world. People—still the most interesting thing there is around."

"What a thing," said Higgins. "People, my God, and anybody thinks you can generalize about them? Well—thank God we got the thing over without the press making a hullabaloo. And look at the *time*, I've got to run—"

"Date?" said Mendoza, Hackett, and Palliser in one voice. If Mary Dwyer ever realized what a good man—

"What? Oh, no, I'm invited to Stevie's Boy Scout meeting," said Higgins, and went out.

"What a *thing*," said Hackett. "Just a—well, you can see the poor woman was a little unsteady upstairs or she wouldn't—"

"No point in hashing it over," said Mendoza sleepily.

"Atwood is what *gets* me," said Palliser. "Everything to live for. Just for *that*, my God. Because that nut, and you don't tell me he's anything else but a nut, got that lunatic notion into his head—"

"'To every thing there is a season,'" said Mendoza surprisingly. "I don't know the answer, John. All we can do is play the hand as we see it, by the cards we get dealt . . . Why don't you take Sunday too?"

"What? You mean it?"

"Why not?" Mendoza stood up and reached for his hat. He was very pleased and content; the contentment emanated from him like physical warmth. The orderly mind was for the moment satisfied: the jigsaw puzzle was all neatly put together and complete. "You've got some sick leave added up. Gamble that you won't get shot up the next year and take some. Take Monday. Even Tuesday." He clapped the Homburg on slantwise.

"I may just take you up on that," said Palliser, grinning.

254

Hackett went home and told Angel about it. "Honestly, people," said Angel. "It does make you wonder . . . Funny how he has those sudden brain waves . . . Have you weighed today? Well, I'm only trying to take *care* of you, Art. Best husband I've had so far."

"I wasn't aware," said Hackett, "that you'd tested out any others."

"That's what I mean," said Angel. "The best there *could* be, darling, if you'd only be sensible and *think* a little."

"And this," said Hackett, "to a senior sergeant of detectives!"

Palliser went home and called Roberta. "It's O.K.—I'm taking Saturday, Sunday, Monday, and Tuesday. We can maybe stay over in Vegas and patronize the one-armed bandits."

"Not if I've got anything to say about it," said Roberta. "A sheer waste of money—gambling a nickel is something I cannot do. We'll come straight back to my place and start to look for a house. To buy. Investment. If we do intend to start a family in a year or so—"

"Yes, darling," said Palliser meekly. "As a sober married couple, we come straight back. And next month maybe a weekend at Tahoe."

"I'll get you trained yet," said Roberta.

Alison was still exclaiming over the avenger as she brushed her hair for the night. "It does make you wonder. I've ceased to be surprised at *anything*, the way people can —can brainwash themselves, so to speak. But you can't help but feel sorry for him—in a way, Luis."

"Oh, can't you?" said Mendoza, unbuttoning his shirt. The four cats were coiled complexly on the foot of the bed; El Señor raised a sleepy head to serve official notice of his disapproval of conversation at bedtime. "Can't you? Me,

255

maybe I've got the occupational disease most cops get sooner or later—seeing it in black and white. There are shades of gray—oh, yes. *De veras*. But you come down to essentials, *cara*, there is black and white, *finis*. And we all have to choose sides. Sooner or later."

"Well—" said Alison thoughtfully. "I see what you mean. Yes." The phone rang in the hall.

"Damn," said Mendoza, and went to answer it. "Mendoza."

"Lieutenant," said Sergeant Farrell, "we've got a kind of funny little thing I thought maybe you'd want to look at. A body, of course, and Schenke says—"

Resignedly Mendoza started to rebutton his shirt. Once a cop, always a cop . . .